INTO THE
WEST

INTO THE
WEST

Max McCoy

AN ONYX BOOK

ONYX
Published by New American Library, a division of
Penguin Group (USA) Inc., 375 Hudson Street,
New York, New York 10014, USA
Penguin Group (Canada), 10 Alcorn Avenue, Toronto,
Ontario M4V 3B2, Canada (a division of Pearson Penguin Canada Inc.)
Penguin Books Ltd., 80 Strand, London WC2R 0RL, England
Penguin Ireland, 25 St. Stephen's Green, Dublin 2,
Ireland (a division of Penguin Books Ltd.)
Penguin Group (Australia), 250 Camberwell Road, Camberwell, Victoria 3124,
Australia (a division of Pearson Australia Group Pty. Ltd.)
Penguin Books India Pvt. Ltd., 11 Community Centre, Panchsheel Park,
New Delhi - 110 017, India
Penguin Group (NZ), cnr Airborne and Rosedale Roads, Albany,
Auckland 1310, New Zealand (a division of Pearson New Zealand Ltd.)
Penguin Books (South Africa) (Pty.) Ltd., 24 Sturdee Avenue,
Rosebank, Johannesburg 2196, South Africa

Penguin Books Ltd., Registered Offices:
80 Strand, London WC2R 0RL, England

First published by Onyx, an imprint of New American Library,
a division of Penguin Group (USA) Inc.

First Printing, June 2005
10 9 8 7 6 5 4 3 2 1

Tatanka lived in the underworld. He saw our nation in a vision. He saw our needs. And for love of us, Tatanka turned his spirit body into a shaggy buffalo. Tatanka came up from under the earth to give his life, again and again, that we could eat of his flesh and make our clothes and tipis from his hide. He called us what we are . . . Buffalo Nation.

—Loved by the Buffalo

Wheelwrights we are, going back to when they invented the damn thing, when a man took his name from what he made. The Wheelers made wheels. But when I was born, it seemed the wheels made the Wheelers.

—Jacob Wheeler

PROLOGUE

Lakota Winter Camp
The Dakotas
The Winter of Deep Snow (1827)

Two Arrows, the keeper of the count, dabbed the chip of porous bone back into the wooden pot for more paint and with quick strokes on the stretched hide indicated even more buffalo raining from the sky.

"The prairie opened up, like a dog mouth yawning."

The ancient holy man Growling Bear was shuffling counterclockwise around the lodge fire in time to the beat of a slow drum, arms outstretched, as he related his disturbing vision to the circle of elders. His flickering shadow on the *ozan*, the lodge's inner lining, resembled a wounded bear.

"The hole was a hundred tipis wide," Growling Bear continued. "I looked down into the darkness. And the buffalo came like a storm cloud covering the plain."

More buffalo appeared on the hide beneath Two Arrows's gnarled hand. He was practiced at depicting *Tatanka*; because the buffalo provided life for the tribe, it was the central image in most of the painted hides, the winter count, and the annual pictorial history that Two Arrows had painted for most of his seventy years. But even as unimaginably old as Two Arrows was, Growling Bear was older.

"I saw the last buffalo going back down into the earth," Growling Bear cried. "I turned and saw our people living in a time to come. After all the four-leggeds went back down into the earth. After the white strangers, the *wasichu*,

wove webs around the Lakota people, like spiders do flies.
I saw our brave and good people starving on the barren
land."

Diving Eagle put a hand to his mouth to hide his smile.
This was only his twenty-fifth winter, but the ambitious
young holy man knew that gloomy predictions were unpop-
ular. What did Growling Bear think he was doing? The old
fool should have died years ago.

"I saw our people in square gray lodges," Growling
Bear said.

Two Arrows faltered. A square lodge? Then he went
on painting.

"They looked no more to the stars, but across the prairie,
expecting the buffalo that would come no more," Growling
Bear said, then dropped to his knees. Tears rolled down
his rugged cheeks as his hands clawed at the earth. "Better
I had died in my mother's womb than bring this vision to
the Lakota people."

Diving Eagle sneered. The gesture drew the attention of
one of the elders.

"Speak your mind," Bull Bear said.

Diving Eagle stood.

"Growling Bear wails like a woman," Diving Eagle said.
"Why? Have not the Lakota kept the sacred rites? Our
prayers have risen to *Wakan Tanka* on the sacred smoke
of our pipes."

With all eyes on him, Diving Eagle beamed with confi-
dence. "Since the grass has grown, *Tatanka* has come again
and again, keeping his promise to sustain us. But the vision
of Growling Bear says that *Tatanka* the compassionate will
give of himself for our needs no more. That would be the
end of the world."

Many of the elders nodded.

"I call upon my protector the eagle to carry a message
aloft to *Wakan Tanka*. If the vision of Growling Bear be
true, take my life. But if it be true, take Growling Bear.
Either Growling Bear has lost his powers," Diving Eagle
said, "or I have found mine."

Growling Bear regarded his young protégé with sad eyes,
then took the finished hide that Two Arrows offered. There
was the buffalo herd flowing down into the abyss, the little

square lodges, the scattered corpses. Growling Bear nodded and handed the hide back to Two Arrows.

Then Growling Bear struggled to his feet. He looked around at the smoky interior of the medicine lodge, at the leathery faces of the elders, at the pile of winter counts that recorded battles both won and lost, horses stolen, winters with snow nearly to the smoke flaps of the lodges, eclipses of the sun and moon, and always and everywhere . . . buffalo.

Growling Bear shuffled to the door of the tipi, then paused. "Let us hope," he said, "that Diving Eagle is right."

He emerged from the dark and smoky lodge into the hard winter sun like a child from its mother's womb. He blinked against the light. The winter air stung his cheeks where the tears had made them wet.

Growling Bear looked at the faces around him. Young and old, they seemed to have been waiting for him to emerge. What event would mark this year? they wondered. What would be painted on the winter count? What would give its name to the year so that it would not dim from memory? He could not tell them.

As Growling Bear made his way through the crowd, the world began to wheel around him, just as the night sky dances around the one star that does not move. The faces were spinning, the hundreds of tipis of the winter camp were spinning, and the great hoop of the daylight sky was spinning. The long night was already rolling down upon them.

ONE

Sixteen-year-old Jacob Wheeler sprawled on the rough planks of the loft, took another bite of the apple, and smoothed the page to better peer at the illustration. The book in his lap was *History of the Expeditions of Captains Lewis and Clark*, by Meriwether Lewis himself, and the sketch portrayed a Lakota warrior.

Jacob had to force himself to breathe.

The explorers had encountered a large band of Lakota, or *Tetons*, as Lewis called them, at the mouth of the Bad River on the Upper Missouri. The Lakota were unhappy that the whites were on their river, unhappy being asked to accept Thomas Jefferson as their leader, and unhappy that the explorers declined to offer their guns in trade. To make up for things, they took one of the explorers' canoes, which prompted Captain Clark to draw his sword—and the Lakota to string their bows. But Chief Black Buffalo smoothed things over.

Jacob had first spied the book the year before, on Independence Day, when his grandfather Abraham Wheeler had brought the book down from his library upon hearing the news that Thomas Jefferson and John Adams had died within hours of one another. Jefferson had commissioned the Corps of Discovery, Grandfather Abraham had said, riffling the pages of the book, making the illustrations dance before Jacob's eyes.

That morning, Jacob had pilfered the book from the library, matched it with an apple from the backyard, and climbed into the loft of the wheelwright shop while every other male member of the Wheeler family toiled below.

From blank wood the men fashioned the felloes and spokes and the hubs, and from strips of iron heated in the forge, they pounded the strakes. When separate, each half looked fragile; the wooden portion was out of kilter, seeming a bit too large for the overall design, while the stave resembled a child's toy. But when the glowing stave was forced hissing and flaming over the wood and then doused with water, the shrinking iron drew everything together in a seemingly magical process that resulted in a perfect wheel. And this the family did, over and over again, as long as there was daylight enough to work.

As the hours passed and the dust mites chased the shaft of sunlight streaming in from the loft window, Jacob was delighted to discover not a single mention of a wheel in the captain's book.

"Where's that Jacob?"

The sound of his own name shattered Jacob's revelry. He closed the book, flopped over, and pressed an eye to a wide crack between the planks. He could see the top of his grandfather's pink head as he quizzed the others, he could see his father shaking his head sadly, and he could imagine the smirks on the faces of his brothers.

"Pity that I was born in a drab age and live in the stifle of a barn where a man is only as good as the horseshoe he makes," he muttered. "Pity my days spent over an ornery anvil pounding dead iron or stoking an infernal forge where there is no glory to be gained."

"Jacob!"

His grandfather's bellow seemed to shake the rafters.

"My grandsire returned a hero from the war," Jacob said to himself. "He crossed the icy Delaware with the Old Fox, had a leg subtracted by a cannonball at Yorktown, came home to have an entire town named after him. He took as his wife the prettiest girl in that town, sired my father and my uncle, and then settled down to make wheels . . . and condemned the rest of us to do the same."

A wooden wheel was laid on the dirt floor of the shop with the smoking strake over it. As Jacob watched, his uncle Benjamin doused the wheel with a bucket of water. As the iron cooled, it hissed furiously but brought all of the parts of the wheel together in a perfect circle.

"Now that's a thing of beauty," Grandfather Abraham said with a tone usually reserved for church . . . or for Grandmother Hannah.

Absorbed despite himself, Jacob brought the apple absently to his lips for one last bite, then paused. "It takes ten years to be a journeyman wheelwright," he said to himself. "Another ten for master. That's twenty years—that's a *lifetime*." Then the apple core slipped from his fingers, tumbled through the crack in the floor, and splattered against the hub of the newly made wheel below.

Jacob groaned and rolled onto his back.

TWO

While Jacob Wheeler was being punished for day-dreaming of Indians, a twelve-year-old Lakota boy named White Feather stood inside his mother's tipi and stared at the winter count of Growling Bear's vision.

The hide was hung at the rear of the lodge, in the place reserved for sacred things, and White Feather was fascinated by the terrifying images. In his hand he held a buffalo rib, but he was more interested in the mystery of the winter count than in eating.

"The dream, Grandfather," he said. "Is it true?"

Two Arrows ignored the question and continued to gnaw on a rib bone. He was reclining on a backrest, in the midst of the other men: White Feather's older brothers, Running Fox and Dog Star, and their father, Good Shield.

The women were huddled around the cooking fire. White Feather's older sister, Thunder Heart Woman, and their mother, Big Rain, were dropping meat, wild onions, carrots, and turnips into a water-filled buffalo stomach suspended from four upright sticks. The water had been brought to boiling by adding heated stones. The younger women worked under the old but watchful eyes of Grandmother Good Path, who idly swatted flies with a buffalo tail.

"Grandfather," White Feather said, "you made no answer."

Two Arrows grunted with displeasure. "No answer is an answer," he said.

White Feather looked to his sixteen-year-old brother, Dog Star. "Is the dream true?"

"Do not speak of evil to the young," Two Arrows advised gently. "It only creates curiosity."

"But why do the buffalo run into the hole?" White Feather persisted. "Have you ever seen a square lodge? What do the *wasichu* look like? Why do we use a sacred name for them if they are wicked?"

"Eat," Two Arrows said.

White Feather looked at the rib bone in his hand and blinked. "But who killed the Lakota?"

While the other Wheeler men took the noon meal, Jacob was left behind to shoe a plow horse. The old horse was as docile as a house cat, but Jacob was having a miserable time.

"Stand still, dammit," Jacob said.

He had tried to hurry the job, but succeeded only in cutting the heels too deeply. The result was that the job took twice as long as it should have; he spent most of his time shaping and trimming. He was on the right foreleg, the hoof between his legs, with a handful of nails in his mouth and sweat dripping into his eyes, while he tried to keep the hoof steady, place the shoe, and drive nails at the same time.

Jacob was still cussing beneath his breath when a shadow crossed the yard in front of the barn.

"That hoss doesn't understand you've had a rotten day, young one. Why don't you take a break before me or him kicks you back into the barn?"

The man was dressed in fringed buckskin and cradled a long rifle. Around his neck was a necklace made of grizzly bear claws. The man offered the gun. "Reckon you can do any better at mending a rifle lock?"

Jacob released the hoof, moved quickly out of range, and wiped his hands on his apron. Carefully, he took the gun. It was a full-stock Pennsylvania rifle with a forty-four-inch barrel in .54 caliber. The curly maple stock had an oblong patch box, a crescent butt piece, and a graceful cheek. A piece of flint wedged in a bit of leather was clutched in the jaws of the hammer, but the pan wasn't primed.

Jacob carefully touched the hammer and drew it back. There was a sharp *click* as the hammer paused at half cock, the gun's safety. Then Jacob drew the hammer back all the way. It wouldn't stay and went back instead to half cock. He glanced up at the rifle's owner.

"You should have treated the old hoss that gently," the man said. Jacob noticed a scar running across the man's forehead, just under the hairline.

"It's the sear," Jacob said.

"I know what it is, son," the man laughed. "What I want to know is, can you fix it?"

Jacob nodded.

"What's your name, son?"

"Jacob," he said.

"James Fletcher," the man said.

Jacob stared at the bear claws. "Sir, might I touch them?"

Fletcher roared with laughter. "Hell, yes, youth," he said. "Grizzly! Stood on its hind feet about where the barn door tops out. Knocked the rifle out of my hands and had to finish her with a pistol. Never felt more like David in my life."

"If I may, sir, is that how you come by that scar?"

Fletcher smiled. "Aw, that was a difference of opinion with a Cheyenne warrior," he said. "The savage thought my scalp might look better hanging from his belt, but I favored where God put it. But then I fancied his locks on my belt."

Fletcher pulled back his buckskin jacket to reveal a glistening string of black-haired scalps. Jacob reached out to touch them, but stopped.

"Call me Goliath," Fletcher said.

Fletcher insisted that Jacob finish shoeing the horse properly; then they went inside the shop. Jacob spread a soft hide on the workbench, took down a few tools, and began to disassemble the lock. All the while, he was thinking about the scalps on Fletcher's belt. He felt both fascination and revulsion.

Jacob bit his lip, then dared more conversation. "They say it's all one big desert."

"It's not, youth," Fletcher said. "It's desert. It's a sea of grass. It's rivers you can just about see across. Lakes like little oceans. Mountains jagged as dog teeth topped with snow. Forests that go on forever. Indians out of the Garden of Eden."

As Fletcher talked, Jacob glimpsed all of these in his eyes.

"Then there's the Pacific," Fletcher said, "unsullied by human hands, just as it was on the eighth day of the world."

Jacob turned his attention back to the gun. He lifted out the lock, turned it over, and examined the sear. He ran his thumb along it. The knife edge was chipped, allowing it to catch on the deeper half-cock cog, but not the shallower full cock.

"I can fix this."

Jacob stoked the forge and thrust the sear into it. When it was white-hot, he withdrew it and began to pound the edge back into shape on the anvil. His hammer blows rang out in groups of three, coaxing the metal, just as his grandfather and father had taught him. Then he cooled it by plunging it into a bucket of water, placed it in a vise, and began to work the knife edge smooth with a file.

"What's this?" Enoch Wheeler asked.

"Young one is mending my rifle lock," Fletcher said, instinctively defensive of Jacob. "Fine young man you got here. He's your son, ain't he?"

"The least of four," Enoch said, then brushed Jacob aside to examine his work. "Let me finish this before you ruin it. We're already behind today because of you." Fletcher made Enoch nervous and he used the excuse of finishing the job so he wouldn't have to make conversation.

Jacob's brothers had returned and were standing some distance away, as if whatever Jacob had might catch.

Fletcher took them in with an easy glance, then said, "Reckon you can put an edge on this? It's gotten a mite dull."

From a holster slung behind his back, Fletcher pulled a heavy knife with a blade that was eighteen inches long. He also passed Jacob a wicked-looking tomahawk.

"You bet," Ezra, the oldest brother, said. He stepped forward, but Fletcher withdrew the knife.

The mountain man offered the handle to Jacob. "Sorry, I was talking to the youth," Fletcher said.

Jacob nodded. As he sat down at the grindstone, he ran his fingers over the blade, gauging the metal. His fingertips came away faintly stained with blood, and he looked up at Fletcher.

"An Arkansas toothpick ain't for cutting your dinner," Fletcher said.

Abraham Wheeler entered the barn, cuffed the older boys to get back to work, then regarded Fletcher. Enoch was still filing the rifle sear and Jacob was patiently sharpening the knife.

Although he was sixty-five years old, Abraham Wheeler still moved with the grace of someone whose survival once depended on an economy and precision of movement. He recognized the same in Fletcher, and was not disturbed, as Enoch was.

"You're far from home," Abraham said.

"Grew up down the pike in Caroline County," Fletcher said. "Thought I'd have one last look at the old place. Sorry I did now."

"Homesick?"

"Yes, by God," Fletcher said, "but not for here. My bed is a mountain meadow and my pillow is the sky. In the morning my washstand is the Platte and when I'm hungry, my larder is the prairie. I just wanted to come back here and remind myself of what a miserable creature I was before I went west."

"I'll thank you for refraining from taking the Lord's name in my shop," Abraham said evenly. "And yes, I suppose you were miserable in Caroline County. But this is Spotsylvania County, and there is a world of difference."

"This town," Fletcher said. "It bears your name."

"It does," Abraham said.

"A bit partial?"

"I am," Abraham said. "Where are you headed, sir?"

"Saint Louis," Fletcher said. "To meet with Jedediah Smith."

Jacob looked up from the grindstone. "Mr. Jedediah Smith?" he asked. "The same Smith who was with General Ashley on the Upper Missouri and who blazed South Pass to the Oregon and California territories?"

"God made just one for us all to look up to," Fletcher said. "And he's looking for some of God's own men to explore the beaver populations around the Great Salt Lake on an expedition that leaves in the spring."

"How much can a man make off beaver?" Nathan asked.

At seventeen, Nathan was the next-to-youngest of Enoch's son.

"Upward of four or five thousand a year," Fletcher said. "That's as long as they keep wearin' beaver hats in New York and London, and I reckon that will be just about forever."

Enoch snorted. "A man doesn't earn those wages in a lifetime," he said as he fitted the sear back into the rifle lock.

"Some don't," Fletcher said. "Some do."

Later that night, while the rest of the family slept, White Feather slipped beneath the tipi cover.

It was colder outside than he expected; he hugged his chest. His mother's lodge looked suddenly inviting. Even in the moonlight he could see the painted horses and stars and crescent moon, and the top half of the tipi's tilted cone, above the inside liner, glowed like a candle. The smoke flaps were set for the night, and a finger of smoke drifted toward the winter sky. The bits of ribbon at the tips of the lodge poles stirred lazily on the waxing north wind.

White Feather walked silently among the lodges, free even of the dogs that usually trailed any movement through the camp, and finally came to a tipi that looked as if it had been abandoned. The wind blew through rips in the cover, the painted symbols were faded beyond legibility by the sun, and the door cover was askew. Inside, he could see Growling Bear lying on his side, wrapped in a robe, shivering. There was no fire.

When White Feather stepped through the doorway, the old man's eyes snapped open. "Who are you?"

"White Feather, son of Good Shield."

There was no recognition on the old man's face.

"Grandson of Two Arrows."

Growling Bear blinked.

White Feather squatted by the fire and blew gently on the ashes, revealing glowing embers. He took some tinder from a rawhide box beside the fire, pressed it to the embers, and blew a bit harder. The tinder flamed with a *pop*.

Patiently, White Feather fed twigs to the fire, then waited on his haunches until the blaze was big enough for sticks. Finally, he placed a log in the fire.

"Your dream," White Feather began, the fire reflected in his deep brown eyes, "was it true?"

The old man nodded. Fumbling, the old man passed a rawhide fringe over his head. He held it out to White Feather, an obsidian amulet swinging at the end.

White Feather took it. The amulet was shaped like a buffalo. As White Feather draped the amulet over his own head, Growling Bear fell back into the robe, sobbing. The boy found a water pouch and offered it to the old man.

Instead of taking the water, Growling Bear seized the boy's hand and pressed it to his face. He closed his eyes. When he stopped breathing, he was still clutching White Feather's hand.

THREE

Jacob was fully clothed beneath the covers, in the bunk above his brother Nathan, staring holes in the ceiling while he waited for his brothers to fall asleep. His cheeks were still hot from the exchange that had taken over Sunday dinner.

As wheels are made of iron and wood, so Jacob thought of his family. One side of the long table—his side—was the wood side. This is where Jacob's father and mother, Enoch and Margaret, sat, with their four sons. Being the youngest, Jacob sat farthest from his father.

The other side was the iron side. It had Uncle Benjamin and Aunt Abbagail, their nearly grown sons, Cyrus and Samson, and their teenage daughters, Rachel, Leah, and Naomi.

Abraham Wheeler presided, with Hannah at his side, and the topic of conversation was freedom. Abraham was passionate about the crop of republics that had emerged in the twelve years since the Napoleonic War had shattered Spanish colonization. Sensing an opportunity, France and Spain (wanting to recapture their old colonies) had courted the backing of Russia to wage a war on the new countries. President James Monroe had proposed a deal: if the rest of Europe would stay out of New World affairs and not join Spain in waging war, then America would not lend a hand to the fledgling republics as they fought it out with Spain.

Having fought in a revolution himself, Abraham was

sympathetic to the emerging republics. He admired Monroe and his secretary of state, John Quincy Adams, for standing up to the European bullies. At least it would give freedom a chance.

"If I were just twenty years younger," Abraham said, "I'd be tempted to go down and lend a hand. I imagine they could use a man with a bit of experience."

"Abraham," Hannah said, "twenty years ago, it had been thirty years since you'd held a rifle."

The old man's eyes flared, then cooled—just like a hot iron wheel doused in water.

"I gave up holding a rifle when I started holding you," Abraham said, causing Hannah to blush. "At any rate, it seems a shame not to lend them a hand when they want freedom so badly."

"If they want it that badly, they'll take it without our help," Enoch Wheeler said in a way that made Abraham wonder whether his son had ever wanted anything badly in his life.

Jacob caught his grandfather's eye, and both knew they shared the thought.

"Perhaps," Abraham allowed.

"We'd do best to mind our own business," Enoch continued. "Leave the west to the Russians and the British. Leave the rest of it to the Spanish."

"Who would want it?" Hannah asked. "Isn't the west one great desert?"

"But that's a common myth, Grandmother," Jacob blurted. "Why, it is all kind of terrain: everything you could imagine—"

"Jacob!" Enoch Wheeler said. "Mind your place."

"Sorry, sir," Jacob said meekly.

"Why, yes," Nathan said, holding his fork in the air. "Jacob has just returned from the western part of the house."

"Jacob has yet to explore the western side of the barn," Jethro said, slapping Nathan on the back. "But he does have maps and has it on good account that it is red and rather broad."

His brothers and cousins laughed raucously.

The laughter was still ringing in his ears as Jacob slipped

down from the bunk, found his boots, and quietly pulled the door shut behind him. He pulled himself into his grandfather's home through a window, then tiptoed to the gun rack on the wall of the great room. He ran his fingers over the rifles until he found the stock of the Pennsylvania rifle his grandfather had carried during the Revolutionary War. His hands closed around the stock; then he paused. He knew he was not worthy of such a weapon. Someday, perhaps, but not now. So he went to the next rifle in the rack, a slightly shorter .50 caliber rifle, and eased it down.

Jacob shouldered it, aiming into the darkness. His cheek felt good against the stock. Then he took a powder horn and bullet pouch, and exited the house the same way he had entered.

In the barn, Jacob hurriedly saddled the fastest horse. He was tightening the cinch strap when he noticed Nathan and Jethro standing in the doorway.

"There's a name for what you're doing," Jethro said.

"It's called stealing," Nathan added.

"I've made my last wheel," Jacob said defensively. "I'm off to catch Mr. Fletcher and see if Jedediah Smith will allow me along. I'll send money after my first season to pay for the horse and the gun."

"You won't live that long," Nathan said. "You were about as quiet as a herd of cows leaving the bedroom. How do you expect to sneak away from a pack of bloodthirsty redskins just itching to lift your hair? Why would any plainsman accommodate *you*?"

"Ask and ye shall receive," Jacob said.

"You go for wool but may come back shorn," Nathan rejoined.

"Or not at all," Jethro said.

"I am certain Mr. Smith's brothers mocked him before he went west," Jacob said. The horse was saddled. He swung up, cradling the rifle in the crook of his arm, and looked down at the upturned faces of his brothers. "But I am equally certain that their mocking turned to green envy when they gazed at his fortune. Nathan, I always thought you had more grit in you. Jethro, you've always been a blade of grass that sways to the will of any little breeze." He touched his heels to the horse and was gone.

"Wait up!" Nathan called as he grabbed a saddle.

Jethro took one as well, but even before he even got to a horse, his will failed. He let the saddle fall to the ground.

While Blue Bird and her sister, Yellow Hawk, were hauling water in buffalo intestines, Dog Star sat atop his horse and leaned forward appreciatively. He smiled at fourteen-year-old Blue Bird, who smiled back.

"The day is beautiful but no more than Blue Bird," Dog Star said.

Standing beside him, his brother Running Fox was holding a freshly skinned rabbit. "Even a night in the moon of the ripening cherries is less beautiful than Blue Bird," Running Fox said, trying to trump his older brother's compliment.

Little Bird, the broad-shouldered father of Blue Bird and Yellow Hawk, emerged from the tipi and looked disdainfully at the suitors.

"When will I have a day when I will not see you two dogs sniffing around my daughters?" he asked. Then, to Blue Bird: "Go inside."

"I have brought fresh meat for your family!" Running Fox proclaimed.

Little Bird took the rabbit, but shook his head. "This is hardly enough to feed an old woman. You are a poor provider. I want neither you nor your brother for a son-in-law. Neither has fought in a battle. Go now." Little Bird stepped back into the tipi.

Running Fox frowned at his brother. "Stay away from Blue Bird."

"I saw her long before you knew that thing between your legs was good for anything but making water, little brother," Dog Star said, then turned his head, his long hair flipping down his back.

Running Fox jumped up and grasped a fistful of his brother's hair. He jerked Dog Star backward off the horse, and they landed in a tangle of fists and elbows in the dirt.

The corpse of Growling Bear lay motionless atop the funeral scaffold, on a rounded hilltop nearest the great hoop of the sky, eyes closed and hands at his sides. Above, a trio of turkey buzzards wheeled in lazy circles, wary of the very much alive White Feather sitting on a rock and sobbing quietly a few yards away. A flock of crows alighted on the scaffold amid a noisy flapping of black wings, and White Feather snatched up a couple of stones and threw them at the birds. The first caused the crows to scatter, but the second thumped heavily against Growling Bear's thigh.

The ghost of Growling Bear sat up. "Your aim is too poor to be a warrior," it said, laughing. The ghost was much younger than the Growling Bear who had died in the ragged tipi, so young in fact that the shaman appeared as he must have in full manhood.

White Feather was a little afraid of the shimmering ghost, but he was not surprised. He knew ghosts walked the earth every day, unseen by most of his people.

"We hunted buffalo on foot until we learned to tame the big dogs that were left to run wild by the Spanish armored ones," the ghost said. "We moved our camp to be near the buffalo. Possessions were a burden, so we left them behind. Now our people have become servants of their possessions and must rely on the big dogs to drag their trash from camp to camp."

"White Feather!" Thunder Heart Woman called from the bottom of the hill. She did not see the ghost of Growling Bear. "Come! The buffalo!"

Below, the tribe was breaking winter camp. Tipis were being collapsed, the lodge hides and household goods were being placed on travois made from lodge poles, and babies were being strapped in wicker baskets the women would wear on their backs.

"I must go," White Feather said.

"Thank you for helping observe the ritual of the keeping of my soul, and for agreeing to keep the soul bundle," the ghost said. White Feather touched the buckskin pouch slung around his neck; the pouch contained a lock of Growling Bear's hair, which had been purified in smoke. "It is the first of the seven sacred rites of the Lakota. Remember, you must keep my soul for one year before releasing it back to the universe, and during that time, you must not wield a knife or even participate in the butchering of the buffalo."

"But I am young and expected to help with the butchering party."

"These are not my rules," the ghost said, and White Feather nodded. "Follow the red path, the straight path that leads from the south, where all life comes from, to the north, which is the abode of the pure spirit. Avoid the black road."

"Why?"

"The black road runs east and west and is the path of those who live for himself and not his people. It is the way of destruction."

"I will remember," White Feather said.

"To remember is good," the ghost said. "Now go. And keep the sacred rites." The ghost vanished.

White Feather stood, stared for a moment at the lonely scaffold on the hill, and then ran for the camp. Thirty hunters with lances and bows and arrows were riding out of the camp. White Feather spotted Good Shield, Dog Star, and Running Fox among them.

Frightened by Thunder, a young *heyoka*, followed last. He was facing backward on the horse and he was shaking a crooked stick for a lance. The holy clown's antics were accompanied by howls of laughter from the women and children.

There were more than a thousand bison in the herd that grazed placidly on the sweet grasses of the gently rolling hillside. Approaching them, beneath heavy buffalo hides, were Running Fox and Dog Star, trying their best to imitate the lurching, ponderous movements of their prey—and guide them toward the cliff that waited at the end of the deceptively gentle slope. Although the elders had denied their request to participate as full-fledged members of the hunting party, they had agreed to allow the brothers a job that in some ways was even more important: to serve as decoys to lure the herd to the buffalo jump.

"No further," Running Fox said when they were within a few dozen yards of the herd. They could hear the snorts and bellows of the animals, smell their fetid breath and matted fur and fresh droppings. If the wind changed, the youths could suddenly find themselves in the middle of a buffalo stampede.

Dog Star ignored his brother and lumbered closer.

Then they heard the sounds of the hunters approaching

on horseback, whooping and hollering, and they knew that arrows and lances were taking the slower beasts. They also knew that the butchering party, which was composed of the tribe's women and bigger children, would already be falling upon the slain beasts to start the serious work of providing sustenance for the tribe for the winter.

It was time for the brothers in bison clothing to run as fast as they could for the cliff, hoping that the herd would follow. With their hearts in their throats and the ground shaking beneath their pounding feet, the brothers reached the cliff. Dog Star was first. He snatched up a sinew rope where it was coiled in the grass and launched himself over the cliff with a great leap.

For a few seconds he was free-falling; then the rope brought him up with a jerk and swung him into a cave below the cliff face. He released the rope and tumbled into safety.

Above, Running Fox fumbled with the rope. The herd was almost upon him when he finally dove over the cliff, but he didn't have enough momentum to swing him smoothly into the cave; instead, he dangled like a fish on a line. Without hesitating, Dog Star took a running start, leaped from the mouth of the cave, grasped his brother around the neck, and swung them both far enough out to bring them back into the cave. A moment later, the air was filled with the bodies of bison falling to their deaths.

"What would you do without me?" Dog Star asked.

Running Fox glanced behind him as the beasts fell like rain. He had no answer.

While Dog Star was saving his brother, White Feather was with his mother and the other women and children of the butchering party. His mother, Big Rain, was expertly butchering a buffalo cow, an ancient flint knife in her hand, blood covering her arms up to her elbows.

"Get to work, White Feather," she said.

But he had not yet touched a knife. Then White Feather felt it. The wind had changed direction.

The herd swerved away from the precipice, where the smell of blood and broken bodies was wafting over the rim, and started back down the way they had come. The hunting party wheeled their horses, with Good Shield far in front, but neither their arrows, nor their lances, nor their war hoops could deflect the herd from the path that would lead them to the butchering party.

White Feather was frozen in terror. While the women and children around him were being trampled beneath the flashing hooves, the herd parted as the largest of the beasts bore down on White Feather. It was a huge animal, with a shaggy coat and rolling black eyes and hooves that struck the ground like thunder. Although White Feather tried to close his eyes, he could not, and while he expected to be trampled like the others, the great beast that bore down upon him was suddenly transformed into the ancient holy man Growling Bear. The wizened sage stretched out his arms, protecting White Feather and forcing the herd to pass on either side.

White Feather was seized by a mixture of terror and awe. Around him were more than a dozen broken bodies, including that of his mother, Big Rain. Only White Feather remained standing. Why had Growling Bear saved him?

FOUR

Inside the darkness of the chicken coop, Jacob and his older brother Nathan were stealing eggs from sleeping hens, cracking them open and downing them raw. As Jacob used the back of his hand to wipe raw egg from the corners of his mouth, Nathan saw a movement in a shaft of moonlight and pulled his knife.

A stave knocked the knife from Nathan's hand, and suddenly Nathan found himself spun around and placed in a headlock. A brown arm encircled his neck.

"A runaway slave!" Jacob exclaimed.

"Get yer nigger hands off me!" Nathan yelped.

Somehow, the runaway had managed to retrieve the knife from the dirt and was now holding it against Nathan's throat. Jacob snatched up the rifle he had stolen from his grandfather and leveled it at the runaway.

"Let go of my brother," Jacob said.

"Only when he lets go of me!"

"Well, you're dead mutton if'n you don't," Jacob said as he cocked the rifle.

Dogs bayed in the darkness.

"Then your brother is just as dead. You're as likely to shoot him as me in the darkness, and even if you miss him and hit me, this blade is likely to finish the job before I die."

Jacob kept the rifle to his shoulder for a moment, then lowered it.

"Go ahead and kill him, if you've a mind to," Jacob said

easily. "He's a pest. You'll be easier shooting without him in front, and I can take my time."

"Jacob!" Nathan hissed.

There were footsteps outside.

"Hush up," the runaway said. "You want to get me killed?"

"Well, yes," Nathan said.

"Who's in there?" a man bellowed outside. "Answer me, by God!"

"Make you a deal," Jacob whispered. "Let my brother go, and we won't tell this sodbuster that you're hiding amongst his chickens."

"Why should I believe you?"

"Because you don't have a choice," Jacob said.

The runaway withdrew the knife from Nathan's throat and melted into the shadows just as the door of the coop burst open. The farmer was carrying a double-barreled shotgun with the hammers pulled back on both chambers.

Jacob shifted his grandfather's gun behind his back and did his best schoolboy impression.

"Who in thunder are you?"

"Just some hungry boys, sir."

"How many of you?"

"Just the two of us, sir."

The farmer looked uncertain.

"What are you doing here in the middle of the night?"

"We were on our way back from a congregational meeting in the next county," Jacob said. "I regret to say the wolf in our stomachs overruled our God-fearing souls, sir."

"We only took enough to keep body and soul together," Nathan said, then offered the eggs they had not yet eaten. "Here's what we don't need."

The farmer scratched his head, then cradled the shotgun in the crook of his left arm.

"Where are you boys from?" he asked. "No, never mind. I wouldn't get the truth anyway. Go ahead. Take a handful each. You only had to knock on my door to discover Christian charity. But I had to admit my hopes were up when I started hearing the dogs howling, what with that big reward for the runaway slave."

"Oh?" Nathan asked.

"A big buck by the name of Benjamin Franklin," the

farmer said. "Got the womenfolk scared half to death, but all I can think of is that reward the sheriff is offering."

"How much might that be?" Nathan asked.

"Three hundred silver dollars."

Jacob shot his brother a withering look.

"With your permission, sir, we will be on our way," Jacob said and grasped his brother by the elbow and guided him toward the door of the chicken coop. "We thank you heartily, sir, and will let you return to your warm bed."

"God bless you, boys, and stay out of trouble."

As the boys walked away from the farmer, Nathan asked, "What objection do you have to three hundred silver dollars in our pocket when all that stands between us and ruination is thirteen lousy dollars?"

"That man kept his word," Jacob said. "I intend to keep mine."

"He ain't no *man*," Nathan said with venom. "He's somebody's property. And that reward money should have been ours."

They had come to the stand of trees where they had left the horses. As Jacob began to swing up into the saddle, Nathan grabbed the barrel of the rifle.

"Let go of my rifle."

"Let's go get him," Nathan pleaded, but could not jerk the weapon from his brother's grasp.

In the distance, they heard the sound of the chicken coop door slam, and then both barrels of the farmer's shotgun discharge.

"There goes our fortune," Nathan said, releasing the rifle.

"Let's go," Jacob said from the saddle.

"Who made you captain of this damned enterprise, anyway?"

"You did," Jacob said. "You were the one who followed me, remember?"

White Feather's eyes were still filled with the vision of Growling Bear, even though he was now looking upon the funeral scaffold of his mother, Big Rain. Beside him his sister, Thunder Heart Woman, cried silently. Around them, the hillside was filled with the funeral scaffolds of the others killed in the stampede.

Diving Eagle let out a cry, flung back his head, and opened his arms. The young holy man had adorned his robe with every power object he possessed: dried snakes, hummingbirds, a bat, frogs, a buffalo hoof.

"Who can doubt that this boy is beloved of *Tatanka*, who came to earth and gave his life that we might live?" Diving Eagle said. "He is White Feather no more. Let him be known as Loved by the Buffalo. May you bring honor to your name as you learn the ways of a holy man."

Two Arrows came forward and placed a hand on his grandson's shoulder. Then, to Good Shield, the old man said quietly, "Diving Eagle made evil against Growling Bear so that only his voice would be heard by the council. Diving Eagle is like a berry that is pleasing to look at, but which is full of worms. We must keep our eyes on the boy."

FIVE

The tribe made a pilgrimage to the *Paha Sapa*, the sacred Black Hills, the center of the world, where the Lakota went to speak directly to *Wakan Tanka*. There, they made a sweat lodge in the traditional way, representing the universe in miniature, and necessary for one of the seven sacred rites.

Young willow trees were used as a frame and marked the four quarters of the cosmos, the rocks to be heated represented the eternal earth, and the path that lead from the lodge's entrance—which faced the rising sun, the direction in which wisdom came—represented the narrow sacred path. After ten paces, the path led to the fire-of-no-end, in which the rocks were heated and taken to the altar in the center of the lodge.

There, Loved by the Buffalo sat naked, legs folded beneath him. He occasionally doused the rocks with water to produce great billows of steam, waiting for a vision. He had not said a word since the day his mother had been trampled by the buffalo and he was saved by Growling Bear. For four days, he sat alone in the lodge and pondered the great mystery that was life, and all the while Diving Eagle watched and waited from outside the lodge.

Then, one morning at sunrise, Loved by the Buffalo emerged purified from the sweat lodge and walked down the sacred path and came to the place of the seven poles. He stood there for a moment, sweat still running down his body even though the morning was cold and he could see his own breath, and he took a little tobacco from a pouch that had been left there for him by his father, Good Shield.

Without speaking, Loved by the Buffalo prayed for *Wakan Tanka* to reveal its presence in the world around him. He offered a pinch of tobacco to the pole that represented the north, the source of the purifying wind; then to the pole that represented the east, where wisdom came; then to the south, which is the source and end of all life; to the heavens, where the sun lives; and below, to Mother Earth.

Then Loved by the Buffalo noticed a dead robin on the ground at his feet. Diving Eagle was watching from above, hiding behind a boulder, as Loved by the Buffalo knelt and gently touched the dead bird with the palms of his hands. Although Loved by the Buffalo's lips did not move, Diving Eagle could distinctly hear the chant of a sacred prayer.

The robin's wings began to flutter.

Diving Eagle blinked in disbelief.

The bird spun in a small circle, then found its feet, righted itself, and flew away.

Diving Eagle pressed his hands to his eyes in jealousy. He had placed the dead bird in the middle of the sacred poles as an evil omen to keep Loved by the Buffalo from achieving his vision. He had known the robin was dead.

SIX

Saint Louis, Missouri
1828 (They Killed Many Mandans)

There were seven thousand residents in Saint Louis, and it was the biggest town that Jacob Wheeler had ever seen or could imagine. The life of the city centered around the Mississippi River landing that Pierre Laclede and his adopted son, Auguste Chouteau, had selected as a French trading post in 1764. Now the former trading post had become the bustling jumping-off point for fur traders, explorers, fugitives, and assorted misfits; Saint Louis was only fifteen miles south of the Missouri River, the inconstant waterway to all points west.

The river landing was the terminus of a few streets upon a natural limestone ledge, which continued south and finally disappeared beneath the mud of Mill Creek, where the United States was building an arsenal south of the city. On the riverfront there was a collection of French-style buildings, with shutters and wrought-iron railings, some along paved streets and others along mud alleyways. The riverfront buildings housed (legally or otherwise) coffee shops, dram houses, gambling rooms, bordellos, outfitters, mercantile stores, and a cabinet and gunmaker's shop.

On the porch of a mercantile store between one of the taverns and the gun shop, James Fletcher was lounging. Around him there was much activity as buckskinned mountain men hauled wooden boxes and cloth sacks of provisions to a waiting wagon.

Jacob reined the horse to a stop in the middle of the

muddy street. His brother Nathan was riding behind him. Long ago, they had lost the other horse on the trail from Wheelerton.

"What's wrong?" Nathan said, annoyed, while the horse turned nervously. The boys were tired, hungry, and very dirty. What had seemed a grand adventure to Nathan when they had first run away from home had quickly become a seemingly unending series of travails.

"Mr. Fletcher!" Jacob called.

Fletcher looked up and regarded the boy on the horse who had called his name.

"Don't you remember me, sir?" Jacob asked as he dismounted. "I mended your rifle and sharpened your knife." Jacob led the horse to the porch railing, looked up at Fletcher, and said: "You said Mr. Jedediah Smith was looking for men, sir, for an adventure in the spring. Well, we made it in time, didn't we?"

"God help me," Fletcher said. "It is the youth from the East. I said Mr. Smith was looking for men, son. *Mountain* men."

"We'd pull our weight, sir," Jacob pleaded. "Do you reckon you could make our introductions to Mr. Smith?"

Fletcher looked at Jacob thoughtfully. "Mountain men are thicker than thieves here in Saint Louis," he said. "Actually, most of them *are* thieves. But they are seasoned men, more red than white. They speak Apache, Cheyenne, Crow, Lakota—not to mention French and some version of English. They do things with powder and ball that are regarded as miracles by mere mortals, they talk to animals and angels in their native tongue, and they can drink rivers of whiskey dry and have spilled lakes of blood. And of these gods among us, son, only fifteen will be chosen."

Nathan gave Jacob a look of disgust. He yanked at the reins of the horse and rode away.

"Nathan," Jacob called. "What are you doing?"

"Trying to forget about you for a while," Nathan said. "Try not to trade the goddamn horse for a bag of magic beans, will you?"

That night, Jacob was sitting dejected on the porch of the mercantile store. The horse was tied at the rail, and Jacob was trying to figure out a way to raise enough money to buy feed. At the edge of the street not far away, some stray dogs were sniffing around the edges of a rough tarp thrown carelessly over a corpse. Sprawled on the porch was a mountain man snoring loudly, sleeping off a hangover.

A drunk Nathan came trudging up the street. He smiled broadly as he approached his brother. He plunged his hands into the pockets of his trousers and shook them, making the unmistakable jingle of gold and silver coins.

"Where in hell have you been?" Jacob asked.

"Winning our fortune," Nathan said. "Saint Louis loves the brothers Wheeler. I couldn't lose a poker hand. Ten times I tried to quit, and ten times they made me stay." From his pocket he drew a parchment and waved it beneath Jacob's nose. "Won me this here *escritura*. That's Spanish for deed. A hundred acres in *Tejas*. That's seventy-five for me and twenty-five for you. What do you say, partner?"

"It's not even in the United States."

"So what?"

"They don't even speak English down there," Jacob said. "And they're papists."

"Our cup runneth over, Jacob," Nathan declared. "With a hundred acres, we don't need to rub elbows with nobody."

"I told you, I'm going with Mr. Smith."

"Who cares beans for that? We've already been told they don't want us. *Tejas* awaits."

"I want to see the Pacific Ocean."

"And then what?"

"I don't know."

"And why should I stick with you?" Nathan said, suddenly belligerent as only a drunk can be. "Know why father made you stoke the furnace while I had the important job of reckoning measurements? It's because you've never had much of a head, except for dreams." Nathan took a few coins from his pocket and tossed them on the porch. "I'm boarding a steamboat within the hour. Come if you want."

Nathan walked off.

Later, Jacob traded his clothes with those of a drunken mountain man. Despite the odor, Jacob delighted in the buckskin hunting shirt and leggings fringed along the seams, and the red flannel shirt where greasy hands were wiped a thousand times.

In a bend of the river outside Saint Louis, thirty-year-old Jedediah Smith was overseeing the unloading of the wagons and the transfer of the goods onto the waiting keel-boat. Smith was tall, with dark hair and strong features. Grasped in Smith's hand was a well-thumbed Bible. The keelboat was twenty-two feet long, with a cabin in the back and a swivel gun near the bow. There were a mast for a square sail and places for oars along the side, but the power for most of the upriver journey would be the cordelle, a heavy rope that would be used to haul the boat upstream by teams of men on the bank.

Smith smelled Jacob before he saw him. Turning slightly, he regarded the youth and his fringed buckskins and red flannel with a mixture of amusement and disdain.

"Mr. Smith, sir," Jacob said, "my name is Jacob Wheeler and I want to see where no white man has seen before."

"We have our crew, son," Smith said.

"If a horse throws a shoe, I'm a first-rate farrier," Jacob said. "I can also repair rifles. Just ask Mr. James Fletcher. And, sir, I'm a hunter."

"Oh?" Smith asked. "And what kind of game do you take?"

"Rabbits, mostly," Jacob said.

When the other mountain men guffawed, Smith gave them a stern look. Then he asked, "Ever kill a man, son? Not out of pleasure, but of necessity?"

"No, sir." Jacob started to leave, then stopped. "All due respect, Mr. Smith, but have *you* ever killed a man?"

Smith smiled gently.

James Fletcher appeared at Smith's side, catlike, from nowhere. "Youth, Mr. Smith cannot count the savages that have fallen to his hand."

"Well, it's pretty easy to kill a savage out to lift your hair," Jacob said, practicing the bluster he had seen so often in the men he admired. "But you ever hunted down an innocent rabbit that has done you no harm, cut it down in cold blood, and then eaten it?"

This time, even Smith laughed. "Do you drink or smoke?"

"No, sir."

"What do you expect for wages?"

"Experience, sir."

"Know your Bible?"

"Tolerable well, sir." Several years of Sunday school haunted Jacob's memory.

"John 3:16?" Smith asked.

"For God so loved the world . . ."

"So He did," Smith said, the Missouri breeze ruffling his hair. He looked up at the sky, but he needed no help with this decision. Then he looked at Jacob squarely. "Master Wheeler, can you write and cipher?"

SEVEN

Lakota Winter Encampment
The Dakotas
They Saw Wagons (1829)

Broken Flower was only thirteen, but she was dying. She lay shivering on a buffalo robe, curled on her side, clutching her stomach. Her forehead was dotted with sweat, her dark hair was matted, and her eyes were sunken beneath her brow.

The girl's family was sitting in a circle around her, and Diving Eagle was moving around her, shaking his charms at imagined malefactors. Loved by the Buffalo was sitting beside the girl, slowly beating a small drum; he was confused that Diving Eagle did not see the sickness that was coiled in the girl's stomach.

Diving Eagle adopted a countenance of wise sorrow. "It is her last winter count," he told her father. "It may be the weather—or her lack of faith."

The girl's father nodded gravely. "Is there nothing we can do?"

"Nothing," Diving Eagle said.

Loved by the Buffalo placed the drum aside. He had fifteen summers, but his eyes seemed much older. As he looked at the sick girl, he saw, in his mind's eye, the broken body of his mother, who had been taken by the buffalo. Then he thought of his sister, Thunder Heart Woman. Their father had given her in marriage (along with thirty-one beaver skins) to the trapper Thomas Lebeck for a cooking pot, glass beads, a few bits of blue-and-red cloth, and a trade rifle that had the symbol of a serpent inscribed on the lock. Lebeck had discovered that it was easier to trade for beaver pelts—which the trappers universally called plews—than to wade into frozen streams, set iron traps baited with stinking concoctions made from animal glands, and constantly expect an arrow in your back from the Blackfeet or some other hostile tribe. Thunder Heart Woman resigned herself to life with the trapper because Lakota girls did not question the wisdom of their fathers. Also, the situation could be much worse; some girls found themselves traded as slaves, won in battle, or worse. At least Lebeck, in his broken Lakota, seemed to harbor some genuine affection for her. There were, after all, other girls in the village who might have caught his eye.

"This is how it is for women," her mother, Good Path, had told her. "I was a mother at twelve summers. You should have three babies sucking at your tits by now. We are born to be of use to men."

Before Thunder Heart Woman left, Loved by the Buffalo had taken the obsidian amulet that Growling Bear had given him and placed it reverently over his sister's head. He did not say a word, of course, but the girl knew the meaning of the gesture. *Remember: you are loved. You are Lakota!* The last time Loved by the Buffalo saw his sister, she had been riding behind Lebeck, one hand on the amulet and the other grasping the waist of the clumsy trapper, the pack mules following behind, laden with beaver pelts.

Now Loved by the Buffalo glanced at Diving Eagle with an expression that betrayed nothing. He leaned forward and placed his hands on the girl's stomach. She did not flinch. Instead, it was Loved by the Buffalo who gasped with pain.

He did not, however, remove his hands. The illness moved from his hands to his wrists, serpentined up his arms, and then slid down his torso to settle in the pit of his stomach.

Beads of sweat formed on Loved by the Buffalo's brow. He closed his eyes tightly, his lips curled back, and he tried to summon an attitude of gratitude toward Buffalo Calf Woman for allowing him to assume the girl's suffering. He failed at first, and for a terrifying moment, the pain stole a reptilian glimpse into his soul. Then, suddenly, Buffalo Calf

Woman was there with him, shining with her own light, and he knew he could finally remove his hands from the girl's body.

The world spun and Loved by the Buffalo fell back into the circle of the girl's family, and a dozen hands caught him before his body touched the floor of the lodge. But his soul was elsewhere, with the stars far above the *Paha Sapa*, the sacred Black Hills, and the earth spun beneath him. The earth wheeled around a hoop of ancient stones that had been placed upon a hilltop, and while the horizon was moving at a dizzying speed, the stone circle turned slowly. The very center of the circle was turning so slowly, in fact, that it hardly seemed to be moving at all.

When Loved by the Buffalo stared into it, time stopped.

It took Loved by the Buffalo days to regain his strength. The girl's family gave Diving Eagle a spotted pony for curing the girl—it was required, after all, because Loved by the Buffalo was his apprentice—but the tribe knew who really had brought the girl back from the land of the dead. And although Diving Eagle had a fine new horse, his soul withered a bit more from jealousy. The sacred song that *Wakan Tanka* had given him during a vision quest, when he was the same age as Broken Flower, became twisted. Now, when Diving Eagle sang it to seek the favor of the buffalo, his voice was not carried by the wind.

Change seemed everywhere.

The Lakota's understanding of time was based on events. Indeed, they had no name for time itself, but instead used the suffix *-etu*, which implied a causal relationship. There were thirteen months, or moons, in the Lakota year, and each was named for something associated with the season— the Moon When the Cherries Turn Black, the Moon of the Popping Trees—but there were no names for the individual days. The years were named for the winter counts, which served as a reminder of the defining event for a year, something that all of the tribe could remember. The names for the winter counts differed from tribe to tribe in the Lakota, even when they referred to the same events. It was as if time ran at different rates around the seven council fires that made up the Lakota nation. A comet that had appeared in the night sky for one tribe might be remembered as appearing a year or two earlier for another.

The earliest winter count, or at least the earliest winter count that Two Arrows could ever recall seeing, was the Winter the People Scattered. A decade later, the Lakota would suffer a war within their own tribes, and it was called Those Who Speak the Same Language Fight. In 1782, measles swept the tribes; in 1789, the winter was so cold that crows froze and dropped from the sky; and in 1804, the Lakota met the expedition of Captains Lewis and Clark in a winter count that would be called the People Came Together with Many Flags.

The winter that Broken Flower was cured was called *They Saw Wagons*. That summer, a white trader the Lakota called Red Lake had arrived with a wagon. While the revolving wheels were fascinating, they also seemed absurd and more than a little sacrilegious to the tribe. Hoops were sacred. To use them for something as earthly as hauling trade goods might be fine for the *wasichu*, but it was unthinkable for the Lakota.

Also that winter, Good Shield learned to use his new gun to take game (and to kill enemies should the opportunity present itself) and Good Path abandoned the use of buffalo stomachs and heated stones in favor of the iron cooking pot from the trapper Lebeck.

EIGHT

Near Mission San Antonio de Valero
State of Coahuila y Tejas, Mexico
1829 (They Saw Wagons)

One thousand miles to the south of the Lakota village, Nathan Wheeler scooped up a handful of water from a meandering creek. The water was sweet. Beside him, his horse and pack mule edged toward the water and he allowed them to drink. From his vest pocket he took an old scrap of paper and compared the rolling grassland, the creek, and the stand of cottonwoods to that indicated on the map.

It was the place.

It was *his* place.

Although the map that accompanied the *escritura* was also in Spanish, Nathan had picked up enough of the language in the journey to recognize the word "*alamo*," penned near the stand of trees, as cottonwood. Back in the village he had passed through, the unfinished and crumbling Catholic mission was commonly called *Del Alamo*, but Nathan did not understand why.

Something moved in the brush a few dozen yards away, and Nathan reached warily for his rifle. After a few moments of watching anxiously, he picked up a stone and threw it in the direction of the movement. A jackrabbit scurried away, and Nathan laughed.

Nathan slipped the rifle back into the scabbard beside the saddle, staked the animals, and withdrew an ax from the mule's burden. The place for the cabin would be well back from the water, on the higher ground near an escarpment, but the trees were located here, near the water's edge.

Nathan weighed the ax in his hands, getting a proper grip on the handle, and looked up at the sky. He felt suddenly and uncharacteristically lonely and wished for a moment that Jacob—or even one of his other brothers—was with him.

Then he shook his head and muttered to himself, "Fools."

Nathan planted his feet, drew the bit in a lazy circle behind him, then sank the blade into the trunk of the biggest cottonwood. He found the action deeply satisfying, because for the first time he was using some of the skills that he had learned in his grandfather's shop to make something other than a wagon wheel.

A while later, a group of riders approached from the river as Nathan was on his horse, dragging a cottonwood toward the home site. He realized too late that he had left his rifle leaning against the low wall of the cabin.

He stayed in the saddle and tried not to glance at the gun as the group approached. There were six riders, two men, a woman, a teenage girl, and two children. All were *Tejanos.* The older man was perhaps thirty, as was the woman. The teenage girl was strikingly beautiful. All were dressed well, and had the air of ranchers—of landowners.

"Hola, amigo," the man said.

Nathan said hello.

"Qué pasa?"

Nathan brought the horse to a stop.

"Esta tierra es mio," the man said with a smile.

"Land? This land?"

"Sí, amigo," the man said, still smiling. *"Es mio."*

Nathan slowly dismounted. He smiled as he reached slowly inside his vest pocket and brought out the papers.

"This is my deed," Nathan said.

The man took the papers and examined them carefully.

"Su escritura es de España," he said. *"El mio es de Mejico. Después de la revolucíon—siete años."*

Your deed is Spanish. Mine is from Mexico. Is is seven years after the revolution. Nathan struggled with what the man was trying to tell him.

"That son of a bitch," Nathan said. "Sorry—that pirate in Saint Louis who tricked me into betting everything on a worthless piece of paper."

"Ah," Juan said, and introduced his family.

"*Mi casa,*" Juan del Campo urged. "*Vamos a comer, amigo.*"

"I will eat with you, yes," Nathan said, then thought: *My grandfather would be spinning if he knew I was taking dinner with papists, but I am mighty tired of rabbit and corn dodgers. What old Abraham don't know won't hurt him, I reckon.*

NINE

Mountain Meadows
Mexican Territory (now Utah)
1829 (They Saw Wagons)

It was as beautiful a spot as Jacob had ever seen. It was twilight, and the stars were coming out one at a time, with the mountains as a backdrop, and the air was as still as the inside of a church on Monday morning.

Jacob was bone-tired, but he kept pace as Fletcher and Jedediah Smith walked the perimeter of the meadow, with Smith occasionally dictating notes that Jacob scribbled in pencil in a pocket ledger. The youth had learned to cradle his grandfather's rifle in the crook of his left arm, while holding the book open with his left hand and the pencil with his right. Behind them, the rest of the company were bivouacked for the night.

"This meadow will make a fine campsite for a larger party," Smith said.

"It gives me an uneasy feeling," Fletcher ventured.

"Explain yourself."

"All of this open space where you expect to find none," Fletcher said. "It may look like the Garden of Eden, but it would be one helluva place for an ambush. Begging your pardon, Mr. Smith, but there is no cover."

"Please make a note of both opinions, Master Wheeler," Smith said. "There is truth in each."

Jacob nodded, and did his best to sketch the terrain. The ledger was already filled with sketches of rivers and mountains and trails; Jacob had carefully noted the distance traveled between each.

From Saint Louis, the explorers had followed the Mississippi only a few miles north to the confluence of the Lower Missouri. While oaring and cordelling their flatboat up the river, they were amazed to see a small packet steamboat pass them going upriver; it was the only steamboat they saw on the Missouri during their journey, but Smith commented that it was a harbinger of the future.

At Arrow Rock Landing, the head of the Santa Fe Trail, they sold the keelboats and bought horses and pack mules. Three of the men got roaring drunk at Huston's Tavern, and Smith fired them on the spot. In the morning, they struck out on the old trail.

The men paralleled the south bank of the Missouri River, passed Lexington and Fort Osage and crossed the Little Blue River. Near the fledgling town of Independence they turned to the southwest and soon had left the young state of Missouri—and the union of states proper—behind. Most of the vast Louisiana Purchase of 1803, which had doubled the size of the nation and caused Jefferson to send Lewis and Clark on a journey of discovery, remained unorganized; although some of it had already been settled by the Spanish or French, the more remote parts still had not been explored by Europeans, much less mapped.

At Council Grove, on the Neosho River, the men rested for the day, in the shade of the great oak where, just three years before, in 1825, three smiling U.S. commissioners had given the Great and Little Osage tribes eight hundred dollars each in cash and merchandise for free passage to Mexicans and Americans through their territory.

The explorers followed the rivers west until the waterways became what Jacob would have called a ditch back home, and then they struck out across the plains, using Smith's encyclopedic knowledge of landmarks to guide them. They fed themselves on elk and bison, which seemed so numerous that Jacob reckoned there were more buffalo in the world than there could possibly be human beings.

Sometimes, usually near the rising or setting of the sun, Jacob would spy on a lonely hilltop a group of Indians enigmatically watching the group of white explorers. Always, they had their backs to the sun so Jacob could make out few details of their dress or demeanor. But Jacob knew that, with the sun at their advantage, they were studying the mountain men in great detail.

Leaving the plains behind, Smith and his troop followed mountain paths that Jacob thought not even a mountain goat could traverse. "Do you think that pass is passable?" he had asked Fletcher when confronted with one particularly treacherous trail.

"Hell, youth," Fletcher had snorted, "that path ain't even jack-assable."

Weeks later, they reached Santa Fe at the base of the Sangre de Cristo Mountains. Santa Fe, the capital city of the province of New Mexico, in the young Republic of Mexico, was already 219 years old—thirteen years older, in fact, than the famous Plymouth colony Jacob had heard so much about while growing up.

Jacob looked around at the sleepy adobe village. It seemed as lazy to him as Saint Louis had seemed frantic. Nothing seemed to be moving, except for the cattle in the town plaza, which was being used as a makeshift corral.

"Beg your pardon, sir," Jacob said, "but why in the world would anybody want to come here?"

Smith had laughed, squatted down, and drew his patch knife from his belt. "Observe, Master Wheeler," he said and then began to sketch a map on the ground with the tip of the knife. "There are two routes to the west, when you boil things down. Both start at Saint Louis, and neither is as the crow flies. You either follow the Upper Missouri, as Lewis and Clark did, which snakes to the northwest and eventually reaches the Pacific Ocean way up here."

Jacob opened the ledger book and began to copy the map.

"Or you take the southern route, which was blazed by the Spanish long ago, and as a trade route by the Indians before them, and meanders because the route is limited to manageable distances between watering holes," Smith said. "You eventually arrive at this crossroads called Santa Fe, about a thousand miles from Saint Louis. Now, up until the Mexican revolution a few years ago, we couldn't take the Santa Fe route because Spain didn't allow trade or colonization with speakers of English."

Jacob nodded.

"If we were headed for Mexico City, it would be a tough route—in fact, the Spanish called it the Journey of Death—but it would be a known route, an established route. But we're not going south. We're now striking off to the north and west, to find a route to California, and between here and there is land that no white man has yet laid eyes on."

Now, as Jacob sketched the meadow on a fresh page in the ledger, he wondered if they were indeed the first mountain men to see it. As he glanced up from the page, he noticed a stirring in the brush at the edge of the tree line, a few dozen yards away.

"Could be an elk," Fletcher said.

Jacob closed the ledger and slipped it into his pocket, cocked his grandfather's rifle, and held it at the ready. When a bear cub darted into the meadow toward them, Jacob laughed and uncocked the rifle.

While Smith and Fletcher stepped back, Jacob stepped forward, intent on touching the animal. Fletcher grasped the tail of Jacob's coat, pulling him back.

The cub raced passed, followed by another. Then the brush exploded as the mother grizzly followed. Her brown fur was tipped with silver, she had a large hump behind her head, and she was moving as fast as a man could ride on horseback.

Smith and Fletcher fired in succession. Both balls found their mark, but failed to slow the bear. They did, however, enrage the animal.

Jacob dropped his rifle and ran. The grizzly was upon the men in an instant, and with a powerful swipe of its paw, it knocked Smith to the ground. He curled into a ball as the grizzly mauled him. Fletcher picked up Jacob's discarded gun, placed the muzzle point-blank against the back of the bear's head, and pulled the trigger.

Jacob watched in horror as Smith struggled from beneath the dead bear. While the cubs frolicked over the body of their mother, Smith stood by his own power.

"Good Lord," Fletcher said.

Jedediah Smith's head was covered with blood, except the places where his skull gleamed white. His scalp and one of his ears hung by a ribbon of skin.

"Indeed," Smith said. "Praise the Lord for providing us

with meat for our supper. Master Wheeler, fetch my saddle wallet. You'll find a needle and thread."

The other mountain men had come running, and Jacob nearly fell before he was steadied by the others.

"Yes, sir," Jacob said.

Smith sat on a rock and took a sip of water from a canteen handed him. Then, he poured the rest of the water over his head, cleaning away much of the blood. Jacob had returned now, and Smith beckoned to him.

"Mend my scalp, Master Wheeler."

Jacob grimaced. Gingerly, he flipped the scalp back onto the top of Smith's head. The mountain men looked away, and even Fletcher had to suck in his breath.

"Sir, I've never done anything like this before," Jacob said.

"Neither have I, son," Smith said.

Jacob's hands were shaking so badly that he could not thread the needle.

"Perhaps Mr. Fletcher . . ."

"No, son, I gave you an order," he said.

"Don't you think that will hurt, sir?"

"I do, son, but I think it will hurt the person being sewed upon more than the sewer."

Smith grasped Jacob's wrists to steady them. Jacob managed to thread the needle, then proceeded with the gruesome task while Smith sat with his open Bible on his lap. When Jacob had gotten the scalp back in the approximate position it had been before the grizzly had removed it, Smith felt it gingerly. His ear was still flapping.

"Don't forget the ear," Smith said. "My wife has grown rather fond of it."

Jacob nodded and touched the needle to Smith's good ear.

"The *other* ear, son," Smith said. "And I should warn you that I'm a stickler about having my ears on straight."

The mountain men laughed, and Jacob nodded.

TEN

The Medicine Wheel
Beneath Sacred Bear's Lodge (Devil's Tower)
Near present-day Wyoming—South Dakota border

The rock was as big as Loved by the Buffalo himself, and as he rolled it closer to the top of the hill, the more difficult the task became. The boulder was shaped like an egg, with a rough and irregular surface that left his palms bloody, and it was so impossible to steady or balance it that the boy came to believe the spirit of the rock was fighting him. Loved by the Buffalo sank to his knees, sweat pouring from his aching body, blood running down his wrists. He was trying to muscle the rock up to the plateau that was home to the sacred medicine wheel, and always he lost his grip and watched helplessly as the rock rolled back down to the bottom of the hill.

Diving Eagle had assigned Loved by the Buffalo this mindless and seemingly unending task to break his spirit. He had been filled with jealousy since seeing the boy restore life to the bird following the sweat lodge ceremony. Diving Eagle had told Loved by the Buffalo that he was not allowed to see the medicine wheel at the plateau atop the hill until he managed to get the rock to the very top. This, surely, would prove too much for the boy who refused to talk.

But to Diving Eagle's dismay, not only was the boy's spirit unbroken, but it seemed to gain strength from the task. Loved by the Buffalo would often take all morning to roll the boulder halfway to the top of the hill, and when it inevitably would roll back down, the boy betrayed no disappointment. He simply started over again.

As the days passed, Loved by the Buffalo moved the rock closer and closer to the plateau that held the great medicine wheel. Then, as weeks faded into months and months turned into a year, the boy became a young man.

One summer, at dusk on the night that light would have its most complete victory over the dark on earth, Loved by the Buffalo—with his new body and the muscles that had been honed from more than a year of mindlessly pushing the boulder uphill—managed to bring the boulder to the very lip of the plateau. Just as he was about to lose control of the boulder for the thousandth time, he turned his back to the stone and braced it with his legs. Finally overwhelmed with the futility of the task, he blinked back tears. He was about to give up and let the boulder roll down the hill one last time when he heard the cry of an eagle. He looked above him.

With outstretched wings, the great bird was wheeling on the thermals, and he began to speak to Loved by the Buffalo. The eagle began to teach him a song, a song that came from *Wakan Tanka*, which gladdened the heart of Loved by the Buffalo and gave him strength. Loved by the Buffalo began to sing the song to himself.

Grasping the largest rock within reach, he jammed it precisely in the spot beneath the irregular surface of the boulder to keep it from rolling back down. He felt the spirit of the rock relent. Carefully, Loved by the Buffalo turned back around, braced his palms against the stone, and gave one last push.

It rolled easily all the way to the top of the hill, tipped over the lip of the plateau, and rolled for a few yards before coming to rest on top of the hill.

Loved by the Buffalo stood atop the plateau, breathing deeply, his body bathed in the last rays of the setting sun. The medicine wheel was before him, and beyond that, the hills and valleys and streams of the sacred *Paha Sapa*. On the horizon, a flock of geese undulated like a ribbon floating on the breeze.

Loved by the Buffalo walked with deliberation to the center of the medicine wheel, then dropped to both knees in reverence before a cairn on which rested an enormous buffalo skull. Eagle feathers fluttered in the breeze from the tips of the great skull's horns, and the skull itself was painted with power symbols: sun, moon, stars, lightning. There were other tokens scattered on and around the pile of rocks: the skulls of lesser animals; bits of bone, some of them human finger bones from long-dead holy men; medicine bags filled with secret things.

Loved by the Buffalo stood and carefully noted the twenty evenly spaced spokes that radiated from the cairn in the center of the wheel. Six smaller cairns were placed at locations around the rim of the wheel, but these weren't evenly spaced. Loved by the Buffalo's brow furrowed in thought. He slowly walked the three-hundred-foot perimeter, examining each cairn.

The great medicine wheel was discovered when the Lakota had moved into this country before memory began, and if it had been built by men—which many doubted—then it had been built at the direction of *Wakan Tanka*.

Loved by the Buffalo threw his head back, inhaled deeply, and filled his lungs with the air of the *Paha Sapa*. He returned to the center of the medicine wheel to give thanks for the magical time between daylight and dark, which was the opening between the worlds of the flesh and the spirit. Tonight was an especially powerful night, because it was the shortest night of the year—the summer solstice.

It was nearly twilight now, and stars were beginning to appear in the sky, with the star that represented Buffalo Calf Woman shining brightly in the east. Opposite, the sun was a burning disk dipping into the western horizon.

As the last rays played on Loved by the Buffalo's face, he realized that the sun was in alignment with the most prominent of the spokes of the medicine wheel. Smiling, he went to the stone he had struggled for so long to roll up the hill. Grasping it in both hands, he lifted it as if it weighed no more than a water skin. He had never before experienced such strength. He walked over to where the last rays of sunlight were following the spoke to the center cairn, and then he carefully placed the stone in line with the spoke, the light, the cairn.

Watching from his hiding spot behind an outcropping of boulders to the west, Diving Eagle clenched his fists so tightly that his clawlike fingernails drew blood from his palms. How had Loved by the Buffalo known where to place the stone without being told? Diving Eagle wept bitterly. Instead of breaking a boy's spirit, he had created a man.

ELEVEN

Bitterroot Range
The Clark Fork of the Missouri River
They Shot Many Buffalo (1830)

The beaver had been caught in the jaws of the steel trap, attracted by the castoreum that had been taken from the sex glands of another of its kind. After the trap closed, the drowning line had taken the beaver underwater. But beavers are semiaquatic mammals and consequently have evolved an uncanny ability to hold their breath underwater; after twenty minutes, when Lebeck came upon it, the animal was still struggling against the line.

The stream was fed mostly by glacial melt and Lebeck, who was wading in water up to his midthighs, was freezing. While he was glad to find another beaver (a pound of plews fetched nearly six dollars now), he was unhappy to find the animal still alive. Taking a hatchet handle from his belt, he brought the trap up and held the writhing animal at arm's length while he clubbed it to death. Thunder Heart Woman, who was heavy with child, looked away as the blood flecked the white face of her husband.

Then Lebeck tossed the carcass of the animal on the bank for Thunder Heart Woman to skin and butcher. Not only did Lebeck expect the animals to provide their fortune, they also provided most of their diet.

Lebeck could not feel his legs in the 40 degree water, but he forced himself to take the bottle of castoreum from his pocket, smear some of the brown substance on the trigger, then set the trap.

Suddenly Lebeck was aware that Thunder Heart Woman was gesturing to him from the bank. She cupped a hand behind her ear, then motioned behind her. Lebeck could hear something moving through the brush on the mountainside far behind her. He saw glimpses of a Blackfoot hunting party riding down the old elk trail.

Lebeck took his rifle from the log where he had stowed it above the water and moved as slowly and quietly through the water as possible toward the bank, even though his heart was in his throat. When he finally reached Thunder Heart Woman, he hid the bloody beaver carcass behind a rock and wedged his Lakota bride beneath a pile of driftwood, while he crouched over her with the rifle. His lips were moving in a prayer that the hunting party had not seen, heard, or smelled them.

That night, in a lean-to that Lebeck had made by throwing logs over a ravine and covering them with dirt, Thunder Heart Woman roasted the beaver over an open fire. Beside her was a pile of beaver plews, which she was preparing to bundle to add to the growing pile, which they would strap to the mule come spring. Meanwhile, Lebeck was stretching a pelt on a wooden frame for drying, and as he did he hummed "O Sussanah" to himself and thought of the riches the plews represented.

"Good as gold," Lebeck said and winked at Thunder Heart Woman.

She smiled, but her eyes showed no joy. It was not that Lebeck treated her badly; she simply missed her family. While one hand cradled her stomach and the baby inside, the other went to the obsidian amulet around her neck.

The day that Lebeck had waded from the freezing water and hidden Thunder Heart Woman and himself from the Blackfoot hunting party, Jacob Wheeler slumped in the saddle and regarded a rock outcrop covered by curious carvings in the middle of the Mojave Desert. It was so hot that Jacob felt as if he had been baked in an oven. The company had been in the desert for weeks now, they had eaten some of their pack animals, and they were running dangerously low on water.

They needed to keep moving, slowly but surely, in hopes of reaching the next watering hole. But Jacob could not resist lingering in the shade of the outcropping and studying the carvings.

The petroglyphs were of human figures, arms and legs outstretched, with curious undulating lines and spirals emanating from them. The faces were distinctly human, but odd, some with bared teeth and fierce eyes, and all with lines and dots on their faces. Jacob wondered if they were meant to frighten interlopers.

Jacob glanced ahead, where through the waves of heat emanating from the desert floor he could see Jedediah Smith sitting ramrod-straight in the saddle. The rest of the party had proceeded forward while Jacob had lingered at the rock carvings. The image of Smith wavered and danced, mimicking the lines that radiated from the stick figures on the rock carving. Suddenly, there seemed to be two Smiths, then four—this time riding toward him. Jacob rubbed his eyes and looked again.

There *were* four riders approaching fast, but none of them were Smith. They rode gracefully, with hands holding bows with nocked arrows pointed downward for the moment, and their faces had the same strips and dots that were on the rock carvings.

Jacob had his rifle across the saddle, and with as little movement as possible, he cocked the hammer. Then the Mojave warriors were upon him, their horses bobbing and weaving around him, and Jacob forced himself to study a point on the horizon with apparent unconcern, even though his heart felt like it would burst in his chest. Then, following his instinct, he shifted the rifle to his left hand, looked the biggest warrior in the eye, and extended his arm for a handshake.

The bows curved and the iron trade points of the arrows came up, pointed at Jacob's chest. He held his hand steady, his hand open, his fingers extended.

Over the shaft of the arrow, the big warrior glanced at the others and met confused faces. Then he glanced back at Jacob and carefully considered the gesture. Slowly, he eased the tension on the bow string, then removed the arrow from the bow and held both in his left hand. He leaned forward and extended his hand in the same manner as Jacob had. Their palms met and their hands closed.

Jacob gestured drinking. One of the warriors handed him a skin of water.

"Thank you," Jacob said and, from his pocket, took a plug of tobacco. "This is from some of your distant relations back east."

Taking the tobacco, the warriors broke out in laughter. Jacob laughed as well, and then drank deeply. The big warrior turned his horse and gestured for Jacob to follow.

An hour later, as most of the company plunged into a river that the Mojave warriors had brought them to, Jacob sketched from memory the petroglyphs, and on the same ledger page wrote:

Today my life was handed to me as a gift.

Smith had told Jacob that the tribe called themselves the People Along the River, while they referred to the mountain men as the beaver eaters. In one of the Mojave huts, Jacob had taken notes while Smith and Fletcher negotiated with the chief the purchase of a half dozen horses to replace the ones that had been consumed. The bargaining was done mostly through gestures, the few words of Mojave that Fletcher knew, and drawings of the number of horses needed in the dirt. The deal was finally made for a bolt of bright red cloth, two dozen trade arrow points, several piles of glass beads, and some cheap Green River knives.

The chief brought out a clay jar, removed the lid, and held it out. Fletcher took the jar and took a whiff. The milky liquid inside, fermented from cactus fruit, smelled strongly of alcohol.

Fletcher smiled, took a swig, and made a face that was a mixture of pleasure and pain. He coughed, wiped his mouth, and asked, "Good Lord, Chief, what is this wonderful stuff?"

"Maricopa."

"Maricopa is just dandy!"

"Dandy," the chief repeated as Fletcher took another swig. Then, as the white liquid dribbled down his chin, he noticed that the chief had pulled a young woman from the darkness of the hut. The chief said something to her, and the woman matter-of-factly shed her buckskins. She was beautiful, with glistening blue-black hair, big dark eyes, and skin that had the hues of the desert at sunset. Jacob had never seen a full-grown woman naked, and for a moment, he forgot to breathe.

"Dandy?" the chief asked.

"Oh, very dandy!" Fletcher said.

The chief said something and two more females appeared. One of them, a beautiful Mojave girl about Jacob's age, took his hand in hers.

The girl attempted to lead Jacob to the rear of the hut, but Jacob glanced back at Smith and saw the well-worn Bible beneath his crossed arms. The girl tugged again and looked at Jacob with pleading eyes.

Jacob waved his thanks at the chief and began walking toward Smith, who was quietly watching.

As the men drank maricopa and swam with the Mojave girls or sought them out in the huts, Jedediah Smith sat on a rock overlooking the river. Jacob sat on a rock below him.

"You are a most unusual young man," Smith said.

Jacob shook his head.

"Then what are you doing up here with me instead of down there with the rest of the men?"

"You did it, sir," Jacob said. "Not until now did I appreciate how much I wanted to be like you."

Smith stared at the sky for a moment. "I'm honored, son."

Jacob shook his head. "But I'm just an ape of Jedediah Smith. I resist wickedness for the moment, but come tomorrow I'll regret it all and wish I had been as dandy about things as Fletcher. So what does that make me?"

"A human being."

"A mighty poor one," Jacob said. "When you ordered me to sew your scalp back on, I knew I was made to drip sweat on a hot anvil for the rest of my life. Sir, I knew I was a coward."

Smith smiled. "But the point is that you did it. You did not allow the circumstance to dictate your action. You overcame your animal nature to run and became something higher. He fashioned us a little above the animals and a little below the angels. The west is a place on a map, not a way to live."

Weeks later, inside a crude lean-to, Thunder Heart Woman stared into the darkness. Lebeck was snoring heavily beside her. On the elk skin between them, their new baby was sleeping quietly. Thunder Heart Woman had named her Laughs All the Time, although Lebeck insisted on referring to her as Marie.

Outside, an owl hooted. Thunder Heart Woman sat up. The owl hooted again, and Thunder Heart Woman decided that the owl call was made by no bird. She shook Lebeck awake, and while he drowsily grabbed his rifle, she took a pistol from the elk skin beside her. It was a .45 caliber single-shot flintlock pistol. As Lebeck went to the lean-to door and removed a thick branch that barred the door, she used both hands to cock the heavy pistol.

Lebeck opened the door a crack and peered out.

There was the snap of bowstring, and before Lebeck could react, the arrow had buried itself deep into his gut. He stumbled back, crying out in pain, then broke the shaft of the arrow and threw it down.

A Blackfoot warrior came through the door, bow drawn and face painted in white clay to resemble a grinning skull. He sent another arrow into Lebeck. This one hit him squarely in the chest with a sickening thud. Lebeck gasped and leveled his rifle and pulled the trigger. The .54 caliber ball blew the warrior out of his black moccasins and out the door.

Then in rushed three more warriors, hair heavy with grease and feathers, faces painted with circles and stripes in white, red, and black.

Thunder Heart Woman positioned herself in front of her baby.

Lebeck still had the full-length arrow ticking from his chest, and no time to reload, so he turned the rifle around and clubbed the second warrior so hard in the forehead with the butt of the heavy rifle that blood and brains seemed to dribble from his temple as he fell to the ground.

With both hands, Thunder Heart Woman pointed her horse pistol at the third warrior, who was advancing with a stone club in his hand. Looking confidently over the barrel, she pulled the trigger. An instant later the warrior dropped dead with a large leaden ball embedded in his heart.

"Good," Thunder Heart Woman said in Lakota.

There was only one warrior left. Lebeck advanced toward him with the rifle over his shoulder, ready to swing. The warrior glanced at his dead friends on the floor and the open door behind him. With an iron trade tomahawk in his hand, he was backing toward the door.

Suddenly the full-length arrow in Lebeck's chest got tangled in some branches sticking from the lean-to wall. He grasped the arrow shaft and tried to break it, but the point was buried deeply in his sternum and the pain was too intense to allow the pressure needed to snap the flexible willow shaft.

The last warrior saw his chance and threw the tomahawk at Lebeck. The blade buried itself in Lebeck's forehead, and as the trapper sank to the ground, his eyes moved toward Thunder Heart Woman and their baby.

The baby was awake and crying. Thunder Heart Woman did not have time to reload the pistol, so she drew the skinning knife from her belt and jerked down one of the heavy traps from the wall of the lean-to. She assumed a fighting position, and as the last warrior approached, teeth bared and hate in his eyes, she kept the blade moving and the trap swinging at the end of its heavy chain. The warrior advanced, but Thunder Heart Woman fought like a whirlwind, and in a moment, he retreated with many cuts and bruises.

About that time, the warrior who had taken the rifle stock to the skull sat up, felt for the bloody mess at his temple, and was surprised to find an ordinary bruise. He took it in stride, just another gift from *Wakan Tanka*.

He managed to crawl behind the woman as she was fighting the other warrior, and quickly grabbed the crying baby.

Thunder Heart Woman threw herself at the kidnapper of her child, flailing and kicking and biting, and managed to bite a chunk of flesh out of his cheek but the other warrior pinioned her arms from behind and forced her down to the bloody elk skin. Then he got her in a headlock that made her feel as if she would suffocate. Her head was jerked back, exposing her neck.

The warrior with the bloody hole in his cheek drew his knife and positioned it to make a clean swipe of her throat. But Thunder Heart Woman managed to get her right hand free and she grasped the blade of the knife, blood running from between her fingers. Even as she refused to let go of the knife, the warrior used his other hand to rip away her clothing. He forced her legs apart with his powerful thighs, then clumsily raped her.

He smiled and said, "A dog Lakota killed my brother."

Thunder Heart Woman released her grasp on the blade of the knife, and the knife fell heavily on the elk skin. The other warrior still had her in a neck lock, and as he tightened the grasp, spots danced before her eyes and her lungs burned for air.

She closed her eyes and said a prayer to *Wakan Tanka* and silently asked her brother Loved by the Buffalo to carry the message.

With her own bloody hand, Thunder Heart Woman sought that hand of her three-week-old baby. But the child had already been taken from the lean-to.

TWELVE

Mexican Province of California

Thirteen weeks after the company had been introduced to maricopa and the other delights of Mojave culture, they reached the Pacific Ocean.

It was a few minutes before sunset, and the sun hung like a ball of molten iron over the lead-colored ocean. Birds wheeled and screeched in the distance, and here and there the waves were capped with silver.

Jacob Wheeler had never seen an ocean before, and while the waves lapped close to his moccasins, he planted the butt of his grandfather's rifle in the sand, rested his arms over the muzzle, and marveled that he had traveled so far west that there was no more west to go. The other men, including Fletcher, were already wading into the water, splashing and cavorting like children.

Jedediah Smith stood behind Jacob and regarded the transformation the young man had undergone since appearing before him wearing stinking clothes in Saint Louis. Jacob's eyes were clear, his jaw was firm, and his body had become as lean and hard as that of any warrior Jedediah Smith had ever encountered. But his will had been sharpened more than anything; it was as if something dull and barely useful had been honed against the wheel of adversity. Jacob was still a boy, and had far to go before he would gain the experience of Fletcher or the courage of some of the other men, but Smith saw in Jacob something he had not found in great supply among the rest: character. Smith moved near and placed his hand on Jacob's shoulder.

"Most beautiful thing I've ever seen," Jacob said. Then, after thinking for a moment, added, "Well, almost."

Smith smiled. "All the work of the Lord."

The men suddenly stopped splashing about. They were standing waist-deep in the water, looking past Jacob and Smith at the beach dunes beyond. Five Mexican soldiers were swooping down upon them.

The mountain men's rifles and other weapons were scattered along the beach, and the horses were staked several hundred yards away. Jacob watched as the soldiers approached, and when Smith could feel his shoulder muscles tense and knew he was about to pick up his rifle, Smith said gently, "Steady, son."

The soldiers wore heavy armor and Spanish-style hats with peacock feathers. They carried shields bearing elaborate insignias. Each soldier was also heavily armed, with lance, saber, musket, and pistol.

The *Soldados de Cuera* leveled their lances at Jacob and Smith, while their commander brought himself to his full height in the saddle.

"Por la autoridad del gobierno, ustedes son nuestros prisioneros," he said. *"Capitán Hernando Espina de Salamanca, sus ordenes."*

The men of the company had left the water and, led by Fletcher, were walking slowly up the beach. They were within running distance of their weapons now.

"This young peacock says his name is Salamanca," one of the mountain men translated. Then he suppressed a smile before he added the rest. "He also says that under the authority of the governor of California, we're his prisoners."

"Tell him that perhaps it has escaped his notice," Smith said, "but that he is outnumbered four to one."

The Spanish-speaking mountain man spoke to Salamanca, then hesitated before translating his reply.

"Well?" Smith demanded.

"He says he'd arrest us even if we numbered a thousand."

Smith looked at the determination in the captain's eyes. "I believe him."

The mountain men were taken to the Mission of San Gabriel and housed in a single spacious room, which would be their prison until their fate was decided. Although they remained under guard, they were treated more like guests than prisoners, and they took their meals at a long table in the courtyard beneath the shade of eucalyptus trees. They were often visited by Padre José Bernardino Sanchez, a fat middle-aged priest who was more interested in learning about their motives than in saving their souls. Unobserved Padre José had examined the company's goods, including their animals; on several of the horses was the brand MSG Mission de San Gabriel.

The lancers had captured—and hanged—a number of Mojave warriors who had been caught with horses stolen from the mission. The last warrior was hanged in the courtyard, within sight of Smith's company, as a warning. At any moment, the Americans could also be hanged for the stolen horses.

Before the body in the courtyard had stopped twitching, Fletcher had guffawed and said, "I reckon the Californios aren't nearly as friendly in their customs as the Mojaves are."

His comment broke the tension. The mountain men laughed. Then Fletcher added, "Don't know about you gents, but when the time comes, I'm going to choose bayonet and ball instead of dancing on air."

That night, in the rectory of the mission, after Captain Salamanca and Padre José dined by candlelight, they played chess and discussed the fate of the Americans.

"They say they bought the horses from the Indians," the soldier said. He pushed his queen across the board in a bold but foolish move. "Check."

The priest made a noncommittal gesture. "I believe them. But that is of no consequence. The danger is that they came here by land and not by sea. For centuries, we have been protected from invasion by the difficulty of the sea journey and the impossibility of crossing the mountains. If we release them, they will tell others, and more Americans might come."

"Not if we kill these first," Salamanca said.

The priest frowned, disappointed in his young friend's failure to think ahead.

"It is your move," Salamanca urged. He had failed to notice that by attacking with his queen, he had unpinned one of the padre's bishops and left his king open to a fatal attack.

"But if we kill them, it is certain other Americans will come seeking vengeance," the priest said. "If we release them, we are only risking a small possibility that others will come."

Deliberately, the priest moved his bishop across the board. His rook was already in place to take advantage of Salamanca's mistake, and the soldier had not even noticed. "Checkmate. That is three games in a row."

Salamanca tried not to betray his frustration.

"Explain to their leader that they are being released through the generosity of the Republic of Mexico," the priest said. "Return all of their animals and weapons to them. But explain that they must depart from California immediately and not return, upon pain of death."

THIRTEEN

Somewhere in present-day Montana
They Shot Many Buffalo (1830)

"How much?" Running Fox asked.

The trapper smiled. It was an old musket, and nearly worthless, but to a young Lakota, it was big medicine indeed. He had already noticed that Running Fox had come prepared to trade, because he had come laden with beaver skins.

The trapper looked over his crude spread. His horses had knocked down the rails of the corral and were grazing free nearby. He hadn't felt like running his trapline in two weeks, and for the past few days, he had been holed up in the cabin fighting a high fever. Now, across his face and beneath his filthy red flannel shirt, he was covered with angry red pustules. It was as if somebody had peppered him with a shotgun, and the birdshot had lodged just beneath his skin and festered.

The trapper knew the disease was smallpox, but he was hanging on to the hope that some had survived. He also knew how contagious the disease was. During the French and Indian War, the British had used blankets infected with smallpox to kill more enemies than bullets ever had.

"Easy there," the trapper said in broken Lakota as Running Fox swung the musket in his direction. "That piece is loaded."

Running Fox grinned.

"Try her out," the trapper said in English.

Running Fox looked puzzled. The trapper held a pretend

gun and worked the trigger. Running Fox brought the gun awkwardly to eye level, pointed it at a branch at the top of a nearby tree, and jerked the trigger. He did not have the gun against his shoulder, so the stock slammed into his face, knocking him to the ground.

The trapper laughed so hard he began to cough; then he wiped his mouth with the palm of his right hand. Running Fox sat up, dazed, his cheek bruised and blood running from the corner of his grinning mouth.

"How much?" he asked.

FOURTEEN

Near present-day Grandy, Utah
1830 (They Shot Many Buffalo)

Relieved that it was almost dawn, the mountain man who had been left to stand the last watch of the night filled his clay pipe and took a burning stick from the well-banked fire. He brought the stick close to the pipe and lit the tobacco. As he sucked the smoke deep into his lungs, the stick flared brightly in time to each puff. It made the perfect target.

A Mojave arrow zipped from the darkness and embedded itself deep in his stomach. As the mountain man doubled over, another arrow struck him in the back, and before he could scream, a third pierced his throat. All of the arrows were tipped with the metal points the company had traded for horses months before.

The sentry pitched forward into the fire, and his clothes caught fire, blazing brightly. His powder horn began to fizz, like fireworks, sputtering and spewing, and then erupted with an explosion that left even the ears of the Mojave war party ringing.

Suddenly the camp erupted in chaos, as the mountain men realized they were under attack. Arrows fell like rain as the company scrambled for their weapons.

Jacob clutched his grandfather's rifle and started to rise, but Fletcher pulled him back down. Meanwhile, Smith threw a blanket over the fire, extinguishing the light, which was allowing the arrows to find their targets.

The warriors were suddenly among them, hacking and

slashing their way through the company. Fletcher pulled Jacob out of the melee and toward the safety of some nearby rocks he sensed rather than saw. As they heard the screams of men whose scalps were being lifted while they still clung to life, Jedediah Smith joined them behind the rocks.

"Shouldn't we fight?" Jacob asked.

"This is no fight," Fletcher said. "It's a slaughter."

Quietly, they made their way up the mountain to higher ground.

When morning broke, they had a good view of the bloody campsite below. The Mojave warriors were dividing up the weapons and the horses, and bloody scalps hung from their belts.

One of the warriors, however, was ignoring the loot. He had noticed that the number of dead did not seem to match the number of places where the men had slept, and as the light grew stronger, he picked up the trail along which the trio had escaped. With a shout, he alerted others.

"Time to move, gentlemen," Smith said.

"Let's go, youth," Fletcher said. "Looks like you're going to get your fight after all. Considering the odds, it would be to our benefit to pick the spot. And dammit, they seemed such a friendly folk."

They moved quickly up the mountain, but the war party below equaled their speed.

"This is it," Fletcher said as they reached a fortresslike rock. "It don't get any better, I'm afraid."

They scrambled behind the rock and Fletcher began placing in front of him the things he wouldn't have time to fumble with: powder horn, balls, ramrod, and a loaded pistol for a final shot. Smith began to prepare as well, but with less hurry.

Jacob looked around him. He felt numb, but something inside him was still working, hoping for a way out.

"Get busy," Fletcher said. "Don't sell your life cheap."

"Look," Jacob stammered. He pointed toward the rock face behind them. It was split vertically, and inside the crevice it seemed as dark as midnight. "I think we could . . ."

"The boy is right," Smith said, gathering up his things. "It's a cave. We just might be able to squeeze into it, with a little help from the Lord. And once we're in, it would be mighty hard for somebody to squeeze in after us without us braining him."

"Damn," Fletcher said. "I knew there was a reason I felt good about bringing you with us from the start."

"I wish you'd left me in Saint Louis," Jacob said glumly.

Smith forced Jacob to slip into the crevice first so that, in the event the bigger men got hopelessly jammed, the boy would not be trapped on the outside.

The cave smelled like mud, bat guano, and darkness but Jacob plunged blindly forward, and as he did, he felt like he left half of the skin on his hands and elbows on the rough walls. After he had traveled for a dozen yards or so, holding his breath, hunching his shoulders, and sucking his breath in, the crevice opened up into a proper cave.

A few moments after Jacob fell on the clay floor of the cave, Fletcher and Smith followed. He didn't understand how the men could have squeezed through so quickly until he heard the war whoops behind them.

Suddenly, a Mojave was inside the cave with them, and then another. The second had a rifle. Although his eyes had not yet adjusted to the gloom, Smith gauged the warrior's position from the sound of his advancing footsteps, drew back his rifle like a club, and drove the warrior to the ground. Then, by feel, Smith was on top of the fallen Mojave and drawing his knife across his throat.

Meanwhile, Fletcher found the rifle barrel of the second warrior and pulled him into the cave. Almost in the same motion, Fletcher had pulled the big bowie knife from its sheath and driven it through the Mojave into the clay below. The rifle went off, momentarily freezing the action inside the cave as if a bolt of lightning had struck, and Jacob saw that the big warrior had managed to pulled himself into the cave. He was on Jacob in a moment, and the youth felt a knife ripping the fabric of his shirt. Simultaneously, the cavern was lit up again as Jedediah Smith blew the warrior's head off. He fell, still gripping the knife in the hand that had once shaken Jacob's hand. Covered with blood, Jacob fell back in horror onto the bloody clay.

The rifle blasts had disturbed a colony of bats on the ceiling of the cave. They began streaming out, creating a rush of wind and a rain of bat guano, and for a moment, Jacob feared his senses would leave him.

The bats and the killing of the three warriors were seen as particularly bad omens by the rest of the war party, and they temporarily ceased their attack.

Fletcher paused. Jacob caught Fletcher looking at him intently.

"You know, I think it's time I stopped calling you youth. I only call one person on earth mister, and that's Mr. Smith. But I'm pleased to call you cousin."

After an hour, the trio in the cave knew the war party had rethought their strategy. Drums and chanting began outside the cave . . . and they smelled smoke.

Fletcher was ripping the tail of his flannel shirt into strips to cover his mouth. Already the smoke was pooling in the roof of the cave. Smith was ripping cloth as well. The smoke brought tears to Jacob's eyes and burned his throat, and to make matters worse, arrows began to whiz through the crevice and land in the clay floor.

"Well, looks like they're coming in after us," Fletcher said. He clapped Jacob on the shoulder. "You're the equal of any ten mountain men on any street in Saint Louie. I'm proud to ride with you, cousin."

"Thank you," Jacob said, blinking back tears.

"Mr. Wheeler," Smith said.

"Yes, sir?"

"The Good Book says that for every thing there is a season," he said. "There is a time to heal, and a time to sow. Now is the time to kill."

The next few minutes were a blur to Jacob, who was temporarily blinded by the smoke. But Fletcher and Smith seemed to know what was coming. A Mojave pushed through the flames with a war whoop, and Smith shot him. Then another came in. Fletcher laid him low with the Arkansas toothpick, and then another warrior jumped Fletcher. The warrior's knife drove deep into Fletcher's ribs.

Jacob seized the Mojave by the hair, pulled his throat taut, and then ran his own knife beneath the warrior's jawline. Then he plunged the knife into the warrior's heart, bathing himself in hot blood.

Smith nodded approvingly. "Bully for you, young man."

The mountain men had beaten the war party back once again, but Jacob knew they could not stand another assault.

Smith had gathered up a bundle of arrows and torn some clothing from the dead warriors to make a torch. He sprinkled it with powder and, using his flint and steel, had it blazing in a few moments.

The torch revealed Fletcher sitting against the cave wall, holding his chest with his right hand. When he smiled weakly, Smith nodded. Then Smith observed the smoke drifting deeper into the cave.

"Mr. Fletcher," he said, "the smoke is drifting."

"What's that mean?" Jacob asked.

Fletcher smiled and Smith replied, "It means there's a way out."

"Let's go," Jacob said, holding his hand out for Fletcher. "We'll help you."

Fletcher shook his head. "I'm a gone beaver. Time to hang up the fiddle. You two follow the smoke. I'll keep our dandy friends amused." In his lap were his pistol and his rifle. With difficulty, he held out the bowie knife and sheath. "Take it, cousin."

"No," Jacob said.

"Better you have it than an ungrateful Mojave," Fletcher said. "Learn to use it. Things get pretty personal out west."

FIFTEEN

The dance looking at the sun was one of the seven sacred rites of the Lakota. It had first been held after Buffalo Calf Woman gave the people the sacred medicine pipe. It was always held during the full moon of the Moon of Fattening or the Moon of Black Cherries—June or July by the white man's calendar. In addition to the sacred pipe, there was a long and exact list of tools required for the ceremony: tobacco, red willow bark, sweet grass, a bone knife, a flint ax, buffalo tallow, a tanned calf hide, rabbit skins, eagle plumes, red earth paint, blue paint, a rawhide bag, eagle tail feathers, whistles made from the wing bones of a spotted eagle, and a buffalo skull.

When the tribe had gathered these things, a very old woman, representing one of the visages of Buffalo Calf Woman, led the people's virgins to a cottonwood tree. While a drum beat time to the universe, the girls stripped the tree of its branches, and when it was bare, the young warriors rushed upon it, symbolically killing it with their arrows. When the tree was declared dead, it was felled; then the warriors hoisted it on their shoulders and carried it to the medicine wheel atop the plateau. There, Diving Eagle indicated that it should be placed into a hole already prepared for it. Twenty-eight smaller posts were set up around the cottonwood posts, and at the top, other poles went toward the center, completing the sun dance lodge. The entrance to the lodge faced east, and the roof and walls of the lodge were left uncovered to the sun and stars.

When the lodge was complete, Diving Eagle made offerings—tobacco, red willow, sweet grass—four times, because all good things came in groups of four.

"Of the many standing trees, you, the rustling cottonwood, have been chosen in a sacred manner and have been placed in the center of the people's sacred hoop," Diving Eagle said. "You have taught us to make our sacred lodges, when our old men watched children make play houses of your leaves. We place you in this spot, where we observe the red and the blue days, which make our people holy, and from this spot, we offer the medicine pipe to *Wakan Tanka*, from which all good things flow."

Diving Eagle nodded at Loved by the Buffalo, who walked forward through the group of dancers to stand barechested in front of the tribe. He was painted red from the waist up, and a black circle was painted around his face. Diving Eagle explained that a circle was used because it, like *Wakan Tanka*, had no beginning and no end.

Loved by the Buffalo had already purified himself by fasting for four days and completing the sweat lodge ceremony.

"*Wakan Tanka*, I speak for Loved by the Buffalo, who cannot—or will not—speak for himself," Diving Eagle continued. "It is here that he shall offer up his body and his soul for the sake of the people. All of this may be difficult, or impossible, for him to do, yet attempt it he must. Help him, O Grandfather, and give him the courage to withstand the sufferings that he is about to undergo! And, Grandfather, should he fail, have pity upon him . . . and us."

Diving Eagle smirked as he pierced Loved by the Buffalo's pectoral muscles with the flint knife, then threaded the rawhide through the wound. Diving Eagle noted with satisfaction that his apprentice grimaced as he secured the tether with a bit of bone. The other end of the rawhide was tied near the top of the cottonwood pole.

Then Loved by the Buffalo began to dance, wheeling and testing the limits of his tether. He danced around the tree to the rhythm set by the chanting of the tribe and the beating of the drum. Loved by the Buffalo, despite the pain, danced in silence.

By the light of the makeshift torch, Jedediah Smith led the way deeper into the cave. Jacob followed, wading through bat guano that was nearly to his knees. The passage began to narrow, and soon they were crawling on their hands and knees through the muck. Jacob was seized by the fear that this would be their grave.

"I can't do this," he gasped.

"You must," Smith said.

A gunshot echoed in the cavern behind them, followed by war cries and the sound of a desperate struggle.

As his fear increased, Jacob found breathing more and more difficult, and as a consequence, his chest and shoulders seemed to swell, wedging him tight against the twisting passage walls. Jacob cried in anguish. "I can't fit."

"I did," Smith said. "You can."

"This doesn't go anywhere," he said. "It's a dead end. I don't want to die like this!"

"The smoke vents," Smith said calmly, holding the torch in front of him. "Believe me. We don't want to go back."

Jacob began to cry. "At least if we had died outside, people would know what happened to us. In here, nobody will ever find out what happened to us. Not my pa. Not Mama—"

"Jacob," Smith said, "remember the story of Jonah—"

"I don't need a goddamned sermon when I am so afraid!"

Unable to turn around in order to slap Jacob, Smith kicked him in the forehead. "Fear of the Lord is the beginning of wisdom. Now take my boot. Exhale and move forward with me."

Holding tight to Smith's boot, Jacob squirmed forward.

"I cried by reason of mine affliction unto the Lord, and he heard me," Smith recited softly. "Out of the belly of hell cried I and Thou heardest my voice. Salvation is of the Lord. Say it, Jacob."

"Salvation is of the Lord." He sniffled.

Hanging at the end of the rawhide tether, Loved by the Buffalo stared up into the empty eye sockets of the buffalo skull. He was dimly aware of the chanting and the beating of the drum. Then the world receded, and his spirit was pulled into the eye socket. From the interior of the skull, he saw trees falling and arranging themselves into an unfamiliar pattern of fourteen spokes. Then he was pulled through the other eye socket, and he saw piles of stone arranging themselves into the twenty-eight cairns of the medicine wheel. Then his consciousness saw the two wheels spinning in opposite directions and coming closer and closer together until their rims finally met. In the place where they met, there were lightning and fire and smoke and the wailing of two peoples.

It was the harshest sound that Loved by the Buffalo had ever heard. He opened his mouth and screamed, and the scream was magically turned into a song by the grace of *Wakan Tanka.*

The chanting and the drumming stopped. The people gathered around him.

Loved by the Buffalo renewed his struggle against the tether, planting his feet and pulling backward, swaying in time to his scream song. The bone hooks threatened to pull the muscles from his chest. Blood streamed from his wounds. His skin was stretched tight into two tipi-shaped cones, and then one of the hooks pulled free, leaving Loved by the Buffalo imprisoned by the hook in his right breast. He twisted and danced, and he hallucinated that an eagle was on his chest, pecking at his eyes and sinking its talons into the flesh beneath the remaining hook, his body throbbing with pain from each blow.

He fought the eagle, trying to break its hold. Just as he felt the eagle was about to peck out his eyes and devour them, he managed to free himself of the eagle's wicked claws. The tether snapped upward and Loved by the Buffalo went limp and fell, but the people did not let his body touch the ground.

Even as they carried him to a bed of sage, Loved by the Buffalo was already deep in the other world—the world that most people only glimpsed in the reflection of still puddles or when staring deep into the hoop of the night sky.

Long before they pushed themselves through the narrowest part of the passage, they could hear water ahead. Then suddenly, they were through, and found themselves in an enormous cavern through which ran an underground river.

Jacob fell to his knees beside the river, and before plunging his hands into it, he looked at his reflection in the light of the flickering torch Smith held above him. Startled, Jacob did not recognize himself. Instead, he was staring into the eyes of a much younger version of his grandfather.

After they both had washed the bat guano from their hands and faces and drunk a little water, they stood and walked toward a faint light coming from the far end of the big cavern. The walls of the cavern were covered with earth paintings of stick men with spears attacking beasts that looked like the elephants Jacob had seen in books.

Absorbed in the paintings, Jacob tripped over something. It was the leg bones of an ancient skeleton wedged against the cave wall. The skeleton wore a tarnished helmet and breastplate; a broken halberd lay nearby. An arrow penetrated the cracked leather strap on the skeleton's right shoulder and exited the other side. The point of the arrow was flint.

"Mojave," Smith said, judging by the arrow's shaft and fletching.

A sword and leather pouch lay near the skeleton's right hand. Jacob picked up the pouch, and the movement caused the skull and its heavy peaked helmet to roll to the ground. The old leather crumbled in his hands. Five gold coins slipped through his fingers.

The doubloons bore the markings of a cross and shield on one side and the Spanish coat of arms on the other. Smith walked over and looked at the coins. He left three with Jacob and pocketed two.

Loved by the Buffalo sat in the middle of the circle of elders in the great lodge. He was furiously trying to paint his vision on a buffalo hide, just as he had seen his grandfather Two Arrows do so many times before. But he had never painted, and he was making a mess. In frustration, he tried to rub away with the side of his hand the marks he had made.

"Can he not speak?" the chief asked.

"Not a word since he became Loved by the Buffalo," Two Arrows answered.

Two Arrows moved forward and offered his grandson a clean hide. He ruined this one, too, and yet a third hide was offered as Loved by the Buffalo attempted to portray the clash of the wooden hoop with the sacred stone circle.

Then he noticed a pile of twigs on the dirt next to the fire. Nearby were scattered pebbles. Loved by the Buffalo abandoned the hides. He took the sticks and portrayed the wooden circle he had seen in his vision.

"What is this?" the chief asked. "A hoop?"

Loved by the Buffalo grunted in acknowledgment. He made a circle of the pebbles.

"Another hoop," Two Arrows said. "Our medicine wheel. Stone."

Loved by the Buffalo cried out in joy. He balled his fists and brought them together sharply, knuckle to knuckle, representing the clash. Then he drew back his hand and scattered the pebbles that represented the stone circle. The meaning was clear. The chief was shocked.

Diving Eagle lunged from his place in the shadows and stood before the elders. "The vision is false. Wood does not break stone. What idiot would believe that? A wicked spirit—perhaps the spirit of trickster Coyote himself—has possessed Loved by the Buffalo. The smallpox has come to the Lakota again, and perhaps he is responsible. After all, his brother Running Fox was first to show it. His father also is on the path of the dead. Loved by the Buffalo is no longer worthy of his name. He has brought bad spirits upon us. And his vision, just as that of Growling Bear, is a lie."

Loved by the Buffalo stood. He was taller than Diving Eagle now, and the word that came to Loved by the Buffalo's lips came from his very soul: "No!"

Diving Eagle snatched up the three winter count hides that Loved by the Buffalo had attempted and threw them into the fire. They burned brightly. "If Loved by the Buffalo does not lie, then let him prove it by healing the people."

Diving Eagle ran out of the council lodge and left the Lakota camp, afraid of both his apprentice and the disease sweeping the tribe.

Sixteen

Loved by the Buffalo walked deep into the *Paha Sapa* and prayed to *Wakan Tanka* to receive all of the tribe's illness into his own body, and his request was granted. He walked for days without food or water, shivering though the sun was shining on his face. He began to stumble. Wolves flanked him and buzzards wheeled above, but he ignored the creatures. Often he was crawling on his hands and knees. An angry rash appeared first on his arms and then spread to his body. Sweat drenched his body. Spots on his skin developed. They progressed from blemishes to bumps to blisters and then to hard, pus-filled berries. His face and hands were covered with these ugly wounds, as if he had been stung by a thousand bees.

He did not know how many days had passed when he rose from his bloody knees and made one last effort to walk. He lurched along, the world reeling crazily around him, and then stumbled on a rock. He twisted as he fell and landed with his back against the ground; his eyes stared into the sky. On the horizon to his west he could see the Great Bear's Lodge, rising toward the sky, like the stump of some great stone tree. As he lay gasping, he could hear wolves snapping and snarling as they came ever closer.

Then he was aware of something large and woolly moving around him, making a protective circle. It was a buffalo—or the spirit of *the* buffalo—and sensing that this person was protected by *Wakan Tanka*, the wolves slunk away.

Loved by the Buffalo's head turned as he watched the sacred animal circle around him. As he watched, the buffalo went from a shaggy brown to red, then white, black, yellow—all the races of humanity. Loved by the Buffalo had never seen a black or yellow human being, but he knew they must exist.

Then, magically, the buffalo became Growling Bear.

"You gave us the sacred pipe," Loved by the Buffalo cried. "You taught us to use it and to pray to *Wakan Tanka*. To ask for help for our troubles. To give thanks and praise. You taught us the seven sacred rites and vowed you would come again."

"I have indeed come again," Growling Bear said without speaking, and Loved by the Buffalo began to cry. "Have no fear of death. You were born to prepare the way for one who is not yet born: a holy one who will teach the true path to all peoples of the earth."

Growling Bear moved gracefully to Loved by the Buffalo. He knelt, then lifted Loved by the Buffalo's head. Growling Bear's touch was the coolness of water and the warmth of a lodge fire all at once. "Behold the future."

The ground shook as buffalo stampeded on either side of them. Some of the buffalo sprouted human heads, and others sprouted human bodies, but all kept running. They were young, old, male, female, but all were fleeing from some mortal danger. Then Loved by the Buffalo heard the gunshots and understood. They were being hunted. White men on horseback surrounded them and every time one of the thunder sticks spoke, one of the buffalo people died . . . and Loved by the Buffalo jerked in agony.

"No," he said, "I cannot watch."

"You must," Growling Bear said.

A beautiful man with the head of a buffalo bull walked unscathed through the melee. The white man's bullets did not harm him. He pulled the men from their horses and broke their guns as easily as a child might break a twig. Then he tore the white men apart, often using his teeth or his horns to spill their intestines and organs onto the ground. When all of the white men had been slain, he walked through the corpses of the buffalo people. He touched all of them, and as he did, they got up laughing. Then the resurrected buffalo people and the beautiful man began to dance and laugh, and the sound of joy echoed across the land.

Growling Bear moved his hands over Loved by the Buffalo's face. The pustules disappeared. Then he backed away through the colors that Loved by the Buffalo had seen earlier: yellow, black, red, white. Then Growling Bear ran into the distance in his buffalo form and disappeared. Loved by the Buffalo's head sank back onto the ground and he closed his eyes.

Dog Star slipped from the back of his horse and knelt beside his brother. He had located him by the buzzards circling overhead, and the approach of the horse had frightened the wolves. He took Loved by the Buffalo into his arms.

"My brother," he said, "please do not leave us."

SEVENTEEN

Five hundred mountain men and nearly as many Indians were camped on the grassy plains below the Sierra Nevada. Tents mingled with the tipis of nearly every mountain and plains nation because the Indians had learned from the whites to set aside their differences for the annual Rendezvous; after all, business was business, and there were pelts to be bought and sold. Also, it was the only location for several hundred miles where one could actually spend any of the year's wages on wares, gambling, liquor, or other diversions.

As Jacob and Smith walked amid the carnival-like atmosphere, the babble of a hundred tongues reached them. In addition to the various English dialects and the Indian languages, Jacob could pick out French, Spanish, and Russian.

"Babylon," Smith said.

"It is a sight," Jacob said.

"Not for my eyes," Smith said. "I shall not tarry."

Both men were emaciated and their clothes had been repaired many times, but they had the walk of men who were afraid of nothing. With the Spanish gold, they had gotten their fill of buffalo ribs and beans and replenished their powder and shot. Now it was time to part.

"Next spring I'm going west again," Smith said. "I could use men I can count on. Saint Louis in March, if you're interested."

"I'll be there," Jacob said.

Smith paused. "I want you to have this." He held out

his well-worn pocket Bible. Jacob took it and placed it inside his shirt. There would never be enough words to express what he felt for Smith. He simply nodded and held out his hand.

That night, as Jacob walked through the camp, a fistfight that had erupted over a game of dice suddenly rolled into his path.

"Here, now," Jacob said easily. The fistfight had turned into a knife fight. "You children are going to hurt yourselves if you aren't careful."

Then somebody placed a hand on his shoulder. Jacob spun, knocking the black hand away, his own right hand already on the handle of the bowie knife Fletcher had bequeathed him. Then he stopped and peered into the face that was grinning back at him.

The black man wore mountain man garb: worn buckskins, a fur cap, knife, tomahawk, rifle. "Rob any chicken coops lately?"

Recognition dawned slowly on Jacob. "I'll be damned."

In a tent that served as a tavern and charged prices ten times higher than those in Saint Louis for whiskey that tasted of gunpowder and rattlesnake heads, Benjamin Franklin threw a silver dollar on the plank bar. Then he held up his glass and toasted Jacob Wheeler.

"I think about you every day of my life," Ben said. "I've been treed by grizzly bears and tracked by Blackfeet. But I was never so scared as when I heard that farmer say there was three hundred greenbacks' reward for a runaway slave."

Jacob took a drink of the whiskey and grimaced. "Always wondered if you got away. We heard shots."

"I run pretty fast," Ben said.

"Why's a man prefer grizzlies to running north like any other runaway?"

"A grizzly is honest," Ben said. "It looks at me and sees belly timber. A man is just a man in the west."

"Or belly timber," Jacob said.

"Where's your brother?"

"Tejas," Jacob said. "Or at least that's where he was headed when I saw him last. Lord, I can't stand any more of this wicked stuff."

They left the tent and were greeted by a man leading a broken-spirited Cheyenne woman away on a leash. Ben's eyes blazed. Jacob nodded toward a group of magnificently frightening Blackfoot Indians who were dragging another captive to the stump that served as an auction block. The girl's hands were bound and she was at the end of a chain, but she was kicking so fiercely that one of the mountain men had to help get her to the stump.

"It ain't always the color of your skin," Jacob said. "Sometimes it's just bad luck."

"Maybe," Ben said. "But you know that money is eventually going to end up in white pockets. No offense meant."

"None taken."

"Here we have a young Lakota girl," a mountain man announced as he circled the stump. "Says her name is Thunder Heart Woman, but you can call her anything you want. She cooks and knows the fur trade. Speaks a little American. She's pleasant and agreeable."

Thunder Heart Woman spat. The trapper wiped the spittle from his face, then drew back his hand to strike Thunder Heart Woman. One of the Blackfeet grasped his wrist and gave him a look that told him not to damage the merchandise.

"Bidding starts at a hundred dollars," the trapper said.

A collective groan rose from the crowd of mountain men over the richness of the price, but they did not leave. Instead, they stood their ground and looked with greedy eyes as Thunder Heart Woman was made to turn in a slow circle on the stump.

"Hundred," a voice called.

Johnny Fox stepped out of the crowd for a better look. Fox had sold more plews than any ten of the trappers combined, and his newfound riches—and a jug of Taos Lightning—had convinced him of his superior worth. He had a brutish, unfinished look to him, and his blond hair had not been combed in months. Fox planted a hand on Thunder Heart Woman's behind.

"Looks like love at first sight!" someone called. The mountain men guffawed.

"Who else is in the bidding here besides our old friend Johnny Fox?" the auctioneer called. "Boys, don't let this little Lakota bitch get away. It gets awfully cold in the mountains, and this little one's sittin' on a furnace."

It didn't surprise Jacob that Thunder Heart Woman was being sold by her enemies. After all, he had grown up with slavery and heard from the pulpit that the Lord endorsed such commerce. But there was a sadness in the Lakota girl's eyes that did surprise him—something that moved his heart in a way that cut through all the roughness he had learned in the west.

Jacob held a gold doubloon in the air. "Two hundred."

"Two hundred from no beard," the auctioneer said.

The mountain men between Jacob and Fox moved back, clearing a path between them.

Fox glanced at Jacob with disdain. "Who is this green-horn? Three."

Mountain men shook their heads in disbelief. Some chuckled. Only Johnny Fox would be crazy enough to give three hundred dollars for a Lakota squaw.

"Four hundred," Jacob said.

Johnny Fox laughed. "This kid has more money than sense." He sauntered over to Jacob. He stood a head taller than Jacob.

Ben put his arm around Jacob. "Boy, you picked a mean one. Johnny Fox can whip your weight in wildcats." Then Ben backed away.

"You want to buy yourself a sister, peach fuzz?" Fox asked. "Or maybe you're looking for a wet nurse. You even know what to do with her?"

"I aim to set her free and send her back to her people."

Fox roared with laughter.

Thunder Heart Woman stood very still. She understood what Jacob had said. Their eyes met, and she knew it was not about love. It was about right and wrong.

"Set her free?" Ben asked. "What are you thinking?"

"If I thought different you'd be back on the plantation."

Fox shook his head. "You gonna back down?"

"Not for flapjacks or French girls," Jacob said.

"Then it's rifles at twenty paces," Fox said, and the crowd cheered at the prospect of more entertainment.

Dawn was breaking as they moved to the meadow beside the camp that would be used as the dueling ground. "Look," Ben told Jacob. "Keep on the move. Even when reloading. Make yourself small. Give him your side. Make your first shot count." Jacob nodded. Then he and Johnny Fox stood back to back with unloaded rifles. Watching from not quite a safe distance were a couple of hundred mountain men. The Blackfeet were also watching, and at the end of her chains, Thunder Heart Woman thought of her brother and prayed silently to *Wakan Tanka*.

"Gentlemen," the auctioneer announced with a theatrical flourish, "we will count off twenty paces. After that, anything goes."

The auctioneer began counting off the paces, with Jacob walking solemnly in perfect time. Fox leaped and pranced, jeering at the crowd.

"Twenty."

Fox did not even glance at Jacob as he expertly loaded his rifle. But Jacob looked over at Fox, and when he did, he fumbled and dropped the ramrod to his grandfather's rifle.

By the time Jacob had retrieved the ramrod, Fox was already loaded and smoothly swinging the muzzle down on him.

"Get down," Ben called, but too late.

Jacob had never expected anyone to be able to load so fast. Fox's rifle broke the stillness of dawn with flame, thunder, and smoke. The ball neatly clipped away the top of Jacob's left ear. Blood ran down the side of his face as he finished loading. By the time the rifle was up, however, Fox was on the run, reloading all the while, and then he was rolling on the ground. Jacob took aim and fired, and Fox's ramrod went to pieces in the air around him.

Thunder Heart Woman lowered her eyes. The white boy was throwing his life away for no reason, because she still would be sold to the loutish one.

Fox finished seating the powder and ball by sharply pounding the butt of the rifle against the ground. Jacob was ramming home his own ball when Fox fired again. The bullet hit Jacob in the left forearm, shattering it. The force of the impact spun Jacob to the ground. The crowd approved with an ugly cheer.

Fox danced a jig as he looked at Thunder Heart Woman. She turned away in humiliation. Then she dropped to her knees and began to chant in Lakota, arms outstretched toward *Wakan Tanka*, her chains jangling.

Jacob got to his feet. He was angry now, and he recalled

what Smith had told him about a season for everything. It was not his time to die. Holding his rifle in his right hand, Jacob charged.

Fox had wasted time by playing to the crowd, and now his composure was disappearing as he attempted to reload. But Jacob was upon him by the time he was raising his rifle. Aiming the rifle with one hand at point-blank range, Jacob fired, and the ball hit Fox in the jaw.

Fox dropped to one knee. When he got up, there was no sound even from the mountain men. His jaw had dropped down to his chest, giving him a gruesome appearance.

Fox brought the stock of his rifle up to what was left of his face and took careful aim. Jacob was frozen. There was no time to reload. It was so still now in the meadow that, in the background, he could hear Thunder Heart Woman chanting and Ben say under his breath, "Move, dammit!"

Jacob dropped the rifle, drew Fletcher's knife from its sheath behind his back, and slammed it into Fox. As Jacob drove the knife up to the hilt into Fox's chest, the rifle went off, skyward. Fox was dead. Jacob placed his foot on the body and withdrew the knife.

One by one, the mountain men removed their hats. With blood streaming down his broken left arm, Jacob walked toward the auctioneer. He withdrew the two gold coins and dropped them, blood and all, into the man's hand.

"I knew you could do it." Ben slapped Jacob on the shoulder. Jacob flinched in pain.

The Blackfoot leader brought himself to his full height and looked Jacob square in the eyes. Jacob stared back. Then he turned, pulled the chain from where it had been staked, and threw the end at Jacob's feet.

Thunder Heart Woman looked at Jacob's arm. "Broken. It must be set." Then she withdrew the buffalo amulet from around her neck and slowly draped it over Jacob's head.

EIGHTEEN

The Winter of Stars Falling (1833)

"There is no lodge among us that has not fed the funeral scaffolds," Diving Eagle told the council. "And the pox is not yet done with the Lakota. Our prayers have been snatched from the air by some evil spirit. That is why we must appeal to the eagle—closest bird to the sun, the messenger between the people and spirit. To carry our prayer to *Wakan Tanka* directly, we must have a live eagle. There is only one among us who is favored. There is only one who can bring us a living eagle."

Diving Eagle looked at Loved by the Buffalo, who glanced at the ground. Diving Eagle had slunk back to the camp like a starving dog after Loved by the Buffalo had returned from surviving smallpox. Now his mentor was giving him another impossible task, another chance to fail in the eyes of the people, another chance to die. The council turned to Loved by the Buffalo expectantly.

"Well?" Diving Eagle asked. "Will you bring us the sacred eagle?"

"Yes," Loved by the Buffalo said.

Two days later, Loved by the Buffalo adjusted the hide bundle on his back and prepared to climb a rocky crag where some eagles had built their nests. He stopped when he saw Dog Star approaching, leading an extra horse.

"I will take you far away from that unholy man," Dog Star said as he slipped from the horse.

"You must have more faith in *Wakan Tanka*."

"My faith is boundless," Dog Star said. "But I also know an eagle is not a sparrow. It will rip your arm off, peck out your eyes, and open up your throat with a flick of its beak. I am prepared to save you, even if you force me to bind you up with this rope."

"If *Wakan Tanka* protects me, then I will know the course of my life."

"And if not?"

Loved by the Buffalo smiled. "Then no man can save me."

Dog Star embraced Loved by the Buffalo. Then, without a word, he mounted his pony and rode back toward the camp.

Atop the crag, Loved by the Buffalo spread out the hide and sat cross-legged beside it. The *Paha Sapa* stretched before him, as beautiful as a bride in the afternoon sun, but he forced himself to close his eyes and look inward. Soon he was in a trance.

Minutes, or hours, later, he felt the shadow of the eagle cross his face. The eagle circled around the crag and then with a cry settled upon the hide beside him.

After Loved by the Buffalo delivered the living bird to Diving Eagle, the older man brought the council and the people together at dusk, the dividing line between the worlds.

"Eagle, patron of councils, overseer of battles and hunts, hear Diving Eagle whisper in your ear, begging forgiveness, pleading that the sacred messenger carry our prayers to *Wakan Tanka*."

Diving Eagle released the eagle from its hide prison. It flapped toward the cobalt sky. "The eagle has spoken to me. The eagle will deliver our prayers, and it has given us a message from *Wakan Tanka*. The buffalo will be abundant this year . . . if Loved by the Buffalo can bring us the beard of a living bull."

The people looked about them for Loved by the Buffalo, but did not find him. Instead of attending the ceremony, Loved by the Buffalo was on the other side of the camp, looking at a cart that his brother Running Fox had bought with thirty beaver pelts. Loved by the Buffalo had never seen a wooden wheel before, and he examined the wheels of the cart closely. He squatted before one and examined the hub, the spokes, and the broken felloes that had been shoddily repaired with strips of rawhide. He moved his hand close to the wheel, allowing his fingertips to brush the hub and spokes.

From behind the spokes, Growling Bear smiled. The sun had long since slipped beneath the horizon, but Loved by the Buffalo could see him clearly because he shone with an inner light.

"Is this the hoop I saw in my vision?" Loved by the Buffalo asked.

"Only you can know," Growling Bear said.

"Give me a sign if it is."

"That is for the weak of faith," he said gently. "You must find the answer yourself."

"Then tell me what I must do to avoid being killed by Diving Eagle."

Growling Bear smiled radiantly. "You must die. You must be dead to the Lakota so that you can live for all peoples. You know the secret power of herbs. The spirits have taught you to slow your heart and stop your breath so that, to the common eye and hand, you are dead and your flesh cold."

"Is this not a lie?"

"Death is an illusion," he said, and Loved by the Buffalo nodded. "When the Lakota leave for winter camp, you must enter into this living death. Then you will be free to seek the holy one. Until then, you must hide where Frightened by Thunder hides."

"As a *heyoka*?"

"Both holy men and *heyoka* are sacred," Growling Bear said. "Diving Eagle will cease to fear you."

At that moment, cries of fear and wonder rose up from the camp and dogs began to bark. Loved by the Buffalo glanced behind him, but saw nothing but rows of glowing tipis. When he glanced back, Growling Bear had turned into a beautiful rainbow-colored mist. Loved by the Buffalo looked up. Above him, the stars were falling.

"Thank you."

On the other side of Lakota camp, Running Fox, his wife, Blue Bird, and their young son, White Crow, gazed at the sky. They were soon joined by Dog Star and his wife, Yellow Hawk, and their small sons, Brings Horse and Sleeping Bear.

"What does it mean?" Running Fox asked.

"Only Loved by the Buffalo will know," Dog Star said.

"Jacob," Thunder Heart Woman said.

He roused, grabbed his rifle, then realized that Thunder Heart Woman was looking skyward. She was wrapped in a horse blanket before the fire, and her dark eyes reflected both the firelight and the lights in the sky.

"I'll be damned," Jacob said. "Wonder if it's the judgment."

"They are the souls of my ancestors."

"How do you reckon that?"

She pointed at the Milky Way. "That is the Trail of Spirits. That is where we go when we die. Do you see where the trail becomes two paths? That is the place where the spirits are judged. If we have walked in a sacred manner, the judge allows us to take the long path that leads to peace. If we have not walked in a sacred manner, we are asked to take the short path, where we fall off the edge and into the forever darkness."

"My folks believe something similar," Jacob said.

"I had a baby," she said. "I called her Laughs All the Time. The Blackfeet killed her. I could live in peace if only I knew she was on the long path."

When a particularly bright meteor streaked across the sky, Jacob asked, "Reckon that was her?"

"I hope," she said.

Jacob took her in his arms.

"What does it mean, Padre?" Salamanca asked.

Alerted by his soldiers, the captain had stumbled half dressed out of his quarters into the mission courtyard. Padre José was already there, his eyes skyward, watching the meteorites as they streaked across the sky.

"I don't know." The padre crossed himself, dropped to one knee, and grasped the sleeve of Salamanca's nightshirt and pulled him to the ground as well.

From the bank of the river, the Mojave chief looked skyward in horror. He was wearing Jim Fletcher's bear claw necklace, and the weight of it suddenly seemed too great for one man.

"The stars are falling," he said. "It is the end of the world."

From the veranda of their ranch house, Nathan's wife, Pilar, sat on a rocking chair and swayed gently as she breastfed the baby. Nathan stood behind her. Both were watching the sky.

Standing in the yard of the old Wheeler place, the women watched the meteors paint the sky as the men stayed inside and argued politics. Margaret and Abbagail, who had married the brothers, Enoch and Benjamin, whispered prayers. But Naomi and Rachel, now in their twenties, gazed without fear at the November sky.

"I wish Abraham and Hannah could have seen this," Rachel said.

The patriarch and his wife had died three days earlier, within hours of one another. . . .

"How do we know they can't?" Naomi asked.

In the house behind them, the women heard the crashing of furniture and the breaking of plates as the argument erupted into a proper fistfight. Later, the men would read in the newspapers that the annual Leonid display—so named because it appeared to come from the constellation of Leo—was the greatest yet recorded.

NINETEEN

Two Arrows held one of the winter count hides that Loved by the Buffalo had painted up to the cart wheel so that the elders could see for themselves.

"This was the vision," Two Arrows said. "This is the circle of wood that Loved by the Buffalo foretold would come and break our stone wheel."

"You grow dim in your old age," Diving Eagle said. "How can this pathetic thing break the sacred stone wheel that sits atop the *Paha Sapa*?"

"You show your weakness when you deny the prophecy."

"Behold the Lakota prophet," Diving Eagle said sarcastically as Loved by the Buffalo shuffled toward them. He was dressed in a comic parody of his mentor, with rodent hides and skulls hanging from his filthy robe.

With a long stick held in his right hand, he approached a puddle of water, knelt at its edge, and proceeded to test its depth. But instead of dipping the stick in vertically, he held it horizontally so that when he withdrew it the entire stick was wet. The tribe laughed.

Bracing himself, he jumped and landed in the water belly first, spraying mud and water everywhere. He thrashed his arms and legs as if he were swimming for his life, and then he acted as if he were drowning.

"Loved by the Buffalo," Diving Eagle said, "has become an imbecile."

*   *   *

As Jacob rode into the Lakota camp with Thunder Heart Woman behind him, children scurried before them and many came from their lodges to gawk. Some of the bigger boys darted out in front of them, lightly striking Jacob with bows, arrows, and sticks.

"They are counting coup," Thunder Heart Woman explained, her arms tight around his waist. "It is braver to sneak up and touch an enemy than it is to kill him."

Soon the two came upon Loved by the Buffalo, who was oblivious to them as he stalked a butterfly with a tiny bow and an arrow.

"My brother, a *heyoka*?" Thunder Heart Woman cried in distress.

Thunder Heart Woman swung down from the horse. Loved by the Buffalo dropped the toy bow and arrow and embraced his sister. Then he spied the buffalo amulet hanging from Jacob's neck.

"Why did you give the amulet to the white man?" he asked.

"Because he was worthy of it," she said.

Loved by the Buffalo noted the scar that ran across Jacob's chest beneath the amulet, and it reminded him of the scars he bore upon his own chest.

The rest of Thunder Heart Woman's family emerged from the lodge. Not a word was said, but she embraced each of them in turn.

"Who is this white man?" her father asked in Lakota.

"Blackfeet killed the trapper Lebeck and my baby. This man found me in the land beyond the Cheyenne, where the Blackfeet were about to sell me to a cruel white man. This man challenged the cruel man and vowed to return me to my people."

Good Shield looked approvingly at Jacob and smiled. "This is a white man who walks in a sacred manner. But what does he want?"

"My father wants to know what your intentions are," Thunder Heart Woman said.

"I want to marry you," Jacob said. "Go on, tell him."

"It is our tradition to trade girls for horses."

"Apologies to your people," Jacob said, "but it's not my way."

"Sometimes two people meet and go off into the wilderness for a week or two," Thunder Heart Woman suggested. "When they return, they are regarded as husband and wife."

"I reckon we already did that."

Thunder Heart Woman smiled. "I am already his wife."

Two Arrows nodded and proclaimed, "Then we must make him a relative."

Thunder Heart Woman translated, and Jacob said, "Hope it ain't painful."

"It is joyful," Thunder Heart Woman said. "It is one of the seven sacred rites, and it was brought to us by Bear Boy, who received this in a vision directly from *Wakan Tanka*."

"From hookah who?"

"*Wakan Tanka*," she said. "The Great Spirit."

"God, you mean."

"Not the white man's god," she said. "Not the one you call Jesus Christ, although he is part of the mystery that is *Wakan Tanka*. It is all gods and all ancestors and all of nature together in one thought."

"And this kin ceremony?"

"We will eat. The men will fill a holy bag that you must protect. Then we will smoke the sacred pipe that is made from the red stone that is brought from far away. Our families will be joined. My father and grandfather will be your father and grandfather, and yours mine."

"That suits me just fine," Jacob said, his eyes tearing up. He already felt at home among her people, but he knew that his folks back in Virginia would be mortified to have what they would call a *soulless heathen* for kin. He reached out his hand for Thunder Heart Woman, but Good Shield slapped his hand away.

Thunder Heart Woman laughed. "It is not manly to show affection for women in public."

Later, Jacob stood over a buffalo cow he had dropped with his grandfather's rifle. Around him were the carcasses of other animals that the people had killed in the traditional way. Thunder Heart Woman had already begun to butcher the kill.

When Running Fox gestured for Jacob's knife, Jacob handed it over.

*   *   *

At the camp, Jacob studied the broken wheel of Running Fox's cart and gathered the materials to attempt a proper repair. He removed the rim, repaired the felloes, adjusted the spokes, and then reheated the hoop in a bed of coals. Using heavy pieces of timber, he beat it back over the wheel, then doused it in water, just as he had done thousands of times back in his grandfather's shop.

The steaming iron seemed to scream in pain. Loved by the Buffalo, who was still fascinated by the wooden circle, recoiled in pain.

"What's wrong with him?" Jacob asked.

"He says you tricked the iron," Thunder Heart Woman translated.

"How can you trick iron?" Jacob asked. "I don't understand."

Thunder Heart Woman conferred with her brother. "You tricked the iron to subdue the wood," she explained. "Your magic wrongs the iron."

"How can you wrong iron?" Jacob asked. "It's dead."

"*Wakan Tanka* cut himself into pieces and put himself in all things," Thunder Heart Woman said haltingly, attempting to accurately convey her brother's thoughts. "When you trick iron, you trick *Wakan Tanka* to obey you."

"Tell him that iron doesn't obey me," Jacob said. "Iron obeys the laws of nature. It's the nature of iron to get bigger when it's heated and to get smaller when it's cooled. That's how we turn iron into rifles to shoot the lead balls."

Loved by the Buffalo listened to his sister translate, and then fell silent.

"Ask him if *Wakan Tanka* is in the stone," Jacob said.

"*Wakan Tanka* lives in every blade of grass, that dog, that mountain, that cloud, your flesh, every star."

"Is *Wakan Tanka* dishonored when you trick an arrowhead out of a stone?"

"Not if it is done in a sacred manner."

Loved by the Buffalo picked up a sliver of iron that had sloughed from the rim, and a sliver of wood from a broken spoke. He held them tightly in his hand and later, when he was alone, he would place them in the medicine bundle he wore around his neck.

"My brother wishes to know the meaning of your name," Thunder Heart Woman said. "Your names are difficult for us to understand because they do not seem to stand for anything. They are simply ugly sounds."

"Tell him that I am named for a man who lived long ago on the other side of the world. Jacob was proud of his wrestling. One night an angel came to this ancient Jacob and wanted to wrestle. Jacob wrestled all night and got the angel in a headlock and wouldn't let him go until the angel blessed him, his family, and his people."

"It is not holy for a man to threaten *Wakan Tanka*."

"This old Jacob was a little better than the rest of us."

"Did your god give you the wheel of wood and iron?"

"Nope," Jacob said. "Just the smarts to make it."

"But still it is made by men," Loved by the Buffalo said. "Now I will show you a wheel made by *Wakan Tanka*."

The trio walked around the rim of the sacred medicine wheel. Loved by the Buffalo was carrying a pair of crow wings that dangled from a strap of rawhide.

"Each of us is born somewhere on the stone hoop," Loved by the Buffalo said. "As a gift, the Great Spirit gives us one of the great powers at birth."

"What powers?"

"Wisdom," Thunder Heart Woman began. "Innocence. Illumination."

"A church without a roof," Jacob said. "I wonder where I am on the wheel?"

Frightened by Thunder rode up to them. He was facing backward on his horse. He jumped down, moved very close to Loved by the Buffalo, and whispered, "Remain a *heyoka* or die."

Diving Eagle was riding close behind.

"You, fool," he called from his horse. "What are you doing up here? This is no longer your place."

"Testing the wind," Loved by the Buffalo said, then swung the crow wings over his back and tied the rawhide across his chest. Then he jumped up on the back of the horse that Frightened by Thunder had ridden up. "The next time you see me, I will be flying like an eagle!"

Loved by the Buffalo put his heels to the horse's flanks and raced off in the direction of the buffalo jump, leaving Thunder Heart Woman looking after him with concern.

When Thunder Heart Woman and Jacob reached the buffalo jump, they found the horse grazing peacefully on top. Below them, at the bottom of the cliff, the body of Loved by the Buffalo was sprawled on the ground. Thunder Heart Woman cried out and fell to her knees.

In the west, storm clouds had gathered. Flashes of lightning jumped from the clouds to the ground, followed many seconds later by the ground-shaking rumble of thunder.

Days later, after the body of Loved by the Buffalo had been left on a funeral scaffold near the sacred stone hoop and Diving Eagle had performed the keeping of the soul ceremony, the Lakota folded their lodges and prepared to move. In addition to the traditional travois hauling the lodges and other goods, the cart of Running Fox creaked along, borne by the wheel that Jacob had repaired.

Two Arrows and Good Path gave away their possessions and gave final instructions to their family.

"Dog Star, you have mixed my paints since you were only five summers," he said. "Now it falls upon you to keep the winter count. Do the same with your sons."

To Jacob's disbelief, the family made a fire and left a little food and water for the grandparents, then bid them good-bye.

"Do not be sad," Thunder Heart Woman explained. "This is our way. They are too weak to make the journey to winter camp and have decided instead to return to the great mystery together."

As the family moved out of sight, Two Arrows and Good Path reclined on their funeral scaffold. It was growing dark and the stars had appeared in the cold vault of the sky.

"We had a good life," Good Path said gratefully.

"I was a warrior," Two Arrows said. "Hard as bone. Swift as the eagle. One man could not count all of the buffalo that fell to my arrows. I was brave and made many children with my beautiful bride. She has many wrinkles now and her breasts are dry. But oh, you should have seen her then! Thank you, O *Wakan Tanka*, for making us man and woman! Teach our grandchildren to live as you have taught us to live."

Then he began his death song. The whistling of the north wind competed with the sound of wolves in the distance.

On a hill near the great medicine wheel, Loved by the Buffalo rose from his own funeral scaffold, scattering the crows that had come there to feast. He did not know that his grandparents were on another hilltop, just a mile away.

Stiffly, he climbed down from the scaffold, dragging the buffalo robe left for him. When he reached the ground, he was greeted by the ghost of Growling Bear. The ghost had been throwing phantom stones at the crows.

"Your aim is no better than mine," Loved by the Buffalo said.

"True," Growling Bear said. "But I had to do something with my time while awaiting you."

"You will wait some more," Loved by the Buffalo said. "It is not my time."

"But Diving Eagle did the soul-keeping ceremony."

"It is a trick," Loved by the Buffalo said. "He does not hold my soul. It is still mine."

"All souls belong to *Wakan Tanka*," Growling Bear said. Then the ghost gestured to the sky above, where the great path flowed across the sky. "I must return to the land of the dead."

Instead of following the broad trail that the Lakota had left behind them on their way to winter camp, Loved by the Buffalo chose the opposite direction. Pulling the buffalo robe tightly around him, he strode happily toward the mountains beyond.

TWENTY

Lakota Winter Camp
They Shot a Fat Buffalo Bull (1835)

"Our rivals are gaining advantage over the Lakota by trading with the whites," Running Fox told the council. "Why do we sit here while they become superior to us?"

In the years since he had left his grandparents on their funeral scaffold, Running Fox had so distinguished himself as a warrior and hunter that he was one of the few young men allowed to address the elders.

"We must go to the fort of the whites, where much trade takes place, where many things are possible," he urged. "Perhaps my elder brother, Dog Star, sees the wisdom in this."

Dog Star shook his head. "I do not allow my wife to cook in an iron pot. I prefer the ways of my ancestors. The white man's road may be good for the whites, but the Lakota ways are sacred."

"What will you do when the Blackfeet and Cheyenne come with the white man's rifles?" Running Fox asked. "You will die and they will have your woman and children."

"I will fight with lance and bow," Dog Star said, "and I will trust the Great Spirit."

"If Loved by the Buffalo had lived, he would have seen the truth of my words," Running Fox said passionately. "We must be more like the whites if we are to resist the whites!"

"And what good is resisting if we lose what makes us Lakota in the process?" His voice was thick with contempt.

"I have lost nothing," Running Fox said, growing angry. "I speak as I do to save the people, not to destroy them. Your voice is the voice of death."

The brothers launched themselves at each other, grappled, and fell in front of the council fire. The elders rushed forward and separated them.

"If we become white so that we can cook in iron pots, or use their weapons, we have lost," the chief said. "If we fight one another, we have lost. Learn to live in peace or go away."

"I will go to the whites, then," Running Fox said, his eyes blazing with hate. "I will take my family with me, and those of our friends who see the truth, and you will see how our people can thrive. You all will see."

Fort William was located on the Laramie River, in the hunting ground used by the Cheyenne and Arapahoe. It was named for the first names of mountain men Bill Sublette and William Anderson. Sublette had been an associate of Jedediah Smith on several ventures, including the tragic Ashley Expedition, and Anderson was an educated man who sometimes wrote his journals in Greek or Latin.

Because of its central location, the fort would become an important stop on the Oregon-California trail; the Gila River was to the south, the Red River north, and the Columbia west.

Running Fox and his clan had never seen anything like the fort. It was a square stockade, with blockhouses that jutted from the corners to afford a deadly cross fire for attackers. Another blockhouse was suspended over the entrance, and the main feature of this defense was a cannon that was sometimes fired to impress the Indians who converged upon the fort several times a year to trade for tobacco, beads, and alcohol. Fittingly, the entrance faced not east, but to the west.

The plaza inside was cramped, and vendors speaking a variety of white tongues competed for the attention of Running Fox and his clan. If the exterior of the fort had been shocking for the Lakota, the interior made their senses reel. Never had they seen so many white people in one place, and never before had they seen a white woman. Here, there were two. They were outnumbered several times over, however, by the number of Indian prostitutes hanging in the shadows beneath the vendor stalls, many of them slovenly, most of them drunk, and few of them willing to meet the eyes of Running Fox.

Running Fox and his seven-year-old son, White Crow, approached one of the stalls run by a white trader. There was a glittering array of knives, hatchets, rifles, powder horns, flints, and lead balls. Nearly every device displayed was not simply a tool, but a killing tool.

The trader's name was Bull Harry and he sized up Running Fox with a single look. "I got too many buffalo hides and beads already," he said derisively. "You got anything I can use?" His head inclined toward the Indian whores. "Any of those you're willing to barter? There's a lot of lonely boys heading out west, and there ain't no preachers or highborn women to tell 'em that a man has no right to his pleasure."

Running Fox did not understand the trader's words, but he got the meaning from the frequent glances toward the Indian women.

"Surely that young boy has a mother or a sister who would provide comfort to some deserving white man with the money to pay," the trader said.

Running Fox's cheeks burned in anger.

"Of course you do," the trader said.

While Running Fox hurried White Crow away, the trader laughed coarsely over the naïveté of the young Lakota.

TWENTY-ONE

Near Mission San Antonio de Bexar, Tejas
1836 (A Boy Killed Blackfeet)

At dawn, the Mexican band struck up a tune that was at least a thousand years old. It was called "Deguello," a name that the Moors had probably conferred on it during their occupation of Spain, but it had become universally known as "Slit Throat."

The meaning was clear. For the 188 *Tejanos* holed up in the roofless Spanish mission and its adjacent palisades, no quarter would be given. Around them, four thousand Mexican regulars, under the command of Santa Anna—"The Napoleon of the West"—were grimly preparing to assault the walls.

When the band had sounded the last notes, the Mexican cannons opened up with an earth-pounding chorus of their own. The concussion of the artillery shook the little rancho of Nathan and Pilar, and dust drifted down from the ceiling of their bedroom.

Nathan was awake, sitting in a chair in the bedroom, watching his wife and baby sleep. Pilar stirred in fear, and the baby began to cry.

"Nathan?" Pilar asked.

"It's begun," Nathan said. "Those poor bastards . . . I wish I could help them."

"Your place is here with us," Pilar said. "The death of one more man will not change their fate. Besides, Houston may reach them with reinforcements in time."

*　　*　　*

At the old Wheeler place in Virginia, Jacob reined in the horses and stood on the brake to bring the wagon to a creaking stop. Beside him was Thunder Heart Woman, holding their four-year-old daughter, Margaret Light Shines. The wagon was loaded with furs and other goods, and behind the wagon were two pack mules.

Jacob jumped down from the wagon and gave Thunder Heart Woman, who was large with child, a quick smile. He strode up the path toward the house, his head taking in the familiar front yard and big porch. He paused for a moment on the porch, listening to music that came from inside.

A woman was singing "Amazing Grace" while accompanying herself on the piano. She had a fine voice. When Jacob knocked, the music stopped. A moment later the door opened a crack and he glimpsed the muzzle of a shotgun.

"I hope you don't shoot as well as you sing," Jacob said.

"I suggest that you not attempt to find out," Naomi said, peering around the door at the lean man in buckskins before her. "Just who are you?"

"Kin."

"I beg your pardon, but we don't know any Indians," Naomi said, glancing at Thunder Heart Woman on the seat of the wagon.

Jacob laughed. "Cousin Rachel? Daughter of Benjamin and Abbagail?"

"No, I am Naomi, Rachel's younger sister."

"My God, I thought you were still a child," Jacob said. "How the years have flowed like snowmelt. I'm Jacob, your cousin. My father is your uncle. And the Indians in that wagon are my family."

"Well, I'll be . . . ," she said. "This can't be. Last month we got a letter from your brother Nathan saying he was in Texas married to a Mexican woman. And now you show up on our doorstep with a heathen family in tow. And I'm to marry the Baker boy from Lancaster County!"

"Mighty pleased for you," Jacob said. "Tell me, do our grandparents still live?"

Thunder Heart Woman gave birth to their second child in an upstairs room surrounded by the Wheeler women. The men waited downstairs, and while Jacob fretted, his father, Enoch, calmly smoked a pipe and his eldest brother, Ezra, whittled.

"One thing I can't get out of my mind is those California oranges," Jacob said, making idle chatter. He held out his hand as if he were grasping a cannonball. "They're this big, bright and shiny. Grow everywhere. I miss them."

"Then why'd you come home?" Jethro asked. He had been uncomfortable since Jacob's return. Every day for the past decade, he had pondered how differently his life might have turned out had he saddled a horse and ridden off with Jacob and Nathan.

"Mexicans pushed us out, just like they're doing in Texas," Jacob said.

"Look at brother Nathan," Jethro said. "He stuck it out in Texas. Now he's got a farm, raising a family. He didn't run back home, tail tucked between his legs."

Jacob looked curiously at Jethro, wondering why his older brother was being so contrary.

"I'll go back someday," Jacob said. "I came close to losing my hair a few times. If it hadn't been for Mr. Jedediah Smith or a fellow named Fletcher—"

"The one whose rifle lock you mended," Enoch said.

"The same," Jacob said. "He's dead now."

"Talked about gold and fortune plenty," his father recalled. "And now he's gone. So much for dreams of glory."

"That kind of life will always carry some risk," Jacob said carefully. "Nothing worth having comes easy. But Mr. Smith is not dead. He's blazing trails, making a name for himself. There's plenty of glory being spread around out there, and Jedediah Smith deserves most of it. Greatest man I ever met."

"So what is it you intend to do for a living?" Jethro asked.

"What we all do, I reckon," Jacob said. "What we always done. Be a wheelwright. If father would allow."

"Of course I'll allow," Enoch said, taking the pipe from his mouth. "Business isn't as it was, with the bank failures and all. People barter for services nowadays, but we'll get by. You'll never lack work. They need wheels in time of peace."

"And they need wheels in times of war."

"You can bunk here if you like."

"Thank you," Jacob said. "That suits me just fine."

"Your squaw feel the same?" Ezra asked as he made a particularly deep slice with the knife.

"She is nobody's squaw," Jacob said evenly. "She's my wife, my woman, my missus. Nothing shameful about it. I lived with her people, hunted buffalo with them, learned to honor their ways. They made me one of their own. It was my hope that you all would do the same."

"We're doing our best," Enoch said. "Give your brothers time."

Suddenly, they were interrupted by the crying of a baby upstairs. Naomi walked down the stairs, wiping her hands on her apron. "A boy."

Jacob grinned, then squeezed by Naomi and took the stairs two at a time.

"Katala . . . Katala-wee . . . whatever her name is," Naomi said. "She didn't cry out. Not a bit."

"How's that possible?" Enoch asked.

"Indians aren't human," Leah said, hovering over Naomi's shoulder. "They don't feel pain like we do."

"They're animals!" Ezra said.

Enoch stood. "No more of that talk. You're talking about my son's wife. That's his child up there, my grandson, born of his seed. I will brook no more of that kind of talk."

When Ezra did not respond, Enoch demanded, "Do you understand?"

"Yes, sir."

In the bedroom upstairs, Jacob held the squealing child in his arms. Jacob's mother, Margaret, sat beside the bed, holding Thunder Heart Woman's hand.

"I will name him for grandfather," Jacob said. "Abraham."

Thunder Heart Woman whispered something.

"And his Lakota name shall be High Wolf!"

When the Mexican soldiers swarmed over the ranch, Nathan studied their uniforms. In contrast to the motley-dressed *Tejanos*, Santa Anna's soldiers wore uniforms that were right out of the Napoleonic wars of a generation before: shakos with a glittering emblem above the brim, coats with tails, white crossed belts. Their guns seemed cumbersome compared to the long rifles carried by Crockett and the other Alamo defenders. The muskets they carried were heavy and crude copies of the English "Brown Bess," with a gaping bore of at least .72 caliber and a seventeen-inch bayonet socketed on the end. Even though the Mexicans had a reputation for being cowardly, most of them were battle-hardened regulars, some with fifteen years of combat behind them.

"Notice to all Anglo-Americans, filibusters, and heretics on Mexican territory," an officer read off a proclamation, his English heavily accented. "Leave your homes, leave your farms, protect your lives while you can. Depart *Tejas*, depart Mexico."

Then the soldiers burned the ranch with ease.

Shaking with rage, Nathan rushed forward and grasped the hand of one of the brightly dressed soldiers as he set fire to the thatched roof of the barn. Another soldier placed the muzzle of one of those clumsy rifles against Nathan's ribs.

"Jefe, por favor!" Pilar cried as she fell at the officer's feet. Their baby was strapped to her back.

The officer made a disgusted sound deep in his throat, extended a hand, and pulled her to her feet.

"Only because you are Mexican, my dear," he told her in Spanish, "I will spare the life of your husband. But you must leave at once. Gather what you can quickly and go."

The soldier removed the musket from Nathan's ribs. From behind Nathan and Pilar came the popping and ripping sound of gunfire. Flames lit the predawn sky.

"The Alamo?" Nathan asked.

"Fallen."

"The garrison?"

"The few left were put to the sword."

"Santa Anna's casualties?" Nathan asked.

The officer shrugged. "A few hundred. It does not matter. Soldiers are made to die."

Nathan saved what he could and threw them into a two-wheeled cart. The good wagon, with the spoke wheels he had crafted with his own hands, was burning to ashes in the barn. The carts were so common that the soldiers had not bothered to destroy it.

After hastily hitching a mule, Pilar climbed aboard the cart with their child while Nathan led the mule to the road.

A line of refugees—on foot, on horseback, in carts and wagons—was streaming away from San Antonio de Bexar. When the wheel of Nathan's cart hit a rut in the road, some of the items fell into the road.

"Leave it," Pilar said.

"My tools," Nathan said. "I need them."

A neighbor slowed his wagon. "Better move, Wheeler. Don't look back and don't surrender. They'll cut your throat."

"I've harmed no one," Nathan protested.

"Tell that to Fannin and the three hundred seventy prisoners they bayoneted at Goliad!"

Nathan carefully stowed his tools on the cart. "I'll get you to your brother's ranch," Nathan said quietly. "You and the baby will be safe there."

"Nathan?"

"I'm going to volunteer," Nathan said. "Help Sam Houston kick Santa Anna and his butchers back across the Brazos."

"No!" Pilar cried.

"I have to fight," Nathan said, "for what they did to us." Then he looked back at the red sky over San Antonio de Bexar. "For what they did to them . . ."

Jacob could not believe the notice in the Wheelerton *Gazette*. He had been working outside, forging horseshoes and then plunging them into a bucket of water to cool, when Jethro had come running to him with the newspaper fluttering in his hand. With hands still dark from work, Jacob read the notice again:

Word has reached the New York journals of the passing of the legendary pathfinder and mountain man Jedediah Smith. The trailblazer was leading a wagon train on the Santa Fe trail last May when the party became desperately low on water. With characteristic disregard for his own safety, Smith rode ahead to the Cimarron River, intent upon returning the life-bestowing liquid to the party. Before completing his mission of mercy, however, Smith was set upon by a band of bloodthirsty Comanches. The evidence at the gruesome scene was that Smith fought valiantly with rifle, pistols, and knife, but that a Comanche arrow in his back finally helped him shuffle off this mortal coil.

"Shuffled off this mortal coil," Jethro said. "That means the great Jed Smith is dead, don't it?"

"You are dumber than dirt," Jacob said, then continued reading.

The trails that Smith blazed continue to provide overland trains with sure routes to the lands of California and Oregon. The point of departure for these adventurous souls is now Independence, Missouri, where experienced pathfinders are in short supply.

Jacob wiped a single tear away with his forearm. Jethro was suddenly sorry for bringing the notice to Jacob's attention.

"I'm sorry," he stammered.

"Mr. Smith was a God-fearing man," Jacob said. "A modest man. He saved my life when we were holed up in a cave by a Mojave war party. That's where Jim Fletcher became a gone beaver. My bones would be rotting there in that stinking cave, too, had it not been for Jedediah Smith. He kept me going. He kept me believing. And now he's dead."

Jacob looked at the sky. "He wanted me to stay out west. Said if I came back home I'd never know the man I could've been, the man God wanted me to be."

"What are you saying?" Jethro asked.

Jacob removed his apron and tossed it over the anvil. "Wheelerton's gone stale. I don't appreciate how my own family treats Thunder Heart Woman or Margaret Light Shines. Or how they'll treat Abraham High Wolf. Can't say I'm surprised by it. This town is mighty small."

"This is your home," Jethro protested.

"This ain't my home," Jacob said. "My home's out west. I ain't found it yet, but it's out there somewhere." Then he paused, and for a moment, Jethro caught a glimpse of the Jim Fletcher that had come to their shop so long ago.

"Hell, I don't know," Jacob said. "Perhaps it's the dare and dash of it all. Perhaps it's that chance of catching a Comanche or Mojave or Blackfoot arrow in the back that makes a man feel alive. But whatever it is, I can't stay here."

"You're touched," Jethro said.

"A man don't make history sleeping in the same bunk he was born in," Jacob said.

Jethro sighed. "Take me with you."

As Enoch and Uncle Benjamin gave the sons a lecture that they could not expect to come back and receive a portion of the family business, because that would now go to Ezra, the son who had always stayed, they loaded the wagon that Jacob had driven into town. Jacob bid a cordial farewell to his father, embraced his mother, then climbed into the wagon seat beside his brother. Thunder Heart Woman was holding Abraham High Wolf in her arms, and Margaret Light Shines was sitting sadly beside, holding a rag doll given her by her grandmother.

"I wish I could have held the baby one last time," Margaret Wheeler said.

Then Jethro whipped the reins and the wagon jolted forward. Jacob touched the brim of his hat in farewell to his parents, and then turned forward and did not look back.

Just outside of town, a rider overtook them. It was Rachel, riding hard like a man.

"Come to say good-bye?" Jacob asked.

"I'm going with you," she declared.

"Not by a damn sight," Jacob said. "You turn around and get back to Pa this damn minute."

"There's nothing for us here," Rachel said. "Besides, we can help with the children. We have grown awfully fond of them."

Jacob peered at her. "What do you mean by 'we'?"

Behind them, on foot, Leah and Naomi were struggling to catch up.

"Damned if it ain't an exodus of Wheeler women," Jacob said.

"Leah goes where Naomi and I go," Rachel said. "And Naomi's bastard fiancé in Lancaster County up and married somebody else. She wants to disappear from the face of the earth. And that's where you're going, isn't it?"

TWENTY-TWO

Western Plains
A Boy Killed Blackfeet (1836)

Running Fox, his eight-year-old son, White Crow, and eight warriors from the renegade Lakota clan, rode hard toward the top of a grassy hill. They had been flanking a small herd of buffalo, and now they readied their bows and lances for the kill.

When they reached the crest of the hill, they were surprised to meet a Blackfoot hunting party that had ridden up the other side. This party was the same size as the Lakota party, but every Blackfoot hunter was armed with a long gun.

"The herd is ours," Running Fox said.

The Blackfoot leader smirked. "Is this the land of the Lakota?" he responded in sign language.

"I speak of the herd, not the land," Running Fox signed back.

"You speak foolishness," the Blackfoot leader said. Then he casually adjusted the rifle across his saddle. The other warriors carried old flintlock trade muskets, but the leader proudly carried a half-stock percussion plains rifle. The stock of the rifle was outlined in shining brass tacks. Eagle feathers fluttered from the ramrod jutting beneath the big .54 caliber bore.

Running Fox guessed that the rifle was a war prize. "We need meat." He wheeled his horse and led his clan away.

The Blackfoot hunting party stood their ground for a few moments, then pushed off in the opposite direction.

Running Fox led his hunting party down a shallow draw, where they attempted to hide themselves from the herd of the buffalo in the distance. Even though he could not see the buffalo, he knew where they were from the great plume of dust the herd sent into the air.

Too late, he noticed a smaller cloud of dust to the east. He knew it was the Blackfoot hunting party. They had doubled back and were keeping pace with Running Fox and the others on the opposite side of the hill.

Running Fox dug his heels into his horse and the rest followed. If he led the hunting party up the hill on the other side of the draw, the Blackfoot guns would pick them off with ease as their horses struggled toward the crest. No, what they needed was speed.

"Ride," Running Fox urged White Crow.

The draw passed over a low saddle between the slopes of the hills, and Running Fox knew if his party could reach it before the Blackfeet, they would be in the open plain. There, they would have a chance of outracing the Blackfeet.

But when they reached the saddle, they discovered another Blackfoot party waiting for them. Then, in the dust and confusion, the first Blackfoot party was upon them as well.

A single shot rang out and one of the Lakota pitched from his horse. Running Fox jumped from his horse to his fallen comrade, but he could offer no help. The warrior, shot squarely in the chest, was dead before he hit the ground.

The Blackfeet stood around the Lakota, rifles held in the ready position. Smoke was curling from the muzzle of the percussion rifle the leader held.

Running Fox glanced at his son. White Crow was sitting calmly on his pony, with no trace of fear. A Lakota warrior made a motion to nock an arrow, but Running Fox shook his head.

Then the Blackfeet turned their horses and rode leisurely away. The message was clear: we can kill you at our leisure, and we turn our back to you because the Lakota can do nothing about it.

"They seek the same herd," Running Fox said. "Tomorrow, they will come to kill the rest of us."

"What shall we do, Father?" White Crow asked.

"What the dogs do not expect," Running Fox said.

"But the rifles," White Crow said.

"We need only fear the rifles by day," Running Fox said.

That night, in a deep ravine near the Blackfoot hunting camp, White Crow held the reins to the ponies. As the warriors prepared their knives and tomahawks, the horses shuffled nervously.

"Keep the ponies quiet!" Running Fox said.

"I want to fight," White Crow whispered.

Running Fox gave his son a stern look. "Should I not return, get on your horse and ride as quickly as you can onto the prairie."

White Crow gave his father a sullen look. Then, with the night breeze in his face, Running Fox inched toward the Blackfoot camp on his stomach. Twenty minutes passed before he was close enough to see that two warriors were talking quietly by the fire while the others slept. The moon was not yet up. Another five minutes had elapsed before Running Fox realized that the leader of the Blackfoot war party was one of the men who slept not six feet away.

Then the wind shifted and the Blackfoot ponies, staked forty yards away, picked up the scent of Running Fox. The animals began to stamp and nicker; the Blackfoot leader sat up and reached for his rifle.

Running Fox was upon him in an instant. As he knelt on the rifle to keep it from the leader's grasp, he clamped a hand over the other man's mouth while at the same time drawing a knife across his throat with the other.

One of the gossiping warriors saw a flash of firelight reflected from the blade of Running Fox's knife. He paused in midsentence. By the time he thought to reach for his musket, Running Fox had the percussion rifle in his hand and was running at full speed toward him.

At point-blank range Running Fox pulled the trigger, knocking the surprised warrior to the other side of the fire. Then Running Fox flipped the rifle around and, using the stock as a club, knocked the other warrior to the ground.

At the sound of the gunshot, the waiting Lakota rushed in on the camp. In the confusion that followed, one of the Blackfoot warriors escaped into the nearby ravine and suddenly found himself in the middle of the Lakota ponies.

He tried to snatch the reins away from White Crow, but the boy would not let go. In irritation, the warrior took the metal trade hatchet from his belt and swung at the boy, but White Crow dodged just in time. The boy tried to run, but before he knew what was happening the Blackfoot had swept his feet from beneath him and then the warrior was on top of him.

White Crow tried to scramble away, but the warrior grabbed his heel and pulled him back. While he was still on his stomach, White Crow drew his own knife. Then the warrior flipped the boy around so that he could see his face. The warrior grinned as he drew back the hatchet . . . and White Crow plunged the knife beneath the man's sternum. The hatchet dropped to the ground as the warrior used both hands to stanch the geyser of blood spurting from the wound. Then his eyes rolled back into his skull. White Crow kicked the dying warrior away.

Running Fox appeared in the ravine. His son was standing over the body of the Blackfoot warrior.

The boy threw his arms wide, the bloody knife still clutched in his right hand, and he sang to the stars, "O Grandfather, *Wakan Tanka*, I am but a boy. Your spirit was with me, and now a warrior's scalp shall hang from my belt. *Aieee!*"

Running Fox was filled not with pride, but with dread.

TWENTY-THREE

Independence, Missouri
1840 (The Winter of the Drunken Fight)

Stephen Hoxie, a marginally competent lawyer but failed politician, was forty-five years old. He had left his native state of Ohio to nurse his disappointment in the anonymous ebb and flow of the border. He had been watching the curious family for some time as they milled about the tents, where immigrant trains were being organized for California and Oregon.

The family was composed of two young men, an Indian woman with a new baby in her arms, two half-breed children, and three white women in their twenties. The men were obviously brothers, so strong was the family resemblance, but they differed in manner. The younger was obviously the leader.

At each of the tents, the "captains" of the trains shouted their intentions and boasted of their prowess. Jacob Wheeler passed by the tents where captains drummed for Oregon and paused instead at one of the California tents.

"Huzzah for California!" the grizzled captain called. "Come with us and find your fortune in the land of the Mexican dons. I offer the safest, the fastest, and the most democratic overland train ever to set wheel upon the great American prairie!"

Jacob listened with jaded disinterest.

"Welcome, friends," Hoxie said. "Where are you from?"

"Spotsylvania County, Virginia," Jacob said. "It's taken us several years to get this little family here. We stopped in towns, settled for a while, worked, then pushed on. A gentleman from Europe wrote a book that said, 'An American will build a house in which to pass his old age and sell it before the roof is on; he will plant a garden and rent it just as the trees are coming into bearing; he will clear a field and leave others to reap the harvest.'"

"Oh, I can relate to wanderlust," Hoxie said. "Is it the golden coast you seek? The paradise of the West? California?"

"Ever been there?" Jacob asked.

"Can't say that I have," Hoxie admitted.

"I've seen it with my own eyes," Jacob said.

Hoxie looked at him carefully. Such a statement he would have questioned from another man. But there was no boast in Jacob's eyes, only fact.

"And what's your assessment, friend?"

"By comparison, everything else is a dung heap."

Hoxie roared with laughter. "Well put. Then we are in agreement, sir. We can use a man who's been down the trail. I have nigh unto the makings of a train here. Don't want too big of a company. We wish to travel light and fast."

"And safe."

"That's it, exactly!"

Hoxie's secretary, a hawk-faced young man named Leland, pushed a contract into Jacob's hands.

Nearby, a black family was listening intently. "Pardon me," the father said. "You accept freemen of color?"

"What's your name?" Hoxie asked.

"Absalom Jones."

"And where you from?" Hoxie asked suspiciously.

"Illinois," the man said. "We are loved as a race there, but hated as a people."

"Have you money?"

"A little, sir," the man said.

"Join us!" Hoxie said.

"You're joining this train?" Jones asked Jacob.

"Thinking on it," Jacob said, regarding the contract with disdain. "A lot of rules and regulations here, mister."

"Hoxie's the name. Stephen Hoxie. I'm providing wagons, horses, cattle, stores. And doing that, I aim to captain this train, not pilot or guide, but captain."

"The man in charge," Jacob said.

"Somebody's got to be," Hoxie said, "might as well be the fellow who can provide for all. We need rules, standards, organization."

"Says here a council is to report to the captain."

"Laws."

"There's a ten-dollar tax per person."

"Paradise ain't cheap."

"And a morals rule?"

"The saying goes that when alien peoples meet, first they fight and then they fornicate. We need to preserve our dignity, our civilized ways. Can't let the savagery infect us."

"The Lakota feel the same," Jacob said dryly.

"You gents think about that contract," Hoxie said. "Come see me if you have questions. I'll be at Colonel Noland's hotel and tavern."

Jacob considered, then nodded.

"That's fair," Absalom Jones said.

In the tent city at the edge of Independence, the Wheeler family discussed the merits of throwing in with the curious Stephen Hoxie.

"What about Missouri?" Thunder Heart Woman asked Jacob. "The land's rich, there's plenty of people, there are farms, settlements, even a couple of cities. Why not stay here?"

"It's swamp country," Jacob said moodily. He was busy writing in his journal, occasionally dabbing the pen back in to the inkwell, the nub scratching across the pages. "Malaria, pestilence—don't want it, don't need it."

"No fever in Californy," Jethro said. I heard a fellow talking, said folks routinely live 150, two hundred years in California. The climate's so good."

"Folderol!" Naomi said. "Nobody can live that long outside of Bible times."

"One old coot," Jethro said, "was 250 years old and he'd plum had enough—just wanted to die."

"What they do, feed him Mexican food?" Leah asked.

"There's an argument for Oregon," Rachel told Jacob. "At least they speak English."

"True enough," Jacob said.

"Who would talk Spaniard if we get to Californy?" Rachel asked. "You, Jacob?"

"Them dons is educated," Jacob said. "They speak English."

Jacob returned to his journal, added one last line, then closed the ledger with a flourish. "California or bust," Jacob said, and walked off to examine the wagon.

Jethro looked at the women and smiled broadly.

Stephen Hoxie and his secretary, Leland, were passing by the coopersmith when Hoxie noticed that Jacob and Nathan Wheeler were expertly working on a pair of massive wagons.

"You boys didn't tell me you were smiths," Hoxie said.

"We're obliged to the proprietor here for allowing us to use his shop. Building another wagon for the journey." Jacob stood and wiped sweat from his brow. "And we're wheelwrights. Been wheelwrights for as long as anybody can remember. Probably were wheelwrights before they even had a damned name for the profession."

"Well, next to pilots and Indian fighters, there're few things as crucial to the success of a train as a skilled wheelwright," Hoxie said. When the Wheelers didn't answer, he continued. "You didn't come by Noland's. We intend to leave day after tomorrow."

"How many wagons?" Jacob asked.

"Eighteen," Hoxie said. "I've hired a pilot named Josiah Bell. He ran with Fitzpatrick trapping beaver, fighting Indians. He's got two scouts with him. Including the others, we have twenty-two armed men."

"Horses or oxen?" Jacob asked.

"Horses for the wagons. Think those wheels can handle the trail?"

" 'Spect so. Iron tires, three-inchers, bolted."

"Now that's a substantial wagon."

"Conestoga, they call 'em," Jacob said. "Well-seasoned wood, falling tongues, well-steeled skeins."

"What about extra axles?"

"Can't do without," Jacob said. "Tires buckle, wagon tongues snap, front axles fail. The lower half of the wagon. That's where all the problems are, Mr. Hoxie. Running gear, they call it."

Hoxie was a bit agitated now. "We sure could use you

folks on this journey. I've got a part-time coopersmith and a half-assed wainwright. But no wheelwright."

"We'd be delighted to come," Jacob said, "but we don't have eighty dollars."

"I'll loan it to you," Hoxie said.

"Won't be indebted, either."

Hoxie threw out his hands. "Then what?"

Jacob smiled, wiped his hands on his pants, and stood to look Hoxie in the eye. "You pay for the extra axles, tongues, spokes, heavy equipment," he said. "And me and Jethro's labor for the journey will come to . . . about eighty dollars, I reckon. Don't you figure, Jethro?"

"Right about, brother," Jethro called from beneath the other wagon. "Yes, sir, eighty sounds about right."

A hundred miles outside of Independence, the twenty wagons formed a ragged line on the prairie. Behind the wagons came the horses, and behind them, the cattle, with riders to the sides, keeping things moving. Away from the wagons, off to one side so as not to choke on the dust, walked the women and children.

Jacob Wheeler drove the Conestoga while Jethro was behind in the old wagon they had brought from Virginia. Absalom Jones and his family were in the wagon just behind, and behind them came a German family by the name of Hobbes.

The Hobbes family made quite a show of being devout, with Preacher Hobbes invoking God's favor at every opportunity, and his wife playing hymns on the piano in the back of their wagon. Preacher Hobbes, who claimed to be a doctor, was quick to give unsolicited medical advice.

The shine of the adventure had dulled and the days had lapsed into a seemingly unending cycle: up at four o'clock, animals saddled and camp broken by five, breakfast at six, and then moving by seven and continuing at a crawl across the prairie while the light held out. When there was no wood for a fire, which was most of the time, the train used the buffalo chips the women and children gathered while walking. Hoxie rode incessantly up and down the train, barking orders, but he was uneasy in the saddle. His pilot was a rough man named Josiah Bell, and the scouts Skate and Meeks. Those weren't their real names, of course, because "Skate and Meeks" had fled their given names just as they had fled states, and for the same reason: to avoid prosecution for a long list of petty crimes. Although they shot the occasional buffalo to supplement the train's supplies, their main interests seemed to be whiskey and women. They had plenty of the former but few of the latter, so when they could, they watched the Wheeler women greedily from beneath their filthy slouch hats.

One afternoon, the scouts dropped a pair of buffalo cows but had to compete with wolves to bring the meat back to the camp. That night, the wolves slunk around the camp, hunger driving their persistence, and occasionally they would let out spine-shivering howls.

"The wolves," Thunder Heart Woman told Jacob as she breast-fed their new baby. "It is a bad sign. And these people you have chosen to lead us—they are surrounded by bad signs. We should go back. Tomorrow."

Jacob shook his head. "These people don't believe in magic or sign."

"Do you?" she asked.

"I can't get them to turn back," Jacob said.

"You won't even try."

A week later, the train was crossing the Smokey Hill River. The pilot had miscalculated and had not reached the river at the rocky ford that afforded easy passage, but had instead struck the river where there was no easy crossing for miles. But the river was not deep and Hoxie decided they had wasted enough time already, so they would risk the crossing.

The smaller wagons crossed it easily, taking the river on the diagonal, the water streaming around the bodies of the animals. The cattle bellowed but crossed without accident. Then came Jacob's Conestoga and the other large wagons, which were too heavy to cross without sinking, so rafts had been made of them by lashing logs to either side, and then they were pulled across with ropes.

Standing in the Conestoga, a long pole in his hand, Jacob gave the wagon a nudge every now and then to keep it headed generally upstream. Behind him, Jethro was struggling to keep the older wagon at the proper angle.

"Let the ropes pull you across," Jacob called, "on the angle. Don't fight it."

"I know," Jethro called as he caught the angle again. "You've told me a dozen times."

Then Jacob noticed the massive Hobbes wagon, fifty yards downriver. All seven family members were in it, the piano was still in the back, and Preacher Hobbes was attempting to drive the wagon straight across. Water was already piling against the side of the wagon.

"Stay on the oblique, Preacher," Jacob called, cussing under his breath. He couldn't mind his own wagon, Jethro, and the Hobbes family all at the same time.

"Watch the current!" the pilot Josiah Bell called. "Angle upriver!"

The wagon bobbed in the water, the wheels spun in the current without contacting the muddy bottom, and then the back end of the wagon spun around. Mrs. Hobbes screamed, and Josiah Bell called for Preacher Hobbes to release the team. It was too late, however, because the wagon had already dipped into the current, and the bed immediately flooded.

With a discordant boom and a shower of ivory keys, the piano toppled into the water. Relieved of the burden, the wagon seemed to right itself for a moment, then was caught by the current again and flipped completely over, scattering the seven members of the Hobbes family into the Smokey Hill. They clung to crates and whatever other of their belongings that floated while the horses screamed and struggled against the pull of the swamped wagon.

"Help them!" Leah screamed at the scouts from the back of Jethro's wagon. Skate and Meeks were sitting on their horses in shallow water near the opposite bank, a hundred yards away from the imperiled wagon, and they spurred their horses up the bank.

"Why don't they help them?" Leah asked.

"They can't," Jacob snapped. "You can't ride a horse downriver. They drown."

While the scouts and the others fished the Hobbes family out of the river, the wheel of Jethro's wagon struck a stone on the bottom of the river and lurched. Leah, who was sitting on the upriver side of the wagon, lost her balance and fell into the water.

Her long dress pulled her under like an anchor, and she could feel herself passing beneath the bottom of the wagon she had called home since leaving Virginia three years earlier. Once on the other side of the wagon, she broke the surface of the water, found her feet briefly, screamed, then was swept under again. She was being swept into the path of the panicked German team.

"Leah!" Rachel screamed.

Jethro pulled his boots off and was in the water in an instant, leaving the long pole in Rachel's hands and Jacob screaming incomprehensible instructions to her from the other wagon. Jethro dove into the muddy water, searching with his hands, hoping he would chance grasping a portion of Leah's dress, but the girl had already been swept far down the river. He came up, shaking water from his eyes, helpless.

Downstream, the Hobbes horses were turning the water into foam as they struggled to break free. For a few moments, the muddy froth turned crimson. Then the horses were free.

Preacher Hobbes huddled beneath a blanket, nursing a tin cup of coffee, with his equally drenched family around him. For the first time since any of the train had known him, he was speechless.

Hoxie was shouting at him. "You were to cross on the angle like everybody else. To wait for the hold ropes. Those instructions were very clear. But no, you wouldn't listen, and you did things on your own. Under the contract, these are grounds to cut you off. Legally, we could leave you right here!"

Jim Ebbetts, a slim and usually quiet rider who helped take care of the riders, glanced at Rachel's grief-stricken face. Then Ebbetts stepped forward and placed a hand on Hoxie's shoulder.

"Dammit, Hoxie. That's enough," Ebbets said. "Nothing can be done now. Leave it."

Rachel was staring downriver, where Jacob was taking Leah's broken body into his arms from the scouts Skate and Meeks, who stood waist-deep in the water. Jacob clutched her to him and rocked the body gently.

*   *   *

By the time a shallow grave was dug and Jacob had prepared a simple wooden cross which said, LEAH
WHEELER 1812–1841, Preacher Hobbes had again found
his voice. By torchlight, he delivered the eulogy for the
twenty-nine-year-old girl to the assembled train.

"God in His greatness, in His mysterious workings, has
taken this child from us," Hobbes intoned. "We weep for
her and her family, and we know that God weeps with us.
Though we know not why this tragedy has fallen upon us,
we thank Thee for Thy blessings and pray that you will
take this child's soul to your tender breast."

Thunder Heart Woman whispered bitterly to Jacob,
"God did not take my sister-in-law. It was his foolishness."

Jacob was silent.

"I do not like this Hobbes," she continued. "His mouth
moves but not his heart."

The service was over in a few minutes, and while the rest
of the train returned to the camp, the Wheelers remained.
Jacob had his old ledger out, and he was sketching.

"What are you doing?" Jethro asked.

"Marking the location," Jacob said. "It's important."

Naomi, who was kneeling beside the grave, stood.

"I've had enough of this business," she told Jacob. "I
want to go back, Jacob."

"Back to Virginia?" Jethro asked while Jacob continued
to draw.

Naomi knocked the book from Jacob's hands. "Back to
Missouri. We're all sick of this. The women, anyway, at
least those of us who are still alive. I know your wife feels
the same."

Jacob calmly picked up the ledger, brushed it off, and
placed it in his pocket. Then, without saying a word, he
turned and strode back toward the camp.

There were wheels to repair. Jacob and Jethro worked
silently the next morning, while Rachel sat alone on a boulder. Jim Ebbetts came up to her awkwardly and removed
his hat.

"Miss Rachel," he said. "I just wanted to say how sorry
I am about your sister."

"Thank you, Mr. Ebbetts."

"Please call me James," he said. "Jim would be better."

"Jim, then."

"I hope what I hear about you going back to Missouri ain't true," Ebbetts said. "I know ten words have not passed between us, but I sure have enjoyed your company on this here train. Your presence, miss, it pleases me." Ebbetts waited awkwardly.

"My presence?" Rachel asked. "The sight of me? I'm twenty-eight years old and feel like I'm twice that. I'd give anything to feel like a girl again: clean hair, smooth skin, wearing my Sunday best, perhaps going on a picnic. That's as much prairie as I'd ever want to see again. And then right back home to a place that doesn't weave and roll and hide wicked things, someplace fixed and permanent. A place to rest."

"Yes, ma'am."

"Leah's resting now," Rachel said. "She's the lucky one."

Rachel began to cry, and Ebbetts was unsure what to do. He reached out for her, but withdrew his hands, afraid someone might see. Then he decided he didn't give a damn and reached for her in earnest; she sobbed against him for a few moments. Then she realized how close they were and abruptly pulled away.

At that moment, Jacob rolled a repaired wheel toward Absalom Jones, who deftly caught it to the delight of his ten-year-old son, Marquis.

"Mister, you have to teach me to fix them wheels right!" the boy said.

"I will, son," Jacob said. "I will."

Days later, a storm came from nowhere. It began as a pounding rain and violent wind, and the wagon train took refuge beneath a copse of trees on the prairie, with the wagons squared and the cattle in the center. Then lightning turned the top of the tallest tree into a ball of flame, showering the train with smoking branches. Margaret Light Shines held her hands to her ears and screamed in terror.

The cattle bolted, knocking over two wagons in the process, and they were followed by some of the horses, scattering in every direction on the prairie.

Ebbetts and the others swung into the saddle, but Josiah Bell called out not to give chase. The animals couldn't be controlled until the storm had passed.

As the other Wheelers huddled beneath the wagons for cover, Naomi followed the cattle. Jethro grabbed her wrist, but she fought him off and ran into the prairie.

"Dammit," Jacob said, then turned to Jethro. "Take care of things here. I'll fetch her."

Jacob slipped in the mud as he chased his sister. She was still running, arms outstretched and mouth open, tasting the rain.

"Naomi!" he called. "Get back here. You'll get killed."

Naomi laughed. "Oh please, God, kill me!"

Jacob reached her but she spun and left him in the mud.

"Strike me with one of your thunderbolts, you old bastard," Naomi challenged. "Take me like you took Leah. What's wrong? Aren't I good enough for you?"

"No!" Jacob said. "Come back."

Then a horseman was upon them and swept Naomi up and across his saddle. It happened so swiftly that Jacob feared it was a Cheyenne warrior and was reaching for his Bowie knife before, through the driving rain, he realized it was the scout named Skate.

Skate rode Naomi back and gently returned her to the waiting arms of Jethro and Rachel. As Jacob ran back to the train, he noticed a knot of people standing around Absalom Jones, who was on his knees. At his feet was his son, Marquis.

"Oh God," Jones cried and drove his fists into the mud. "Cattle stomped my boy. Ran right over him."

At that moment the boy's mother, Sally, appeared. She glanced at the dead boy, then looked with hate at his father. "Why did you have to bring us here? Why couldn't we have stayed in Illinois? What kind of life is this? It's no life for our son—that's what it is. 'Betterin' ourselves,' that's what you called it. Why can't a nigger know his place? Tell me that. Why can't a nigger know his place?"

She threw herself against Absalom so violently that she drove him to the ground. The men had to restrain her from kicking his brains out.

Still being held by Jethro and Rachel, Naomi watched as Skate promised to help the distraught woman find the grave again anytime she'd like.

TWENTY-FOUR

*Encampment of Running Fox Band
They Captured Many Hourse (1841)*

Zebulon Gates was a whiskey trader by profession but was not above dealing in a few cheap rifles, if the profits were good enough. And the little Lakota band he had stumbled upon had more than enough Blackfoot ponies to trade to make it worth his while.

"Four muskets for four ponies," Gates said. "Good?"

White Crow, who had picked up English quickly after his first exposure at Fort William, translated for his father. Running Fox considered for a moment, then shook his head.

"No," he said. "Twelve muskets for four ponies."

Gates laughed. "Hell, I wouldn't give you that good of a deal even if'n you was white. But I tell you what I'm going to do, because I like you and because you are one smart savage. We'll split the difference and make it eight muskets for four of the best ponies."

Running Fox nodded, but White Crow shook his head. "No, Father. The white trader will show us how to use these rifles as well and give us enough of the thunder powder for many shots."

Running Fox peered at Gates, and Gates asked incredulously, "All of you?"

"No," White Crow said. "Teach me. I will show the rest."

"Why, I expect that can be done," Gates said. "Why not?"

"Yes," White Crow said. "Why not?"

TWENTY-FIVE

The Plains
1841 (They Captured Many Horses)

"Nice moon tonight," Ebbetts said.

Rachel looked up. She had been sitting by herself in the shadows while the rest of the train danced by firelight to a pair of fiddles. The train was smaller now, only a dozen wagons and less than half the cattle. By the light of the full moon, the Rockies seemed to loom large in the west, but were still three weeks away. Rachel was thinking of all the things she could do in three weeks in Missouri.

"Nice enough," Rachel said.

Then she looked at Ebbetts. It was the first time she could remember seeing his long hair combed and his clothes not coated with trail dust. She suppressed a laugh, because he looked like a little boy being forced to go to Sunday school.

Ebbetts offered his arm. "Would you dance with me, Miss Rachel?"

"No," she said.

Rachel moved farther into the darkness. Then, impulsively, she stopped and called over her shoulder, "Let's just walk a bit."

Ebbetts trailed after her. "Would you consider getting married?"

"I beg your pardon."

"I mean, would you ever consider getting married," he said. "Someday, of course."

"Someday, I imagine," she said. "Wouldn't you?"

Ebbetts stopped. "Why, that's why I asked."

"What do you mean?"

"Well," he said awkwardly, "what I'm trying to ask is this: would you consider marrying me?"

"You mean someday."

"No, miss," he said. "Now."

"Now?"

"Well, not right this minute of course," Ebbetts said. "But perhaps in the next couple of days, when time and weather permit."

When Rachel stared at him, he said apologetically, "I know you don't know much about me, but we'll have plenty of opportunity for that. Once we get to California, I intend to farm. I heard the grass is so good, you don't even have to put up hay."

Rachel felt like laughing again. "Hay?"

"Well, yes."

Rachel looked at the sky. She felt that she had to start living or else she would suffocate. The moonlight glistened in her eyes. "All right, Mr. Ebbetts, I'll marry you."

Ebbetts smiled. "That was easier than I thought."

She smiled shyly, waiting for him to kiss her. It took Ebbetts a moment to recognize the opportunity, and when he did, he pulled her close a little too roughly and kissed her hard, full on the mouth, but she did not resist. She was returning the passion when she realized that Ebbetts had stopped responding. His eyes were open, looking beyond her.

"What now?" she asked, then turned to see.

An Indian on horseback was silhouetted against the night sky. The moonlight caused his feathers, his lance, and his shield to glow eerily.

"Don't move," Ebbetts whispered.

The horse snorted and pawed the ground. Then the warrior spoke to them in his own language. When they didn't answer, he turned the horse and rode slowly away.

"What did he say?" Rachel asked.

"Damned if I know," Ebbetts said. "I reckon he was Kaw, a friendly enough tribe, and interested in what we could give him. If that's what he was indeed asking, we don't have an infernal thing to spare."

Two nights later, under a canopy of stars, Ebbetts and Rachel stood hand in hand before Preacher Hobbes. He pronounced them man and wife, and Ebbetts knocked some of the wildflowers from Rachel's hair as he roughly kissed her.

"Who's next?" Hobbes called.

Naomi and Skate stepped forward.

"Do you have a ring?" Hobbes asked.

"Yes, sir, we do," Skate said. He removed from his pocket a ring woven from beads and horsehair.

"That goes in your nose," his friend Meeks called, and the assembly guffawed.

Jacob Wheeler stepped up beside Meeks and grasped the drunken scout's right arm just above the elbow. He pressed hard enough to make Meeks squirm.

"A wedding is cause for celebration," Jacob said, "not ridicule. Something about the plains makes dissimilar people cling to each other in order to leave grief behind. We move on, toil and drive, plod and push, and just keep moving. Grief is a luxury none of us can afford. You distract my cousins from their happiness and I will make sure you never use this arm again to lift another jug."

TWENTY-SIX

Dog Star stared in disbelief. The wind whistled through skeletal lodge poles that hovered over cold ashes. The ground was littered with dead warriors and the bodies of many women and children, all surprised by a middle-of-the-night ambush.

Dog Star sat very still atop his horse for several minutes, fixing the scene in his mind, because he knew that he would need to summon the image when the time came. Then he made a motion with his hand, and one of his scouts dismounted and examined the victims.

"Crow," the scout said, examining one of the arrows protruding from the back of a Lakota child.

"Crow did this?"

The scout snapped the shaft of the arrow and brought it to Dog Star to examine the fletching. "With thunder sticks they killed our warriors," the scout said. "Then arrows and knives for the women and children."

Dog Star ground his teeth in rage. "Now that the Crow have rifles they invade our hunting ground and kill the Lakota. Why? Must I make war upon them to know the answer?"

"We cannot make war against them," the scout said. "Not without rifles."

Dog Star clutched the broken shaft. "I have heard that the ghost of my brother, Loved by the Buffalo, still roams the *Paha Sapa*. I do not understand how this can be. But if this is true, we must find the ghost of my brother. He will be able to counsel us from the land of the dead. And if we are indeed able to speak with him, I know there is only one place where we will find him."

The wheel had rolled over Rachel's leg quicker than anyone could shout to her to jump out of the way. They had been negotiating a sharp downslope when one of the wagons had broken free of its draglines and tumbled down upon her, first knocking her to the ground; then a heavy iron-rimmed rear wheel crushed her leg.

Ebbetts had prayed all the way in the thirty seconds it took to ride to her and jump down from his horse, but as soon as he lifted her skirt he knew his prayers had gone unheeded: a splinter of white bone glistened in the bloody mess below her right knee.

Now she lay in the back of the Wheeler Conestoga, crying out in pain as if the wagon was still bumping along on the uneven trail, even though the train had stopped for the night. Her eyes were closed, her face was covered in perspiration, and she clutched Thunder Heart Woman's arm.

Holding a lantern, Preacher Hobbes pulled back the canvas and stepped into the bed of the wagon. Jacob and Ebbetts were behind, and Hoxie waited outside.

"She can't sleep," Ebbetts said. "Says there's something crawling in there."

Hobbes grabbed the edge of the blanket and drew it roughly back from her leg. He lowered the lantern, and the warm light revealed a swarm of maggots over the wound.

"Oh, God," Ebbetts said.

"Jim?" Rachel asked.

"Lie back," Ebbetts said. "Just lie back."

The men withdrew from the wagon.

"Gangrene," Jacob said.

"What can we do?" Ebbetts asked.

"Very little," Hobbes said, "except pray."

"How about surgery?" Ebbetts offered.

"You mean amputation?" Hobbes asked.

"You're the one who claimed to be a doctor," Ebbetts said bitterly. "You tell me."

"You did claim to be able to doctor," Hoxie said. "It's in your contract."

Hobbes was silent.

"Can she be saved?" Jacob asked.

"It's gone too far . . . ," Hobbes said.

"We've got to try," Ebbetts said.

"She's suffered enough, Jim," Jacob said. "There's no point in putting her through more."

"So we're just going to let her die?" Ebbetts asked.

"Keep your voice down," Jacob said.

"She's my wife!"

"Well, she's my cousin," Jacob said.

"Gentlemen, it is *her* leg," Hoxie said. "I think we should leave the decision to the owner of the property. Ebbetts, you're her husband. You ask."

Ebbetts blinked and swallowed. Then he entered the wagon and asked Thunder Heart Woman to step outside.

"I heard you foolish men talking," Thunder Heart Woman said. "You do not understand. The worms are a good thing. They are eating the sickness."

"It's disgusting," Hobbes said.

"It is the only chance she has," Thunder Heart Woman said.

A kitchen table was taken from one of the Hoxie wagons and placed beneath a tree limb from which a half dozen lanterns swung. On a bench beside the table were placed a washbasin and rags, and hidden beneath a blanket were an arsenal of butcher knifes, awls, and a handsaw. Then Rachel was brought outside and placed on the table and Hobbes uncorked a little brown bottle and brought it to her lips. She moved her head away at the smell.

"Drink," he said. "Laudanum."

She took a couple of swallows. Then the men strapped her down with harness leather. She struggled involuntarily, and Ebbetts took her hand and squeezed it tight.

"You're gonna be all right, moonlight," he said. "We're gonna fix you right up."

Hobbes drew back the blanket and picked up the handsaw. Rachel screamed. Hobbes nodded. Then Meeks stepped forward and placed a belt in Rachel's mouth, stifling her screams. Her eyes were wide with terror, and Ebbetts had to look away.

It took Hobbes an hour and a half of cutting and hacking

to remove the leg. By the time he was done, he was covered in blood and sweat, and Rachel was dead. It had not occurred to him to use a tourniquet.

Alone at the medicine wheel at the center of the world, Dog Star made an offering of tobacco, cloth, and sage. Then he sat with his back to the cairn, closed his eyes, and prayed fervently. When he opened his eyes, Loved by the Buffalo was sitting in front of him.

His brother was dressed in worn robes, his face was weathered, but his eyes were bright. Dog Star regarded him for many minutes to make sure that the apparition would not vanish.

"Are you indeed my brother's ghost?"

"I am indeed your brother," Loved by the Buffalo said. "My spirit has not fled."

"How is this possible?"

"It is the will of *Wakan Tanka*," Loved by the Buffalo said.

Dog Star nodded. Nothing more needed to be said of this. "Running Fox, our brother, has left the tribe because he believed we would only be able to resist the white man if we learn their ways. I insisted that we remain true to the Grandfather spirit, to the ancient ways of the Lakota." Dog Star paused. "Was I wrong?"

When Loved by the Buffalo did not answer, Dog Star asked, "Does *Wakan Tanka* speak with you?"

"I seek him every day," Loved by the Buffalo said. "Sometimes, yes. Sometimes, no."

"Then tell me," Dog Star pleaded. "Must we change our ways?"

"No," Loved by the Buffalo said. "Never."

"You are sure of this?"

"Do not ask me how I know this," Loved by the Buffalo said solemnly. "But believe that I know. It is my mission to do this, and I shall live long enough to accomplish this mission and no longer. It is written on my heart and it is as plain to me as this hand that I hold out."

Dog Star reached out and grasped Loved by the Buffalo's hand and squeezed tightly. His brother was indeed flesh.

TWENTY-SEVEN

The Plains
1841 (They Captured Many Horses)

Sally Jones died of cholera. The Jones wagon had been in the rear of the train, and Hoxie declared that the train would separate to keep the disease from spreading; those who had had immediate contact with the dead woman and her family would stay behind, while the forward part of the train proceeded. When the rear part of the train moved, in a few days, it would go its own way.

The three wagons ordered to stay behind belonged to the Wheelers and Absalom Jones.

The only Wheeler in the forward portion of the train was Naomi, with her husband, Skate. As she waved good-bye to her clan, smiling and waving, she choked back the fear that it would be the last time she would ever see them.

"Fear and death," she said to herself as she turned west. "Fear and death."

Before the three wagons moved an inch, Jethro Wheeler became ill. He retched violently and could not control his bowels. Jacob threw a blanket around him, tossed some sugar and salt in a bucket of water, and helped Jethro to the top of a nearby hill. There, he waited with him for the sickness to either pass or to kill them both. Jethro protested, and Thunder Heart Woman pleaded from the bottom of the hill, but Jacob refused to leave his brother.

"I want my husband," she said.

"What else am I to do?" Jacob asked. "He is my brother

and I cannot leave him. You are my wife and I must protect you and our children. If I get sick, you are better off without me. At least you will have a chance to survive."

"But what would we do without you?"

"Boil your water."

"You know what I'm asking."

"Go on without me. Catch up with the others."

"But they won't take us back," she said. "It is not just the sickness. It is the color of my skin and of our friend Mr. Jones."

"Then go your own way. Find your people. They will take all of you in, just as they took me in."

"Is that what you brought us out here for?" she asked. "To seek my own people? You and our children are my people."

"What do you want from me, woman?" Jacob asked angrily.

"I want my husband," she pleaded.

While Jethro shivered and often doubled over in pain, Jacob kept him drinking the water that was laced with sugar and salt.

"Leave me," Jethro urged. "Go to the others."

"We've lost too many already," Jacob said. "Leah. Rachel. We're losing no more."

"I don't think that's for you to decide," Jethro said through chattering teeth.

"The hell it's not," Jacob said. "I shouldn't have let them come in the first place. I should have left them in Virginia, running home to Pa and Uncle Ben, where they would have been scolded but in a week would have been singing hymns in church and pining for the boys in Lancaster County."

"They didn't exactly give you a choice." Jethro was shaken by a fit of coughing and dry heaves. When he could speak again, he said, "I always wanted to be like you."

"You *are* like me," Jacob said.

Jethro smiled weakly. "That's the nicest thing you ever said to me, brother."

Jacob mopped his brow. "You're gonna get through this. I know it. We are going to be living out west, you and me, farms beside each other. You'll be raising a family next to mine."

Jethro nodded. He had lost all hope, but he was content

to allow his brother to hope for him. Two days later, Jacob returned from the hilltop . . . with his brother walking beside him.

"How is everybody?" Jacob asked.

"We are well," Thunder Heart Woman said, and Jacob nodded.

"What now?" Absalom Jones asked. "We are supposed to go our own way, but to where?"

"The sickness is over," Jacob said. "We pose no danger to them any longer. But we are too few to be caught in the mountains alone. Get moving and follow the ruts. I'll ride ahead, find them, and make them slow up. Fetch my rifle."

Thunder Heart Woman touched his face. "Do not forget about us."

He looked at her silently, then turned to saddle up.

The wagons were still burning when Jacob found the rest of the train. Some of the wagons were on their sides, their contents spilled, clothing and household goods tossed about. The horses were gone. Scattered about the mess, full of arrows, were the bodies: the Hoxie family, Hobbes and his brood, Josiah Bell. All had been stripped, most had been scalped, and the men had been mutilated in particularly humiliating ways.

Jacob walked from body to body, his grandfather's rifle cradled in his arms, aware that the war party who had done this would not be far away. Finally he came to the body of Skate, whose bloody knife and shattered rifle were beside him. Four dead Indians were at his feet. Jacob knelt and talked to Skate as if the dead man could hear him.

"Fought them hard, didn't you, cousin? Took more than your share. These are Cheyenne, and they don't come any tougher than that. You turned out not to be such a bad one after all." Jacob glanced about. "Was it because they took Naomi? Is that why you killed so many, cousin? God, I wish you could tell me which way they went." He paused. "Maybe to finish off the wagons left behind."

Jacob ran to the horse and jumped into the saddle. There was no need to bury or burn the bodies of the people he had known. The wolves and the birds would clean up the massacre site soon enough, and what was shocking to the senses would, in time, become one with the earth.

TWENTY-EIGHT

"Listen to 'em howl," Absalom Jones said. "It's enough to make your skin crawl."

"It's meant to," Jacob said.

The wagons were drawn together in a triangle and the men watched over their rifles at the eight Comanches slowly circling.

"Well, are they going to come or not?" Jethro asked.

"Maybe they just want to frighten us a bit, and then be on their way," Jones said optimistically.

"With each circle they come closer," Thunder Heart Woman said matter-of-factly while she clutched the baby, Jacob Jr., to her breast. "Do you see? They are testing the range of our weapons."

"Let them come," Jacob said coolly. "Wait until they are bold enough to rush us. Then sure shots only."

"Can I have a gun, Daddy?" Abraham High Wolf asked.

"Not today, Abraham," Jacob said, and Thunder Heart Woman pulled the boy back down.

Suddenly, the warriors rode straight for the wagons, screaming and letting arrows fly. When they were twenty yards away, Jacob said, "Now."

Jacob and Jethro fired simultaneously. Two of the warriors were knocked from their saddles into the dust. Jones fired and missed. As arrows fell into the protective triangle and thudded against the sides of the wagons, Jacob quickly reloaded, brought the rifle up, and shot a warrior in the face at a distance of three feet.

Spooked, the Jones team bolted, taking the wagon with it. Then an arrow struck Absalom Jones in the throat. He dropped his empty gun and fell. He clawed at the dirt, trying desperately to talk, but unable.

"Damn," Jacob said. He jumped into the breech, bowie knife in one hand and rifle in the other, and took broad swipes of the legs of the nearest Comanche horse. The animal screamed in pain and reared. The warrior fell to the ground, and Jacob clubbed him with the stock of his grandfather's rifle. Then, taking the lance from the unconscious Indian, he spun and impaled the next horse warrior bearing down upon him.

Jethro watched, mouth agape. Then an arrow pierced Jacob's back, near his armpit. The arrowhead protruded from his chest. He staggered. The warrior jumped from his horse, a knife at the ready to take Jacob's scalp.

Jethro brought his rifle up, but Thunder Heart Woman was already holding a muzzle-loading pistol in both hands. The baby was at her feet. She pulled the trigger, missing the advancing warrior's chest, but hitting him in the kneecap. He dropped, and then Jethro blew the top of his head off.

The two remaining Comanche warriors wheeled their horses, surveying the damage to the war party. Then they rode away from the wagons, yipping and hanging on to the sides of their horses.

Jacob staggered toward his brother. His eyes were wild and blood dribbled from the corner of his mouth. "Pull it out."

When Jethro hesitated, Jacob demanded, "Pull it out, damn it!"

Jethro shook his head and stepped back, but Thunder Heart Woman stepped forward. She snapped off the arrowhead. Then, bracing one hand against Jacob's back, she pulled the shaft out the way it had come. Jacob gasped, sank to his knees, then stood unsteadily. He nodded his thanks, but when he breathed, there was a terrible gurgling sound.

Jacob looked down at the body of Absalom Jones. In the dirt, the other man had managed to write *Sally*.

Naomi's hands were bound with rawhide, her face was covered with grime, and her dress was in tatters. She was staring at the ground. The warrior called Bear Blood grabbed her hair and pulled, forcing her chin up.

"Her face is ugly, like all white women," Bear Blood said. "But she is strong and has a pleasing figure. Certainly she is worth more than five horses to a great chief."

"Five horses only," Prairie Fire said. "It is a fair offer."

"Fair?" Bear Blood asked. "For whom?"

"To help your chief past the grief of losing Shadow Woman."

"Ah, but my chief's generosity should overshadow his grief," Bear Blood said. "After all, I was the one who led the attack on the whites. I dared much."

"And you gained much glory," Prairie Fire said. "What is this woman in comparison?"

Bear Blood nodded. He placed a hand in the small of Naomi's back and shoved her toward Prairie Fire. She stumbled and fell in the dust, not understanding.

Prairie Fire gestured to an old woman named Burned by the Sun. She stepped forward and beckoned to Naomi.

"How are you called?" the old woman asked in English.

"Naomi," she said. "Naomi Wheeler. Er, Burns. Mrs. Skate Burns. He was my husband." Then she turned to the chief. "Your warriors killed him."

Prairie Fire simply stared at Naomi, and Burned by the Sun said, "He, too, has lost a loved one. Come, you will now be called Five Horses."

"Oh, thank you kindly," Naomi said, "as if I didn't have enough names now to remember . . ."

Burned by the Sun drew a knife from somewhere within the folds of her robe. Naomi closed her eyes. The old woman severed the rawhide that bound Naomi's wrists.

Then the old woman smiled. "You will learn. I envy you. Come, you must prepare."

She pulled Naomi into a lodge, stripped her, and washed the dirt from her face and body. Then she began to massage her with fats and scented oils.

Naomi sniffed, then grimaced. "What is that?"

"It will make Prairie Fire burn all night." The old woman laughed at her own joke.

After the beads and feathers had been woven into her hair, and a bone necklace placed around her neck, Naomi began to understand. "Am I to be married tonight? Is that it?"

"There are worse fates," the old woman said.

"Hell, I've been married," Naomi said. "There ain't nothin' to it. You get so lonely on the trail you think you're going to go out of your mind, and then you spark with somebody you wouldn't have looked at in a million years back home, and then you're happy for about the time it takes to blow out a candle. And then you're staring at your man, dead on the ground."

When the old woman gathered her things and backed out of the tipi, Naomi asked, "Did I say something wrong?"

Then Prairie Fire entered. "I have never seen such a beautiful white woman."

Naomi, of course, did not understand.

Prairie Fire climbed on top of his property. He felt none of the tenderness he had felt toward Shadow Woman. Naomi did not resist, nor did she allow herself to feel pleasure or pain. To keep her mind intact, she began to recite the first thing that came to her: nursery rhymes.

"Hey diddle diddle," she said, "the cat and the fiddle, the cow jumped over the moon. . . ."

Disconcerted, Prairie Fire stopped.

"Little Miss Muffet sat on a tuffet, eating her curds and whey, along came a spider and sat down beside her and frightened Miss Muffet away."

Prairie Fire left the tipi. He returned with Burned by the Sun, Bear Blood, and the tribe's shaman.

Naomi leaned forward. She brushed her beaded hair from her face and locked eyes with the shaman. "Little Jack Horner sat in a corner, eating his pumpkin pie. Put in his thumb, pulled out a plum, and said, 'Gee, what a good boy am I.' "

Prairie Fire stared in fear at her.

"Old King Cole was a merry old soul, and a merry old soul was he. He called for his pipe and he called for his bowl, and he called for his fiddlers three."

The shaman spoke sternly and shook his rattle.

"He believes you summon evil spirits with these rhymes," Burned by the Sun said.

"I'm not summoning evil spirits. It's more like keeping

evil spirits away." Then Naomi turned to the shaman. "Old Mother Hubbard went to the cupboard to fetch her poor dog a bone, and when she got there, the cupboard was bare and so the poor dog had none."

The shaman recoiled, but Prairie Fire smiled.

At the head of the hunting party, Running Fox regarded the lone Conestoga in the valley below them. A team was hitched to the wagon, but it was motionless.

"Let us take them, Father," White Crow urged. "They are weak. It is the natural order of things."

"Let us pretend for a moment that you are the leader of the clan and not I," Running Fox said. "Would you throw a band of warriors against one buffalo? Or would you wait and stalk the herd?"

Running Fox did not wait for his son's response. Instead, he turned his horse and led the band in the opposite direction.

In the back of the wagon, Jacob Wheeler was in agony. "Leave me here."

"We won't," Jethro said.

"I can't take the wagon no more," Jacob said. "I don't want to die like my cousin Rachel died, fighting and kicking. I'd rather die in peace, looking up at the sky."

"We will camp here until you are well," Thunder Heart Woman said.

"Winter's coming," Jacob said. "You must get through the pass and over the divide before it hits. Nobody has ever survived winter in the high mountains. Go with Jethro. Take the children. I will find you."

"Lord almighty. How can you ask me to abandon you?" Jethro asked. "How?"

"Because the road will kill me quicker than leaving me behind," he said. "At least here I can rest up, heal . . . if it's the Lord's will."

Thunder Heart Woman cried in exasperation, and Jacob said to her, "You know what you must do. It's what your people do. It is more important that our children live than we do."

Jacob clutched the buffalo amulet over his chest, then

with a jerk snapped the rawhide. He held it out to Thunder Heart Woman. "You gave this to me the day we met. It's yours again."

"I want you to keep it." She folded his fingers back over the amulet and held his hand tightly. "Thank you for finding me. Thank you for saving me. Thank you for loving me."

"Hell," Jacob said, then coughed, "loving you was the easy part."

When Thunder Heart Woman began to cry, Jacob said, "I'll see you and the children again. I know it."

"Yes," Thunder Heart Woman said, "but on which path?"

White Crow slid from his horse and cautiously approached the white man who was sprawled facedown in the dirt. A dark brown stain covered one side of his buckskin shirt. His belongings were scattered around him: a blanket, a massive knife, and an old-fashioned flintlock rifle.

The boy put a moccasin on the man's shoulder and pushed him over onto his back. The man's face was badly blistered. His eyes were clouded.

"He lives, but not for long," White Crow said as Running Fox knelt beside the man. "Arrow wound. He has a rifle. We can take it. It is old but well-made. It will be one less rifle the whites—or the Blackfeet—can use against us."

Running Fox unclenched the white man's right fist and found the buffalo amulet.

Josh Brolin as Jedediah Smith.

Jessica Capshaw as Rachel Wheeler
(*on left*); Keri Russell as Naomi Wheeler.

Matthew Settle as
Jacob Wheeler.

Kurt Markus

Kurt Markus

Jacob and Jethro Wheeler (Skeet Ulrich) oversee their
homestead.

Zahn McClarnon
as Running Fox.

Simon R. Baker as Loved by the Buffalo.

Tonantzin Carmelo as Thunder Heart Woman, who is enslaved by a white trader.

From center to right: Dog Star (Michael Spears), Loved by the Buffalo, and Running Fox celebrate a successful hunt with their infant sons.

Dog Star and Running Fox honoring the bones of the sacred buffalo.

Jacob Wheeler and Thunder Heart Woman pause on their journey west.

Kurt Markus

Jethro Wheeler picks through a streambed, looking for ore during the gold rush.

Chris Lange

Jethro and Martin Jarrett (Sean Astin) at the miners' camp.

Chris Lange

The Lakota take to the plains to hunt buffalo.

The Wheeler family mourns around the grave of their kin Leah.

Loved by the Buffalo rides into his tribe's village.

The tribe's medicine man conducts a hallowed ceremony.

Elder of the Lakota tribe.

A Lakota runner brings news back to the tribe.

The Treaty of Fort Laramie is read to the chieftains of various tribes.

A Pony Express rider dashes across the prairie to deliver important letters.

Lakota warriors ride out to confront settlers.

Jedediah Smith leads his men as they ford a river.

Conestoga wagons, or "prairie schooners," served as the primary mode of transportation for settlers moving ever westward.

Naomi and Rachel struggle with the hardships of life on the move.

Jacob and Thunder Heart Woman at the head of a group of Lakota.

Chris Lange

Naomi Wheeler captured by Lakota braves.

Chris Lange

Naomi assimilates
to life with the
Lakota.

Chris Lange

Naomi struggles with soldiers as the U.S. Army moves on the settlement.

The Lakota village is razed in the night by the Army.

Lakota warriors set out to exact retribution.

The cameraman donned a special wet suit to capture this scene in a frigid river in Alberta, Canada.

The crew films Matthew Settle and Tonantzin Carmelo out on the open plains.

TWENTY-NINE

Jethro drove the Conestoga over another endless mile of wheel-rutted road that led up a gentle slope. Thunder Heart Woman walked behind the wagon, carrying the baby, Jacob Jr. Abraham High Wolf and Margaret Light Shines walked behind in the daze they long ago had adopted on the trail, their minds elsewhere.

Then Jethro topped the rise. He reined the wagon to a stop and allowed the others to catch up.

"It's too beautiful to be real," he said.

California spread before them like a never-ending green carpet.

"What is it, Mama?" Margaret Light Shines asked, watching the tears roll down her mother's face.

"It is everything that Jacob said it was," Thunder Heart Woman said. "Do you see?"

"I see," the little girl said.

Abraham High Wolf took it in, then asked, "Will Pa ever see it?"

Inside Prairie Fire's lodge, Naomi lay on a buffalo robe, a piece of rawhide between her teeth. She was struggling loudly to give birth.

"You must remain quiet," Burned by the Sun said.

"To hell with that," Naomi managed in English through the rawhide. "Where I come from, women *scream*."

And she did. Outside the lodge, Prairie Fire smiled. Soon a baby cried, and the chief entered the lodge. Burned by the Sun had offered the umbilical cord to Naomi to cut with her teeth, but she had turned away and the old woman was severing it with a knife instead.

"What shall we call your son?" Burned by the Sun asked.

"My son—our son—shall be called One Horn Bull. When he grows to manhood, he will be as brave as his father . . . and as smart and proud as his mother."

Naomi held the baby to her breast. "Hickory dickory dock, the mouse ran up the clock. The clock struck one, the mouse ran down. Hickory dickory dock."

The baby cooed.

"Another," Prairie Fire said. "Please."

"Old Mother Hubbard went to her cupboard to fetch her poor dog a bone," she said. "When she got there the cupboard was bare and so her poor dog had none."

THIRTY

From the journal of Jacob Wheeler:

For three days, the renegade band of Lakota led by my brother-in-law Running Fox cared for me. It was a gift from Wakan Tanka. There is no other way to explain their finding me, or Running Fox recognizing the amulet I still clutched in my hand. Just as easily, they could have killed me as an act of mercy and taken my grandfather Abraham's rifle. But they did not.

When my strength returned, I set out into the mountains. I was weary unto death of the ways of civilization, both white and Indian, and wanted only to converse with nature.

And so I became a creature of the wilderness. Not a soul to answer to, and God's finest sculpture around me. Out of contact with whites, Indians, humans of any kind or color. The weeks passed. And then months.

I built a hut for myself in the mountains and passed the winter. I ran out of powder and shot and strapped Jim Fletcher's bowie knife on a pole to make a spear and hunted with that. I also set traps for rabbits and other small critters. I fished in the frozen streams. After a spell I got into the habit of talking to myself. Hermits, sooner or later, always go a little bit crazy. And I suppose I was crazier than most.

My little hut became crowded with silent ghosts: Leah still in her drowning clothes. Rachel broken and bloodied by the wheel. The Jones boy, Marquis, and his parents, Sally and

Absalom. Hoxie and his family, Josiah Bell, and Naomi's husband, Skate Burns. They all stared at me with accusing eyes. Why didn't you know your place? they asked with their looks. Why didn't a Wheeler know he was supposed to stay in Virginia? Look how we have paid for it.

In all, I stayed for two years up in the mountains. I could not force myself to leave and seek out Thunder Heart Woman and my children. I knew they were alive—and Naomi as well—because their faces did not peer at me from the darkness of the hut. But at the same time, I could not force myself to leave the stinking hut. I was convinced that everybody I had ever loved was better off rid of me. Considering all I had gone through, and put others through, I reckon I had gone a little bit insane.

And I had no answers.

The Creator himself perhaps knows the whys and wherefores, but I am a mere mortal and lack the reasons for all that has become of my lost and wayward life. I had run out on everything and everyone I had ever loved or ever valued. There was no use in waiting any longer, and there was nobody to say good-bye to.

I burned the hut to the ground.

Then I walked to the top of the highest bluff I knew. Below stretched a valley with a river snaking through it, like many Mr. Jedediah Smith and I had stood before, and I appreciated the handiwork of the Almighty. I figured that I was one of the few things created by the Lord that had come out wrong, and it wasn't His fault. It was mine. It is our responsibility to care for the gifts we have been given, and what had I done with mine?

I called to Thunder Heart Woman and Margaret Light Shines and Abraham High Wolf and Jacob Jr., and I asked the Lord God to help them remember who they are. They are Wheelers. And they are Lakota. And then, just as I adjusted myself to take that long step into that beautiful valley the Lord had made, my hand touched the buffalo amulet around my neck.

It was as if someone had nudged me from a long sleep. I stepped back from the ledge and pulled from my pocket this ledger that Jedediah Smith had given me so long ago. I read again what Mr. Smith had said about west being a place and not a way of life.

Somehow, I had allowed the worst part of the west to seep into my soul, the empty part, where things are deadly dull until they just turn deadly. My pain had blinded me to the grandeur of what the Lord had created and I was dwelling on the hardship and the sorrow. Like many souls, mine had been broken on the wheel of the journey of life, and I had not counted as gifts those who had been lost to me. It dawned on me that allowing ourselves to be driven crazy with grief is neglecting those gifts the Lord has given us, even if we only know them briefly: friends, family, those we meet and who show us some small kindness with no expectation of anything in return. Leah and Rachel and the others had died seeking something that I had first longed for reading the journals of the captains in my grandfather's loft. They may not have found their place, but they had died trying, and my Lakota family would have said those deaths honored Wakan Tanka.

My death would only have dishonored their memory.

So I climbed down from the lonely crag and continued the journey I had begun so long, as a child in Virginia. I was thirty-two years of age. And I realized that all along, it was not a direction I had sought, but a way of life.

THIRTY-ONE

The Northern Plains
The Winter of the Sacred Arrow (1843)

The people of the Cheyenne band were moving slowly, their lodges packed on travois and being pulled by dogs and ponies, the women walking beside. One Horn Bull walked alongside his mother, Naomi Five Horses.

They did not know that a family of white settlers had lost a cow to a starving band of Lakota the week before and that a detachment of dragoons had been sent out from Fort William in retribution.

The dragoons were led by a young lieutenant named Jenkins, who drew his saber and ordered the soldiers to prepare their carbines. The soldiers were also armed with a new kind of pistol, the Paterson Colt. Instead of having only one shot before reloading, the soldiers could fire six .36 caliber balls as quickly as they could pull the trigger on the revolving pistol.

When an older trooper pointed out to Jenkins that these Indians were not even of the same tribe that had slaughtered the cow, the lieutenant had frowned.

"It matters not," Jenkins said. "They are savages, and a lesson to one is a lesson to all. You will do your duty, Sergeant Johnson."

Prairie Fire saw the soldiers approaching, but thought at first that their horses were kicking up dust because they had some urgent message. By the time he saw the sun glinting from the outstretched saber of the young lieutenant, the first shots had rung out. Bear Blood was the first to fall.

Prairie Fire and other warriors fought with bow and lance, trying to allow time for the women and children to escape, but the fight did not last long. After the soldiers had fired their short rifles with the deep voices, they drew their short guns, which never seemed to run out of fire or lead.

Naomi Five Horses fell to the ground, One Horn Bull beneath her. The boy was wide-eyed and screaming in terror at the sight of his father lying dead before them, his head a bloody mass.

"That didn't take long," Lieutenant Jenkins said as he dismounted to inspect the body of the chief. Jenkins cocked his head at the sight of Naomi Five Horse's blond hair. "I'll be damned. A white woman." He removed his cap and offered his hand. "Are you all right, ma'am?"

She spat on his boots. For the Cheyenne, it was a greater insult than spitting in the face.

"Where's your family?"

"Here," she said.

"What's your name?"

"I am Five Horses, wife of Prairie Fire, mother of One Horn Bull."

Jenkins gestured to the soldiers to take her. "She's coming with us, Sergeant Johnson."

Naomi Five Horses fought, but three of the soldiers finally managed to separate mother and son. All of their faces, including the sergeant's, were bloody with claw marks. One of the Cheyenne women swept One Horn Bull away.

"They want to take their dead with them," the sergeant said, interpreting the gestures of the other women.

"Tell them they must leave them," Jenkins said, "or join them here forever."

"Leave me," Naomi Five Horses pleaded. "Leave me with my husband. Please, if you have any compassion in your heart, kill me now."

"Gag her," Jenkins said.

That night, as the dragoons camped by the riverbank on their way back to the fort, Johnson was left in charge of watching their white prisoner. She was tied to a willow tree near the water so that she could relieve herself when needed, out of sight of the men.

Johnson felt the scratches on his cheek. "I've never seen a blond squaw before. You are quite something."

She nodded.

"If I remove your gag, do you promise to behave?"

She nodded again, more slowly.

The sergeant removed the gag. While leaning forward, he paused and touched her hair.

"Perhaps we could talk more comfortably if you would unbind my wrists," Naomi said.

"Can't." Still leaning forward, the sergeant released the woman's hair and ran his hand down her shoulders and inside her buckskin dress. Suddenly, he kissed her, and she kissed him back, but awkwardly because her hands were still bound to the tree.

He stopped, looked at her heaving chest, then kissed her even harder than before. This time, he pulled her to him.

Naomi yelped in pain. "You're breaking my arms."

The sergeant pulled his knife and cut her free.

He raised her skirt and moved against her.

Then Naomi found the knife he had dropped and slowly brought the point up to within inches of his side.

She clapped one hand over his mouth while she slipped the knife between his ribs and twisted the blade, forcing it deeper. By the time she kicked him off her, he was dead.

Running Fox threw thirty buffalo tongues on the ground.

The trader whistled and pushed his hat back. "What you want for 'em, Chief?"

"The hand rifles," Running Fox said.

"Hand rifles?" he asked. "Oh, you mean pistols. Yeah, we can fix you right up, Chief." From a box below the counter he brought out an old single-shot flintlock. "There you go. Forty-five caliber. Blow a hole in something as big as your thumb."

Running Fox shook his head. "No. We want the short guns that shoot many times in a row."

"Oh, you mean Colts," the trader said. "Now you do know your weapons, don't you? I'm sorry, but we're fresh out of wheel guns. The other tribes beat you to it."

Running Fox was crestfallen, but the trader said, "Don't be so glum, Chief. Tell you what I'm not out of, and that's whiskey." He pulled a jug from beneath the counter and placed it in front of Running Fox. "Have a pull on me, Chief. Then, if you like it, we can talk about getting you fixed up with some more."

That night, Running Fox and White Crow and the other men of the clan were sitting around the campfire with their jugs. They were laughing and dancing, drunk out of their minds, and one of the younger men fell into the fire. He had spilled alcohol liberally across his shirt and pants, and he instantly erupted into a ball of flame.

Screaming, he vaulted out of the fire and rolled on the ground while the others watched stupidly for a moment. Some laughed. Then Running Fox and White Crow came to their senses and began to throw dirt on the man. The smell of burning human flesh and hair turned White Crow's stomach, and after the flames were out, he stumbled to the edge of the firelight, fell to his knees, and vomited.

The warrior's name was Younger Bear, and he cried in pain as he lay on the ground. Running Fox knelt beside him, unsure of how to help.

Loved by the Buffalo stepped out of the darkness into the firelight and looked sadly around him. Then he knelt beside the writhing Younger Bear and placed his hands upon him. Younger Bear looked at Loved by the Buffalo in thanks as the pain disappeared. And then the young warrior died.

THIRTY-TWO

California
1846 (The Winter of Soldiers Marching)

John Charles Fremont pulled the company to a stop in front of a well-kept adobe ranch house and addressed the Indian woman who watched warily from the front door.

"Madam, I am Captain Fremont and these are my volunteers," he said, sweeping the dusty cap from his head. "We would be obliged if you would allow us to fill our canteens at your well?"

Thunder Heart Woman was wary of soldiers, and as she rocked newborn Corn Flower in her arms, she pretended not to understand the request.

Jethro Wheeler squeezed past her. "I'm the lady's husband." He regarded Fremont. "Are you the Pathfinder? The hero of Monterrey?"

"Some call me that," Fremont said.

"Seen this?" one of the volunteers called as he unfurled a flag that had a crudely painted bear and star on it. "That's the flag of the California Republic! Made it myself. The border's out of an old red flannel shirt, and I used some pokeberry juice to paint the grizzly and the star."

"Looks like a damned hairy pig to me," Jethro said.

Jacob Jr., now eight years old, walked down the line of soldiers, offering them fruit from a basket. In the back of the column, driving the wheelwright's wagon, was Jacob Wheeler. Beside him was his partner, Pedro.

When the boy reached the end of the column, he looked

in his basket. "Only one orange left. Which one of you wants it?"

"Go ahead," Pedro said.

Jacob Wheeler sighed. He glanced up at Thunder Heart Woman and at his brother Jethro, who was absorbed in a conversation with Fremont. He had come a long and round-about way to reach California, and now that he had, his heart told him that he was no longer needed.

The boy held out the orange and Jacob took it. Jacob gouged a slice out of the orange with his thumb and placed it in his mouth.

"Say, boy," Jacob said.

"Yes, sir?"

"This is the best damned orange I ever had," he said. "I wish to give you a prize in return."

"A gift?" the boy asked.

Jacob took the buffalo amulet and dropped it over the boy's head. Then he leaned down and touched the boy's face gently.

"You take care of that," he said. "It has brought me luck and I'm sure it will do the same for you."

"Thanks, mister," the boy said.

"But you have to remember it's a magic necklace."

"Magic?"

"Yep," Jacob said. "And the magic works best if you don't tell anybody about it."

"Lie?"

"Not lie," Jacob Wheeler said. "Just keep it to yourself."

The boy nodded.

When the column moved again, Jacob lagged behind a bit as he looked over the ranch. It was everything he could have hoped for for Thunder Heart Woman. Then he flicked the reins and the wagon moved on.

"Are you not well, my friend?" Pedro asked.

"As well as anybody could expect," Jacob said, then changed the subject. "What do you think of California becoming part of the United States, amigo?"

"You Americans are like an ocean wave," Pedro said. "You will win the war with Mexico and she will be forced to give up her right to all of her lands north of the river you Americans call the Rio Grande. You cannot be stopped until you fill in all of the land between the oceans."

"Does that make it right?"

"It depends on whose side you are on," Pedro said. "Whose side are you on, senor?"

Jacob grinned. "It seems, for now anyway, you and me are on the side of the hairy pig."

While the baby slept, Thunder Heart Woman was mending some laundry by the light of the fireplace. Jacob Jr. walked past, and she noticed something peeking from beneath his shirt.

"Jacob."

"Yes, Mama."

"What do you have around your neck?"

"One of the men gave it to me."

She reached inside his shirt, but the boy pulled back.

"He said it was a magic necklace," Jacob Jr. said.

"Come here," Thunder Heart Woman ordered.

Dutifully, the boy approached, and his mother studied the buffalo amulet.

"Mama, are you all right? You look sick."

"This man," Thunder Heart Woman said, "what did he look like?"

"I don't know."

"Describe him to me," she said forcefully.

"He was tall, like Uncle Jethro."

"What did he say? Did he know you?"

"He said he liked my orange." When tears formed in Thunder Heart Woman's eyes, the boy asked, "What's wrong? Don't you like the necklace?"

"No," she said. "It is precious. Keep it."

Running Fox stood at the edge of the Lakota village, at the head of his small band, waiting for permission to enter. He had been standing there for an hour before Dog Star finally came out to greet him.

"It has been many years, brother," Dog Star said.

"In our shame, Loved by the Buffalo came to us in a vision," he said. "He told us to return. But we must ask permission and forgiveness to pass through the horns of the camp."

"You are welcome here," Dog Star said. "You are family. You may always share our lodges and our meat, even if we disagree."

"We disagree no longer," Running Fox said. "Brother, you were right so many years ago. The whites' meager scraps will not sustain our people. Only the ancient ways can be relied upon."

"Did you see him?" Margaret Light Shines asked. She was holding the amulet in her hand.

"No," Thunder Heart Woman said.

"Then how do you know it was my father?" she asked. "It could have been anyone. Someone may have killed him and taken the buffalo amulet and as a whim given it to Jacob Jr."

"That does not make sense," Thunder Heart Woman said. "Perhaps, if it was any boy, but Jacob Jr.? No, it had to be him. Who else could it have been?"

The girl nodded. She was sixteen now, and as a Wheeler, logic was one of the things that she had learned to prize. But as a Lakota, she was also required to listen to her heart.

"So he's alive," she said, "and knows we're here."

"Yes, and he wishes to leave us in peace," Thunder Heart Woman said. "I've asked myself why that would be a thousand times, but I have no answer."

"Does Uncle Jethro know?"

"He saw it on the boy," Thunder Heart Woman said. "It eats at him inside. I should have buried the amulet, kept it from him."

When Margaret Light Shines placed the amulet over her own head and stood, Thunder Heart Woman asked, "What are you doing?"

"I must find him," she said. "He's my father."

Jacob Wheeler stumbled through the burned-out remains of the village, stepping over the fourteen bodies of the Klamath men. The women and children were huddled together, under guard.

The smoking village provided a stark contrast to the eerily placid Upper Klamath Lake in Oregon territory. At Jacob's feet, a warrior groaned. Jacob knelt, cradled the man's head, and gave him a sip of water from his canteen.

"These aren't the Indians who killed your men, Captain," Jacob said. "Those were Modoc. These are Klamath."

"This chastisement will serve as a warning to all renegade tribes," Fremont said stiffly.

Jacob turned to Fremont's scout. "You scouted the wrong band, Mr. Carson."

"Stand away from the prisoner," Fremont ordered.

When Jacob didn't move, Fremont nodded toward Carson. Carson pushed Jacob away with his foot, then drew his pistol and shot the wounded man.

"I've had my bellyful of soldiering," Jacob said. "Captain Fremont, your only cause is yourself, and it is innocent folks like this who have paid for it with their own blood. I once swore to myself that I'd never again be part of killing innocents. Well, Captain, you can go to war without my wheels."

THIRTY-THREE

The American River, California
1849 (The Winter of Cholera)

The news that a crew building a sawmill for John Sutter near Sacramento had discovered gold sparked one of the largest migrations in human history.

But Jethro Wheeler, who lived scarcely thirty miles away from Sutter's mill, had no idea that a half million people would eventually fill the Sacramento Valley. He had thrown some belongings in a pack, bid Thunder Heart Woman and the children good-bye, and promised he would be back in a couple of days. He soon found himself walking down the muddy main street of a tent city.

Merchants and hustlers hawked their wares from the backs of wagons and beneath flapping canvas, and every one of them had a scale on which to weigh nuggets or dust panned from the stream. From atop an apple crate, a traveling preacher chastised his unrepentant flock.

"Think on the Lord's words, brother," the preacher called as he thumped his Bible. "What should it profit a man to gain the world, but lose his own soul? Turn back now, brothers. Turn back before the wages of sin exact their fearful toll."

"Move on, preacher," one of the grizzled prospectors called. As others jeered and catcalled, the prospector kicked the crate out from beneath the preacher, who fell into the arms of Jethro Wheeler.

"Whoa, there," Jethro said.

"Thank you, son."

"It's none of my business, Reverend," Jethro said, "but it seems to me that if the Lord didn't want a man to profit himself and his family by those rocks He put in the ground, He wouldn't have put them there in the first place."

"I'll pray for you," the preacher called as Jethro moved on.

"I'll take all the help I can get," Jethro shot back.

"Hey, Reverend," a prostitute called from beneath the flap of a tent brothel, "come on in here and I'll show you something that will bring you to your knees."

The crowd roared.

That afternoon, as Jethro stood up to his shins in the freezing water and panned for gold along with a hundred other aspiring millionaires, he reckoned the preacher's prayer must have done some good: glittering in the sun on the rim of the pan was a bit of color.

Margaret Light Shines stepped out of the second floor of the boardinghouse carrying a pail full of dirty water, passed a window with a sign that said NO MEXICANS OR INDIANS. She emptied the bucket over the rail and into the street. Below her, Charles Fremont looked up to see where the filthy water had come from.

Fremont frowned up at her, then continued to wave to the cheering crowd with his dusty cap. Beside him rode his scout, Christopher "Kit" Carson, in dirty buckskins and with a half-stock percussion rifle across his lap. Behind them, the troopers were spread out on their horses. Margaret scanned the faces of the men passing below.

"Quit gawking and get back to work," the landlady called from behind her. "There's beds to be made. I run a respectable house and you'll see to it that it looks respectable."

Margaret took one last look at the men before returning to the house. The landlady watched her go, then slammed the door shut.

On a promontory above San Francisco Bay, Ethan Biggs ducked beneath the dark cloth and framed the upside-down image of the Presidio on the ground glass at the back of the heavy box camera. The camera was a Giroux, signed by Daguerre himself, and would record, on a glass plate coated with silver iodine, an image that would magically appear when exposed to mercury vapor.

Ethan had a good view of the old adobe ruins and windswept parade grounds where Fremont's troops were garrisoned, and he noticed a young woman walking among the tents.

"Lookin' for someone, gal?" one of the troopers asked. "You just ask me. I know everybody."

Margaret ignored him, but the man blocked her way. "Please step aside, sir. I have business with your officer."

"Well, I'll say you have some *business*," the trooper said.

A kindly-looking corporal approached. "Stand aside, trooper. Can I help you, miss?"

"I'm looking for a man named Jacob Wheeler," Margaret said. "He served with Captain Fremont."

"Wheeler?" the corporal asked, scratching his beard. "Sure, I know him."

"Really?"

"Of course," he said. "Come with me."

Margaret followed the corporal away from the parade grounds and into the ruins of the old Spanish fort. They passed through several walls, then emerged into a scrubby area where a remuda of horses was staked.

Margaret followed the corporal toward the ruins of a stable. The corporal doffed his cap and allowed Margaret to enter first, and then he stood in the doorway as she peered at the empty interior.

"Before I do for you," the man said, his friendly attitude transforming into something crude, "you've got to do for me."

"You are not a very nice man," Margaret said.

The corporal laughed. Margaret walked toward the door, but the corporal held his ground. Then she darted toward one of the stable's open windows and jumped through it, knocking the old shutters away, before lifting her skirts and running across the scrub. The corporal was right behind her. Margaret tripped, and he was on her in an instant. Nearby, the horses shuffled nervously.

"Come on," the man said, pulling Margaret along by the

hair at the nape of her neck. "Let's get on with our business." He threw her down behind a dune near the horses. While straddling her, he ripped Margaret's dress away.

Then there was a *thwack!* as a piece of fence rail connected with the back of the corporal's head. His eyes, which were momentarily wide in surprise, rolled toward the back of his head and he toppled over.

Ethan Biggs dropped the rail. "Come, lass. The whole bloody lot of 'em will be here any moment."

Ethan pulled her to her feet. "Let's arrange you." He straightened Margaret's dress. "There, now. Let's do our best to run, shall we?"

Ethan's studio was covered from floor to ceiling with framed photographs of Western landscape. Clutching her torn dress, Margaret stared at the panoramas. After a few minutes, Ethan reappeared from the back room, holding a fine dress.

"This one appears to be your size."

"It's too pretty," Margaret said.

"Nonsense," Ethan said. "I only use it for sittings. I don't *wear* it."

Margaret smiled and took the dress. "Thank you, Mr. Biggs."

"Please call me Ethan. And I shall call you Margaret. Is that all right?"

"You're very kind."

Ethan directed her to a folding screen at the back of the studio. He chivalrously turned his back as Margaret changed.

"Are all of these photographs yours?" she asked.

"For reasons of economy, I am compelled to do portrait work," he said. "But yours is a magnificent country, which I hope one day to document in its entirety."

"It's a hard country," Margaret said. "Dirty."

"Dirty or not, we're meant to experience life," he said. "Have adventures."

"The wealthy have adventures," Margaret said. "Those without are too busy surviving."

Ethan nearly turned around, then caught himself. "Are you always so direct?"

"I'm sorry," Margaret said. "I didn't mean to—"

"It's quite all right," Ethan said. "In fact, it's one of the

ings I like most about your country. None of that closeted
ritish reserve."

Margaret stepped out from behind the screen. Ethan
rned. He thought she looked extraordinarily beautiful in
e dress.

"You must allow me to make your portrait sometime."

"I couldn't," Margaret said.

"Oh," Ethan said, "I think you could."

He smiled at her, and Margaret was completely disarmed.
he blushed, but smiled back.

Jethro placed his gold nugget on the kitchen table. While
hunder Heart Woman cooked dinner, Abraham and
acob Jr. clustered around.

"It's not very big," Abraham said.

"If you knew what you were talking about," Jethro said,
then you'd know that right there's worth probably thirty
ollars."

"You have found more of this?" Thunder Heart
Woman asked.

"Not yet," Jethro said, "but I will."

"Can I hold it?" Jacob Jr. asked.

"Sure you can, Jake." Jethro dropped the nugget into
e boy's hand.

The look of fascination in the boy's eyes made Thunder
eart Woman uncomfortable.

"You've never seen anything like it," Jethro bragged to
hunder Heart Woman. "Hundreds of 'em in the river pull-
g out a fortune without even trying. Nature's bounty and
's right here for the taking."

"It cannot be so easy," she said.

"I'm telling you, it's just sitting in the water waiting to
e found, and I'm by God going to find it."

Thunder Heart Woman looked skeptical and even a lit-
e scared.

"I want to do what's right by all of us," Jethro said.

"You have."

"A man can always do better," Jethro said. "And I mean
do just that."

"You could fix wheels again," she suggested.

Jethro scowled. "I'm no wheelwright. Neither was Jacob.
ou know that."

Thunder Heart Woman dismissed the gold with a wave of her hand. "Your brother would not care about such things."

"Hell," Jethro said, "he could be out there in some stream right now making his fortune. He sure ain't *here*."

It was Thunder Heart Woman's turn to scowl.

Inside a tent saloon along the American River, Jethro warmed himself with a whiskey. He had stood knee-deep in the ice-cold water all day, elbowing a hundred other prospectors for the best spots, and he had come up with nothing.

His friend Jarrett manned the rail next to him, listening to the band of fiddle, guitar, banjo, and harmonica play discordantly.

"I've looked after them since me brother—" Jethro could not finish the sentence and instead scratched his scraggly beard. "Like I said, they're not gonna want for anything when I'm through here."

"Me, I'm headed upriver," Jarrett said. "Spent most of that four hundred I panned on supplies. There's more coin in selling a man his three squares than standing in freezing water all day."

"Gets right into my bones," Jethro said. He downed the rest of the whiskey, then slapped the shot glass on the bar and wiped his mouth with the back of his hand.

"Ought to get yourself one of these," Jarrett said, pulling a small flask out of his coat pocket. "Every now and again warms the body and the spirit." To the bartender he called, "Dig out one of these special flasks for my friend here."

The bartender reached under the bar, withdrew a flask, and placed it on the bar in front of Jethro. "Fifteen dollars."

"Robbery," Jethro said. "That's what it is."

The bartender reached to take the flask back, but Jethro grabbed his wrist. "Doesn't mean I don't want it."

That night in the living room of Jethro's family ranch, the Rancho Paradiso, Jethro poured himself a drink from the flask. Thunder Heart was mending clothes and pretended not to notice.

"The winter will be hard," she said. "If the new barn isn't finished, our animals will have no shelter."

"Got no time for that," Jethro said.

In the boys' room next door, Jacob Jr. was asleep, but Abraham was listening to the argument. "I just found gold," he could hear Jethro say, "and you're wanting me to hammer and nail?"

Abraham walked to the living room doorway. Thunder Heart Woman and Jethro suddenly stop arguing. Abe stared stonily at Jethro, unnerving him. Abe addressed his mother in Lakota.

"This man has no right to speak to you like that," he said. "Father would know what is right."

"Go back to bed," Thunder Heart Woman said in Lakota.

"What's he saying?" Jethro demanded.

Thunder Heart Woman shook her head. Jethro, however, sensed what was bothering Abe, and he made an effort to explain himself.

"When I strike it," Jethro said, "it'll be for all of us, son."

"I'm not your son," Abe said.

The words cut Jethro to the core. He became angry. "You mind your manners or I'll take a strap to you."

"You ain't my father and you ain't strapping me," Abe said.

Thunder Heart Woman turned quickly to Abe. "Go. Now." When he stared defiantly at her, she added in Lakota, "Do as I say, High Wolf."

The boy retreated to his room and slammed the door.

"Boy's got no call to behave like that," Jethro said. "I've treated him like he was my own."

Jethro and Thunder Heart Woman stared at each other. Jethro sat back down, picked up the flask, then pushed it away. Instead, he fished the nugget out of his pocket and studied it. The gold gleamed in the lantern light.

"Here we hunted our first buffalo," Running Fox said and knelt at the edge of the cliff. Two dried-out buffalo hide ropes, perhaps the same ones they had used as boys, hung limply over the edge.

Dog Star's mind was flooded with memories.

"Remember what you told me?" Running Fox asked his brother. "When you run and jump, you must not stop. Otherwise, you will not swing into the cave below. The run, the jump, and the swing must be one motion."

"Why have you brought me here?" Dog Star asked.

Running Fox pointed beyond the cliff. White settlements dotted the horizon. In the middle ground, a wagon road sliced across the land, resembling nothing so much as a brown scar.

"When we were boys," Running Fox said, "you guided me onto the right path. Now, my brother, it is you who has lost the way."

Jethro dipped his spoon in the watery stew and his face was filled with disgust. Abraham High Wolf, Jacob Jr., and Corn Flower were carefully watching him.

"There is no meat," Jethro said.

"The miners have chased away all the game," Thunder Heart Woman said.

"That," Jethro said, "or Abe here isn't much of a hunter."

The teenager gave his stepfather a wicked look. Jethro reached for the bottle of whiskey at his elbow and poured himself a drink.

"You'd better start doing a better job of providing for your mother," Jethro said.

"Like you are?" Abraham said beneath his breath.

"What did you say?" Jethro demanded.

"Nothing."

"Time you learned some respect," Jethro said.

Seeing the confrontation brewing, Thunder Heart Woman leaned forward and pushed Jethro's bowl a little closer to him.

"Enough," she said. "Eat."

Jethro swept the stew off the table, splattering Thunder Heart Woman with scalding broth. Immediately remorseful, Jethro jumped from his chair and reached for her.

"Stay away from her," Abraham said. The boy launched himself at Jethro.

They wrestled on the floor. Jethro pushed Abe, and when Thunder Heart Woman tried to stop him from striking again, he threw her off. Then Jethro drew his pistol and leveled it at Abraham.

"Come on, boy," Jethro taunted.

The family froze. Corn Flower began to cry. Then Jethro

realized what he was about to do. Slowly, he holstered his gun and walked out.

Later, Abraham threw a blanket over the back of a pony.

"Where will you go?" Thunder Heart Woman asked.

"Away from here," the boy said.

"He does not know what he is doing, Abraham High Wolf," Thunder Heart Woman said. "The yellow dust he seeks poisons his mind."

"Leave him, Mother," Abraham said.

"He is my husband," she said. "I cannot go."

"You don't need him."

"No," she said, "but he needs me."

Abraham struggled to understand, then shook his head. His mother stepped close enough to touch her son.

"It is hard for me to remember that you are no longer a little boy," Thunder Heart Woman said.

"Don't worry on my account," Abraham said. "There's always work for a good rider."

"We cannot know what has been chosen for us," Thunder Heart Woman said.

They embraced. Thunder Heart Woman pressed money into his hands. "There are only a few coins, but I give them to you. Always remember that Lakota blood is in you and will give you strength."

"Sure is good, ma'am," the young man in his twenties told Thunder Heart Woman. "I haven't eaten like this for a month of Sundays."

Jethro was sitting across the table, the ever-present bottle of whiskey at his arm. He looked in wonder at his nephew David. The son of Jethro's eldest brother, Ezra, he bore a strong resemblance to all the Wheeler men.

"How'd you find us?" Jethro asked.

"Just asked around Sacramento," David said.

"Ain't exactly down the road from Wheelerton," Jethro said.

"The family got a letter from Margaret," David said, referring to his cousin Margaret Light Shines. "She had a notion Jacob was alive and wanted us to know she was looking for him if he came home."

"Girl got it into her head that he didn't die," Jethro said. "Then Abe got it into his head not to mind me. Both of 'em are crazy."

"Came west to make my fortune," David said. "I intend to die a rich man, not an apprentice wheelwright pounding iron." When Thunder Heart Woman went into the other room to tend to Corn Flower, David grinned at his uncle conspiratorially. "You've sure done all right for yourself. Can't be an easy thing, marrying another man's wife and raising her kids."

"No, it ain't." Jethro handed his nephew the bottle of whiskey.

David took a pull, then grimaced and wiped his mouth with the back of his hand. "How much you pull out of that river?" the young man asked, motioning vaguely with the bottle.

"Some here, some there."

"I was hoping we could partner up," David said.

"You got anything to invest?"

David placed the bottle on the table and held up his hands. "I've got these. Willing to blister and crack them until I hit pay dirt."

"It helps when a man has a partner he doesn't have to worry about showing his back to."

"So what do you say?"

"Well," Jethro said. He took another drink. "Yes. Hell yes."

A bolt of lightning splintered the top of a pine tree on the opposite bank, and the concussion was followed by a downpour that lashed the American River like a whip.

Knowing that wading shin-deep in water was not a safe place during a thunderstorm, hundreds of prospectors left the river and sought the protection of the bars and brothels in the tent city.

David shifted the shovel to his other hand and shouted to Jethro above the pounding rain, "Shouldn't we quit for a spell?"

They had spent the last week on the river. Elbow to elbow with the other gold seekers, they had not found enough flake to even pay for the whiskey that Jethro drank.

"No!" Jethro shouted. "When do you think we'll have another chance to have the river to ourselves?"

"I suppose," David said, glancing at the sky from beneath the brim of his hat. "But we're risking getting lit like a couple of Lucifer matches."

Jethro pointed at random to a spot on the riverbank. "Dig here!"

David shook his head, but drew back the shovel and drove the blade deep into the gravel. Jethro stood with the gold pan in his hands, waiting for David to drop a shovelful of mud and gravel in it.

With a *clank*, the shovel hit something hard. They looked at each other. David fell to his knees and clawed into the gravel.

"Oh, Lord," he said.

"What?" Jethro asked.

"Help me," David said. "I can't lift it."

Jethro tossed the pan aside, dropped to his knees, and began to claw into the hold. Together, they brought up a rock the size of a man's head . . . and in the side of the rock was a glittering nugget the size of a fist.

"We're rich," David said excitedly. "We're stinking rich!"

He threw his arms around Jethro, but his uncle threw him off and clamped a hand over his mouth. "Shut up! You want the others to kill us?"

David looked around him, suddenly paranoid. It was difficult to see through the rain, but the river appeared still to be deserted.

"Quick," Jethro said. "Give me your shirt."

That night, with rain beating on the roof of the ranch house, Jethro slammed the bundle onto the kitchen table. Then he pulled back the shirt to reveal the big gold nugget.

"Just look at that," Jethro said admiringly.

"Is it real?" Jacob Jr. asked.

Thunder Heart Woman was frightened. "You must take it from here. Quickly."

"She's right," David said. "We've got to get it assayed."

"The river'll be up," Jethro said. "We'll carry it through the forest to the river, go downstream to Sacramento. There's banks there. Jake, fetch a knapsack."

When the boy ran off, Jethro uncorked the bottle of whiskey and took a slug, then passed it to David.

"We'll set out at dawn," Jethro said. "We'll move fast. Might have Jake cover our backs until we reach the lake."

"He is a boy," Thunder Heart Woman said.

"Old enough to make sure we keep what's ours."

"This is not his doing," she said. "Please do not make him a part of it."

Jethro waved her off. "You never were for this and even now you ain't happy about it. I know I'm not Jacob—"

"No one's ever asked you to be."

"—but I've tried to do my best. I've made mistakes, I know that. Things are gonna be different now."

Thunder Heart Woman fought back tears. Suddenly, Jethro was overcome by a wave of tenderness. "If you were white, you'd know that having that rock means everything. It means the life I've always promised you. Give me the chance to prove it. You'll see."

Thunder Heart Woman nodded. "I will pack food for you." She turned.

Jethro poured whiskey into two glasses, then handed one of them to David. On the table, along with the rock in a knapsack, were several revolvers. Jethro cradled a shotgun in his lap.

They toasted.

"Think I'll buy me a grand city house with servants to wait on me hand and foot like the plantation owners back home," David said.

Jethro nodded, and David asked, "What about you? What'll you do with your half?"

"Half? What are you talkin' about, boy?" Jethro poured himself another drink. "That was my claim. You'll get your reward, but you ain't gettin' half. I'd say your take is . . . one quarter."

"I'm the one who found it!" David shouted. "You owe me at least half, you son of a bitch!" David grabbed one of the pistols from the table.

Jethro cocked both hammers on the shotgun. "You being family, I'll make it a third. Take it or leave it. Now sit down and have a drink."

Jethro woke with a start. He had drunk himself into a stupor, and he did not know if it was minutes or hours later. What he did know was that David and the knapsack were gone.

Carrying the shotgun at the ready and a pistol in his belt, Jethro ran through the night. The rain had stopped. Fifty yards ahead, he could see David struggling with his burden.

Jethro brought the shotgun up and fired one chamber. Up ahead, David weaved, then drew his pistol.

"Dammit," Jethro muttered as he ducked behind a tree. At the pistol's report, the bark splintered.

Jethro darted out and fired the other barrel of the shotgun.

Buckshot splattered in the mud a few yards behind David.

Then Jethro pulled the pistol from his belt and both stood their ground as they emptied their revolvers at each other, to no discernable effect. It was dark, both had been drinking, and neither was a crack shot.

When his hammer clicked on an empty chamber, Jethro charged. David turned to run, but the weight of the knapsack allowed him no speed.

Jethro tackled David, they slammed into a tree, then fell fighting to the ground. David finally got a hand around Jethro's windpipe. Blood flowing down their faces, they writhed in the mud. David rolled free, Jethro grabbed him by the throat from behind, and then David sank his teeth into Jethro's forearm. Jethro drew back and landed a stunning blow against the side of David's head, knocking him to the ground. Then Jethro straddled him and delivered a volley of punches that ended only when David kicked him in the groin.

Jethro rolled away, gasping in pain. David struggled to his feet, pulling the knapsack along with him. He stumbled to the river, where he found a dugout canoe waiting upside down on the bank. He flipped the canoe over, slid it into the water, and jumped in. He started paddling madly away. He still wore the knapsack.

Behind him, Jethro dove into the water and began swimming after the canoe. As he neared the side of the boat, David lunged to strike at him with the paddle . . . and realized too late that the movement had caused the canoe to tip too far over to recover. The canoe capsized, throwing David into the water. The weight of the knapsack carried him under so quickly that he did not even have time to cry out.

"No!" Jethro cried. He dove beneath the surface, reaching not for his nephew but for the knapsack. His fingertips found it for an instant, and it dragged him toward the bottom. Even though David was drowning, he fought off Jethro.

Choking, Jethro broke the surface, then reached for the overturned canoe. It slipped beyond his grasp. He went under in the freezing water once more, kicked to the surface, and when his head broke the water this time, it occurred to him that the nugget was found in freezing water . . . and now had returned to it.

Then the water closed above his head. After that, the lake was silent.

"Like this, perhaps?"

Ethan and Margaret were sharing a picnic blanket on the beach, the camera nearby. Ethan showed Margaret the sketch he had been working on. It was a portrait of her father.

"I think so, yes," Margaret said. "I was so young. But I still see that face sometimes. If only I had a photograph, something for people to see."

"We'll get this sketch engraved and post it everywhere."

"I've almost given up hope," she said.

"You will find him, Margaret," Ethan said. "*We* will find him."

Ethan traced the bridge of her nose and the shape of her lips with his finger. Margaret embraced him.

"You're a good man," she said.

"You're only now finding that out?" he asked, laughing.

"I knew it that first day," Margaret said. "I just didn't want to need anyone."

"Well then," Ethan said, "when are you going to introduce me to your mother?"

"When am I going to meet yours?" Margaret asked.

"That's a bit more difficult, wouldn't you agree?" Ethan asked. "You aren't ashamed of me, are you?"

"Ashamed?" Margaret asked in surprise.

"Well, I am a foreigner."

"That's not it," Margaret said.

"Well, what then?"

Margaret stared out at the ocean. "There are things about me that you do not know."

"Tell me," Ethan said.

Margaret nodded, then finally found the words. "I'm not pure white," she said. "My mother is Lakota." Margaret looked expectantly at Ethan.

"Is there anything else?" he asked. When she shook her head, he said, "None of that matters. Out here, we all have a clean slate." Then he grinned. "I suggest I meet this mother of yours. You know what they say. Meet the mother and you'll see the daughter in twenty years."

Margaret melted with relief, and they kissed.

"Now go stand by the water," Ethan said. "This picture requires some scale."

While Ethan thrilled Jacob Jr. and Corn Flower with a succession of glass-plate vistas, Margaret Light Shines sat huddled with her mother in a corner of the sitting room.

"Leave this place, Mother," Margaret urged. "Come back with us to San Francisco."

"This is our home," Thunder Heart Woman said.

"There is nothing here but suffering," Margaret said.

"The grizzly bear spoke to me in a dream," her mother said. "He said if we leave here, your father will never find us again."

"A dream?" Margaret asked. "A dream cannot keep you warm or put food on your table. A dream cannot keep you safe."

Thunder Heart Woman addressed her daughter in Lakota. "You have gone to the city, Light Shines, and it has taken you from the ways of our people."

"The ways of our people must change or they will die," Margaret answered in Lakota. "That is what I have learned in San Francisco."

Then Thunder Heart Woman turned to Ethan. "I see that you hold my daughter in your heart, Ethan Biggs, but the new ways are not always better."

Ethan smiled. "I make no such claim, but it is indeed true that I do hold your daughter, as you say, in my heart."

"So it is with my own husband," Thunder Heart Woman

said. "Even when I was wife to his brother, I was bound to him alone. If *Wakan Tanka* blesses you with such a bond, there is nothing that can destroy it."

Ethan nodded. "We call that destiny, things that are meant to be. That's how Margaret and I found each other."

Thunder Heart Woman searched Ethan's face and found sincerity. Then she looked at Margaret and again spoke Lakota. "You have chosen well."

THIRTY-FOUR

Fort Laramie, Nebraska Territory
1851 (The Winter of the Big Handout)

The plain near the fort was covered with ten thousand lodges. Twenty-one chiefs, all in their most impressive and important ceremonial dress, assembled under the watchful eyes of two thousand soldiers. An additional three hundred clan leaders, including Dog Star and Running Fox, looked on.

Assorted Indian agents and civilian commissioners sat at a long table with papers, pens, and inkpots before them. Behind these civilians stood the Army officers, including a wary young Army lieutenant, John L. Grattan.

Indian agent Thomas Fitzpatrick, known as "Broken Hand" by the Indians because of three missing fingers, read the terms of the treaty in his best oratorical voice.

"The aforesaid Indians do hereby recognize and acknowledge the following tracts of country, included within the metes and boundaries hereinafter designated, as their respective territories, viz . . ."

"What does it mean?" Dog Star asked his brother.

"Broken Hand, who speaks for the white father, has divided the earth among the nations," Running Fox said wisely. "Each is given one part to be forever protected from whites by the soldiers. There will be peace among the nations and with the whites who travel through our lands. In return, the white father will give us many animals and fine things. For any wrong the people commit, we will make payment."

Dog Star nodded, and Running Fox added, "The Washington father has promised food and supplies for fifty straight winters."

"That is a promise no man can make," Dog Star said.

"Many whites cross our land," Running Fox said. "They kill our game and we go hungry. Our people need food. The soldiers will protect the land that we keep from the other whites."

"The earth is not ours to sell for white man's food or supplies," Dog Star said. "If we give them what they want, they will only want more. That is how they are."

"We must give them the chance to prove their honor," his brother said. "If we don't, there will never be peace."

At the long table, a Brule elder named Conquering Bear was handed a pen by Fitzpatrick. While Grattan watched with obvious skepticism, Conquering Bear made his mark on the treaty.

"You cannot put stock in an Indian's word, Mr. Fitzpatrick," the young officer said.

"I can assure you, Lieutenant Grattan," Fitzpatrick said, "that if these people had wished us harm, we would all be quite dead."

Conquering Bear placed the pen on the table. Fitzpatrick offered his good hand. The two men shook warmly; then another chief took Conquering Bear's place.

"Once they've collected all of their trinkets," Grattan said, "they'll be back to pillaging."

"Tell me, Lieutenant," Fitzpatrick said, "how long have you labored to keep our frontier safe?"

"This is my first posting."

"West Point, is it?"

"It is, sir."

"Out here, things don't always obey regulations," Fitzpatrick said. "You'd do well to remember that, young man."

"I can see why a man might live up here," Ethan said, looking at the Sierra Nevadas with an artist's eye.

Margaret Light Shines and he had been married less than two weeks when a settler had recognized the sketch of Jacob on a handbill and rushed to the photo studio with news that the man they were seeking *might* be living near Yuba Pass.

"And never see his children again?" Margaret asked.

"He must have had his reasons."

"What if he doesn't want to be found?" Margaret asked.

Near the summit, they found a cabin. Smoke plumed from the chimney. While Margaret held the reins to the horses, Ethan approached the cabin door.

The door was suddenly jerked open from the inside. The muzzle of a rifle peeked out. The voice of a forty-year-old man called, "You don't look like a thief."

· "No," Ethan stammered, "I'm . . . well, I'm a photographer."

"Don't know much about the woods—that's for certain," Jacob said. "Announced yourself a mile off."

The man stepped outside the cabin, keeping the rifle trained on Ethan. His hair was long and dirty, and whiskers covered his jaw, but beneath it all Ethan could recognize the man in the sketch.

"We're looking for Jacob Wheeler," Margaret called.

The man glanced over at the young woman. She dropped the reins and took a step forward. The man peered at her as if through a fog. Margaret pulled the amulet from beneath her collar. The man lowered the rifle and stepped toward her. He touched the necklace, then looked into her face.

"Margaret Light Shines?" he asked. "Is that you?"

"Daddy," she said. Then she fell into Jacob Wheeler's arms.

Bundled in buffalo robes against the cold, Running Fox and his son, White Crow, warmed themselves at a campfire. Behind them, a tipi glowed.

"You will know now what it is to be a father," Running Fox said. "It is not an easy thing, but it is good."

"I have asked *Wakan Tanka* to make me the father you have been to me," White Crow said.

"You have been a good son," Running Fox said. "You will be a good father."

White Crow glanced away. "Have I caused you much trouble, Father?"

"So much has changed since you were a boy," Running Fox said. "I hope life will be easier for your son."

"And if it is a daughter?"

"Then you will make a son after."

They grinned. Then they heard a baby cry. From the door of the lodge, Blue Bird beckoned to her son.

"It is a boy," she said.

After White Crow had a chance to admire his son, his wife, Dancing Water, asked, "What shall you call him?"

"His name shall be Red Lance," White Crow said.

"It is a good name," Running Fox said.

The Rancho Paradiso had become a watering hole and coach stop for a horde of fortune seekers. Jacob Wheeler sat down at a long table beneath the trees, appearing to be just another down-on-his-luck prospector, while Thunder Heart Woman shuffled among the tables, filling plates and mugs, a shotgun slung over her shoulder. Near the barn, Jacob Jr. washed laundry in a tub.

Across from Jacob, a scruffy prospector and his fat partner watched as Thunder Heart Woman worked an adjacent table.

"Fine-looking squaw," the thin one said. "An' she's got a good-looking daughter, too."

"Sure would like to make her acquaintance," the fat one said. "Might even take me a bath."

Jacob's eyes narrowed as the fat man continued. "Never did know an Injun gal could do wash like that. Her husband must have had clean breeches every day."

"And twice on Sunday," the thin one said.

"Man don't need breeches with no Indian woman," the other one said. "I'll bet she ain't got nothin' on under that skirt."

"Guess we're just gonna have to find out."

When Thunder Heart Woman reached their table, Jacob risked a glance, and she returned the look over her ladle. She began to move on, then Jacob grasped her hand. Thunder Heart Woman gave him a fierce look and reached for the shotgun with her free hand.

"Oh, mind that scattergun," the thin prospector said. "She knows how to use it."

Jacob kept his grip on her hand, forcing her to look at him more closely. Believing that his mother was threatened, Jacob Jr. left the washing and rushed to her aid. "Mister, you just get along and leave us alone."

"Well, ain't he just one tough little half-breed bastard?" the fat prospector said. The other one stuck out his foot and tripped the boy. Both laughed.

Jacob launched himself across the table, knocking both men to the ground. Before they could reach the butts of their revolvers, Jacob had his own in his hand. "Hand over those pistols and clear out."

"You got no call to take our guns," the fat one protested.

"You're lucky I don't kill you for sport."

"And just who might you be, friend?" the thin one asked.

"I'm the man that's going to wing you both so's I can carve your scalps while you're awake and hang 'em on that fence before I finish you off."

The prospectors laid down their guns and backed off. Then Jacob called, "Next time you talk about a man's wife, you'll show her some respect."

"Papa?" Jacob Jr. asked.

Jacob fired into the ground at the prospectors' feet. Then the fat man and the thin man took off running, to the delight of the other customers, who laughed and cheered. Jacob took the shotgun from Thunder Heart Woman and fired both barrels into the air.

"The name's Jacob Wheeler," he said. "From now on, any of you sons of bitches steps out of line, you'll answer to me. Any questions?"

There were none.

THIRTY-FIVE

Nebraska Territory
Conquering Bear Was Killed (1854)

Eight miles east of Fort Laramie, a Mormon wagon train passed near a large village of mixed tribes. Lagging behind the last wagon, a young man drove a sick, half-crippled cow forward by beating it with a stick.

The cow bawled and suddenly bolted away, straight for the village. The rampaging animal knocked over cooking pots and brought down tipis before getting its horn entangled in one of the lodge skins. The young man chasing it stopped at the edge of the village.

A Minneconjou man called Straight Foretop grabbed the cow and called out, "Come. Take back your cow before it does more damage."

The young man stared for a moment, then turned away. He ran to catch up with the wagon train.

"Do you not want your animal?" Straight Foretop called.

The next morning, while Loved by the Buffalo watched, Lieutenant Grattan rode into the village with twenty-seven men. A twelve-pound cannon and a mountain howitzer followed in the rear. Beside Grattan was Lucien Auguste, a French trapper.

"Conquering Bear," Grattan said without ceremony, "a cow was taken from the wagon train that passed here and I demand you return it and turn over the thief."

Auguste translated. From his slurred speech, it was obvious to both parties that the trapper was quite drunk. "He wants the thief who stole the cow."

"The cow was not stolen," Conquering Bear said. "It ran into our village and did much damage. Straight Foretop called to the white man to take it, but he walked away. He left the cow as payment. Straight Foretop killed the cow and we feasted on its bad meat."

Auguste turned to Grattan. "The one called Straight Foretop killed the cow and they ate it."

"You tell the soldier chief all that I say," Conquering Bear urged, but the trapper ignored him.

Sensing trouble, warriors began to gather around their chief. Meanwhile, Grattan's fresh recruits glanced nervously about them. Their horses were skittish and Grattan's bluster was not helping.

"We will give payment for the cow," Conquering Bear said. "It was old and injured, but we will give a good mule in its place."

"Lieutenant, they won't give you this man," Auguste said. "They will give something for the cow."

Grattan tried his best to look fierce. "Tell him the man who took this cow will go to the stockade. Tell him he must give me this man now."

Auguste turned to Conquering Bear. "Straight Foretop must be put in the iron house."

Conquering Bear turned to Man Afraid and a group of elders. They came to an agreement. One handed him five sticks, which Conquering Bear placed on the ground in front of Grattan.

"Tell Little Soldier Chief we will sit and smoke a pipe and settle this payment," Conquering Bear said. "We will give five horses for the old cow."

"He says he'll sit and smoke with you," Auguste said.

"The United States does not bargain with thieves."

Auguste shrugged and told Conquering Bear, "He will not smoke."

Grattan drew his saber. "Unlimber those guns!"

"It's just a cow, Lieutenant," one of the gunners said.

"Ready that howitzer on these lodges or I'll have *you* in the stockade for insubordination," Grattan said. Then he turned back to the chief. "Conquering Bear, you are hereby ordered by the Army of the United States to surrender this cow thief or face the consequences."

"Five horses," Conquering Bear said. "It is a good payment for an old cow."

"What's he saying?" Grattan demanded. "Will he give me this man or not?"

Auguste shook his head. Conquering Bear stood with the elders, not knowing what to do.

"Fire!" Grattan ordered.

"Sir?" one gunner asked.

"We're too close," said another.

"Fire, damn you!"

The howitzer barked, cutting off the tops of several tipis behind the council of elders, followed by a scattering of rifle shots from the troops. Conquering Bear dropped dead at the feet of the council, a gaping wound in his chest.

Loved by the Buffalo looked on in horror.

Straight Foretop screamed and shot Lucien Auguste from the saddle. "Fire at will!" Grattan screamed. A storm of arrows rained down while the soldiers loaded and fired as quickly as possible.

The Indian warriors from the village quickly armed themselves. They used guns, arrows, lances, tomahawks, knives, clubs, and stones.

When the fighting stopped, Grattan was as dead as Conquering Bear. The lieutenant's body bristled with twenty-four arrows.

Loved by the Buffalo fell to his knees and looked skyward. "The people's pain is deep. The white man has shown himself to be without honor. The Treaty of Long Meadows is no more. The wrath of the white father in Washington will become a flood that cannot be stopped. It was his purpose to exterminate the people and destroy everything that belongs to us. But there is no reason to destroy everything when you have already stolen it."

THIRTY-SIX

Lawrence, Kansas Territory
1860 (Many Children Died)

Samson Wheeler, the son of Benjamin and the grandson of Abraham, was a master wheelwright and staunch abolitionist. Knowing that Virginia was forever lost, he had brought his family to the free state capital of Lawrence to help bring Kansas into the union as a free state.

Kansas was part of the territory ceded by Mexico a decade and a half earlier, and as the territory came closer to statehood, the delicate balance of power between free and slave states began to tip. Both sides fought fiercely for control. While proslavery "border ruffians" crossed over from Missouri to vote illegally in the territorial elections, organizations such as the New England Immigrant Aid Society organized the relocation of abolitionist families to Lawrence.

When Lincoln was elected in the fall of 1860, Samson was forty-nine years old and his wife, Susannah, was forty-six. Their family consisted of two sons, Aaron and Jeremiah, twenty and seventeen, respectively, and an adopted daughter, fifteen-year-old Clara. The boys became wheelwrights, as were expected of them. Clara spent most of her waking hours sketching hats and dresses.

Although Samson was worried about the lack of practical skills displayed by his only daughter, he found it difficult to deny her anything. He was somewhat more stern with his sons. He required them to work hard and to examine their consciences.

When the talk in the wheelwrights' shop turned to war, and his sons debated the merits of joining the army, Samson shook his head sadly.

"Make wheels," he urged his sons. "Both sides have enough men to make war. But wheels are needed in times of peace."

"And wheels are needed in times of war," Aaron and Jeremiah replied in unison.

Brings Horse, the son of Dog Star, heard the pounding of hooves before he saw the rider. When he spotted the rider on the horizon, he called out for his father and uncle to come out of the lodge and see for themselves.

"Here is something new for you to paint, brother," Running Fox said as he watched the fleet Pony Express rider cross the prairie, leaving a cloud of dust behind.

Brings Horse ran for his horse, but Dog Star stopped him. "But we can catch him," Brings Horse protested.

"No," Running Fox said. "A man like that must not be killed."

On the back of the Pony Express horse was Abraham High Wolf Wheeler, now twenty-three. Abe was unaware that some of his relations were watching from the cluster of tipis on the horizon.

At the relay station, Abe jumped down from the lathered horse and handed the mailbag to another rider, who took off on a fresh horse to continue the journey.

Abe removed his rifle and uncinched his saddle from the tired horse, then turned the animal over to the wrangler. He plunged his head into a water trough and came up with his hair dripping. Then he shouldered his rifle and saddle and headed inside the station. A group of wire-thin young men in their late teens or early twenties sat at a communal table.

"Any sign of Indians?" Abe asked.

"Not until just now," one of the riders said, and Abe stared, uncertain if the rider was making a joke.

One of the other riders offered a friendly warning. "Careful. Abe Wheeler here's seen the back of every station from Saint Louis clear to Sacramento. More'n once, too."

"Is that so?" the first rider asked. When Abe didn't answer, he said, "I rode sixty miles today. How many did you make?"

"I do my talking in the saddle," Abe said.

They stared at each other across the table until the first rider smiled and said, "You got yourself a race there."

The next day, Abe beat the other rider easily, raising his rifle in exultation. The other rider grudgingly raised his own rifle in acknowledgment. Then Abe continued and, in a few days, found himself crossing the Nevada territory, following a line of telegraph poles to the next relay station.

As he rode up, he was surprised to find nobody rushing out to greet him. "Goddammit!" he said, calling to a station hand. "Fetch me a horse!"

"Ain't no rush," the hand said. "We're closin' down."

"What?"

"You pick up your pay in Sacramento," the station hand said. "We're done in."

"We've only been in business for eighteen months," Abe said.

The station hand pointed at the telegraph pole and the wire strung overhead. The wire stretched across the desert, in both directions, for as far as Abraham could see.

On the snow-covered plain, Running Fox stared up from the saddle of his horse at the telegraph pole. With him were his son, White Crow, and his nephews, Brings Horse and Sleeping Bear.

"They talk over that?" Running Fox's grandson, ten-year-old Red Lance, asked.

"Somehow," Running Fox said.

Brings Horse drew his knife, put it between his teeth, and shinnied up the pole. At the top, he straddled the crosspiece and put his ear to the wire.

"Do you hear anything?" Running Fox asked.

"No," Brings Horse called. "It is a dead thing."

"You do not have the magic," Sleeping Bear said.

"It is not magic," Running Fox said. "It is clever, but not magic. Cut it."

Brings Horse severed the wire with his knife. Then, as blood misted from his chest, he fell from the pole. The sound of the rifle shot came a fraction of a second later. Red Lance watched in horror and fascination as the body landed in a tangle of wire on the snow-covered ground.

On a hillock the better part of a mile away, a sharp-shooter with a buffalo rifle and a telescopic sight took aim again and squeezed the trigger.

The bullet split the air near White Crow's head and *thwacked* into a telegraph pole behind, followed again by the sound of the shot. Before the Indians could take cover, another warrior lay dead in the snow.

Although the telegraph had branched like a river in its course across the country, it had not yet reached Lawrence, Kansas. What news came to the free state capital was delivered by newspapers from the bigger cities or in the long-standing American tradition of political rallies.

Kansas had been admitted to the Union—as a free state—on January 29, 1861, and James H. Lane, a forty-seven-year-old Jayhawker from Lawrence, had been elected as one of its first senators. Shortly after Lane's election, the Samson Wheeler family turned out to hear their new senator address a gathering at a local livery stable.

"There are those on our borders who seek to deter us from the great cause to which we have dedicated our lives," Lane said, gesticulating madly. He was cadaverous and wild-eyed. "We will defend our homes and beliefs and we will not shy from blood until every godless, slaveholding citizen of Missouri is cast into a bit of burning hellfire."

The doors of the livery burst open and a dark-haired young man in his thirties rode his horse into the gathering. He wore a black slouch hat, a brace of pistols, and a necklace of Yankee scalps. Outside, a knot of scruffy riders stood guard.

"I reckon you were talkin' about me, senator," the young man said, then removed his hat and bowed from the saddle. His long black hair swept forward, hiding his face. "Allow me to introduce myself. My given name is William Anderson, but most folks call me Bloody Bill."

A ripple went through the crowd. Clara Wheeler pressed a little closer to her mother, trying to hide from the man.

"You have some gall," Lane said.

"I'll say I do." Anderson placed his hat back on his head.

"You'd best save your jayhawkin' trash for all of your Yankee friends back east, because me and Captain Quantrell are keeping our eyes on you."

Just the mention of the name of the guerrilla chieftain Quantrell nearly sent the crowd into a panic.

"We ain't going to stand you coming here and dictating to us with your nigger worshipping," Anderson declared. "I reckon we'll make this place hot for you soon enough—that's a fact."

The crowd began to stir, but Lane held out his hands. "Do not be intimidated."

"I've seen your faces," Anderson said. "And I'm gonna kill you. I will hunt you down and murder you—and like it, too."

Anderson looked around him, as if to burn each of their faces into his memory. He paid particular attention to the Wheeler family, and his eyes lingered on Clara.

Then Anderson turned his horse and rode slowly out of the barn.

THIRTY-SEVEN

Wyoming Territory
A Boy Was Scalped (1862)

The Lakota man was on the ground, his hands tied behind his back. A dozen cavalry horses and an Indian pony were hitched outside the trading post while a corporal and nine other soldiers loitered nearby. While Jacob Jr., now twenty-two, dismounted and tied off his horse, a lieutenant and a sergeant exited the post with a white trader.

"Give me some water," the prisoner pleaded in Lakota. "I'm thirsty."

"What's he saying?" the lieutenant asked.

"Hell if I know," the sergeant said.

"He's thirsty," Jacob Jr. explained.

"Well," the sergeant said, hitching up his belt, "the folks he killed won't be drinking today, will they?"

Jacob Jr. paused for a moment to reflect on what his father would have done. Then he remembered the story of his father's act of kindness at the Klamath massacre. Without hesitation, Jacob Jr. took a canteen from his horse. He held it to the lips of the prisoner as the soldiers watched. The thirsty Lakota took a long drink, the water running down his chin.

"Thank you," he said in Lakota.

"Take as much as you want," Jacob Jr. replied.

It seemed to Jacob Jr. that even though his father was more than a thousand miles away, in California, he was still in daily contact with him: through the journal his father had carried with Jedediah Smith, which his father had given him on the day he decided he must make his own way; and every time he looked at his own reflection in a mountain stream. The face that stared back, wreathed in blue sky and clouds, was that of his father as a young man.

"You speak their language," the lieutenant ventured.

"What of it?" Jacob Jr. asked.

"Half of the problem out here is that we can't communicate with them," the lieutenant said. "We have to use their own people to do it, and they're unreliable. The Army could use a man like you, if you've a mind to help these people."

Since the day that Samson Wheeler had hired the black freedman named Henry Foster to help at the shop, Susannah Wheeler had worried. Noble causes were well and good, and of course slavery was evil, but to actually invite the wrath of others by treating a black man like an equal was another thing entirely.

So it came as no surprise when one morning the Wheelers discovered that the windows of the shop had been smashed. The equipment was broken and strewn about, and NIGGER LOVERS had been painted across the front of the shop.

"I expect I'll be moving on, Mr. Wheeler," Henry Foster had told Samson.

"To give in to such terror is to admit defeat," Samson Wheeler told him. "You are a good worker and a good man. I'll not have any more of that kind of talk. From anyone."

Inside their lodge, Dog Star and Yellow Hawk shared a meal with their grandchildren. Wind in the Trees was eleven years old and it would not be too many years now before she took a husband; White Bird was thirteen and was already becoming a man; but Morning Star, at seven years old, still lived in the magical world of childhood.

Morning Star lay back on a buffalo robe and stared up, past the funnel of lodge poles and skins, to the oval of stars beyond the smoke flaps.

"When I was in my mother's belly," Dog Star said, "she looked up at the night sky and found the brightest star in it. You see? Right there."

He pointed upward. All the children stared.

"You see how that star and then another and another form the shape of a dog?" When the children nodded, Dog Star said, "That is the name she gave me: Dog Star."

The youngest grandchild smiled brightly. "I was named after the morning star," he said.

Dog Star smiled at Yellow Hawk, sharing the warmth known to grandparents.

"And someday," Dog Star told his youngest grandchild, "when you are a grandfather, you too will look up at the night sky with your grandchildren and tell them about your name and about the name of your grandfather and that together we looked up at the night sky."

Before dawn on August 21, 1863, William Clarke Quantrill led a band of three hundred fifty from Missouri to the town of Lawrence, beside the Kaw River. The guerrillas set fire to the town and killed one hundred fifty men and boys. Senator James H. Lane, who hid in his cornfield during the attack, was not among them.

At the edge of town, the Wheeler family woke to the rattle of gunfire. Samson Wheeler and his sons armed themselves and stood guard over the house and the shop. "You and Clara take to the fields," Samson Wheeler told his wife. "These marauders will not outrage us again."

Susannah and Clara ran toward the corn, but Susannah lagged behind.

"Hurry, Mama!" Clara urged. She carried a carpetbag.

"This is my home," Susannah said, hesitating. In her hands was a shotgun.

"It's mine, too," Clara said.

"Do as I say," Susannah ordered. "If anything should happen, get yourself to Omaha. Cousin Daniel will care for you."

"Please, Mama," Clara said. "Come with me."

Susannah hugged her daughter, then pushed her toward the field. "Go," she said. "Run."

Clara hid in the tall corn while Anderson and his men came down the road from town, hunting down stragglers. She recognized his voice as he barked orders, and through the stalks, she caught glimpses of him atop his horse, his face contorted in madness, a pistol always in his hand.

She watched in horror as Anderson shot a fleeing man in the back of the head, then laughed. She heard Anderson and his men launch the assault on her home. It seemed as if the gunshots would never stop, and when they finally did, they were replaced by the crackling of fire and a horrible stench that drifted on the wind.

When Clara emerged from the cornfield, clutching her carpetbag, there was nothing left of the Wheeler place. Both the house and the shop had been burned to the ground, and the only thing left standing was the chimney.

Soot from a hundred ruined homes drifted down from the sky.

The corpses of her father and brother were in the yard. The body of Henry Foster, the freedman, swung from a tree overhead. And in the ashes of the house, the only thing left of her mother was her left hand, the wedding ring still on her finger.

THIRTY-EIGHT

Loved by the Buffalo traveled across the nations, seeking the prophet who could make false the terrible vision of the white man's wheel. He sought the signs that would lead to his people's salvation, but found only reminders of those who had come before and gone into darkness. He did not know their names, but they had left their clues across the land, in the rock carvings and empty cities of the desert, in the great mounds beside the rivers, even in the places where no trace remained.

Years passed. The war among the whites raged. And always, the wheels kept rolling.

When Loved by the Buffalo touched the earth—while running his hands over ancient petroglyphs, for example—he not only felt the creaking of the millions of wooden wheels flooding the west, but the hammer and hum of something new, of great iron wheels that rode on endless iron rails.

In Omaha, Nebraska, a dirty young woman carrying a carpetbag stepped into a wheelwright shop. "Pardon me," she said to the youngest of the four men working furiously. "Could you please tell me who owns this shop?"

"That would be my father," he said.

"No handouts here, girl," Daniel Wheeler called. "Get yourself along now!"

The girl cleared her throat. "My name is Clara Wheeler, sir. My father was Samson Wheeler. Your cousin."

Daniel Wheeler stared in amazement. That night, Daniel

Wheeler argued with his wife over the girl's fate. He was for sending her back to Virginia, but Esther said it was unthinkable to send the child into another state that had turned into a battleground.

"Then there are places across the river in Saint Joseph where the girl can be with her own kind," Daniel said.

"What do you mean, own kind?" Esther asked. "She is a Wheeler, not an anonymous dweller of some dark slum. It is our Christian duty to care for this child. We're the only people she has left."

"Don't talk to me of blood," Daniel said. "The girl's not even Samson's natural child, just a foundling he took in—as was his wont. We owe her nothing."

Robert Wheeler, the teenage boy Clara had first spoken to at the shop, had been listening while his parents argued. "Mother's right."

Daniel Wheeler turned a steely gaze toward the boy.

"We can't turn our backs on someone looking for our help," Robert said, "not after what she's been through. Think if it was one of us."

"Charity always costs those who give it," his father said. "You'd bear that expense upon yourself, I take it?"

"Pardon, sir?"

"Be responsible for her."

"That's right," Robert said without hesitation.

His father considered the proposition. "Very well, the girl's in your care. You'll answer for her, for good or ill. Understand?"

"I understand," Robert said.

The contractor pushed the roster across the desk and offered a pen. Abe looked over at the policeman who had hustled him over from the jail.

"Sign it," the policeman said, counting the money the contractor had just handed him, "or you go back where you came from."

Abe touched his cheek. It was still swollen from the punch he had received in the drunken fight that had landed him in jail. After being released from the services of the Pony Express, he had found it difficult to make a living when his only talent was riding faster than anyone else. Abe took the pen and signed his name.

"Congratulations, Mr. Abraham Wheeler," the contractor said dubiously. "You are now the property of the Central Pacific Railroad and you will remain our property until such time as you have repaid the debt incurred by this railroad to the State of California and the County of Sacramento for their recruitment efforts."

"You sold me?" Abe asked.

"This is a respectable city," the policeman said. "We don't shanghai people here. We just don't like vagrants, and we like some vagrants less than others. We've got laws to keep your sort in line." The police shoved the money in his pocket.

"Your pay is two dollars and fifty cents a day," the contractor said. "Board and grub is twenty dollars a month, taken out of your wages on top of the aforesaid debt. There's a wagonload of workers leaving for the Sierras at sunrise. Be on it."

"I'll see the merchandise gets delivered," the policeman said.

The dumping boss was a burly Irishman named Patrick Donovan. He indicated with a shovel where Abe was to empty the contents of the wheelbarrow. Abe did so, then started back down the grade.

"Come back here, Chief," Donovan called.

"Name's Abe."

"One of the lost tribes of Israel, are we?" Donovan asked. "Well, my Old Testament friend, have a glance at that offering you've just brought me."

Abe peered down at the pile of dirt below. He shrugged. Donovan kicked at the chunks of root and rock in the dirt.

"Don't want the grade to be uneven, do we? Better clean it up."

"That's your job," Abe said and turned.

Donovan picked up a root and threw it. It bounced off Abe's back. Abe glared at the big Irishman, then charged without warning. They rolled down the grade, trading punches.

Graders up and down the line dropped their picks and shovels to cheer the fighters on. The eye-patch-wearing and ax-handle carrying boss, James Strobridge, strode over and took in the scene with his one good eye.

"Break it up, you goddamned gandy dancers!" Strobridge called.

Strobridge whacked Donovan in the ribs with the ax handle. Donovan rolled off Abe, and both men rose painfully to their feet.

"That's cost both of you sons of whores a day's wages," Strobridge vowed. "Now get back to work. That goes for the rest of you as well."

The graders reluctantly turned back to their tools. While Strobridge continued to cuss beneath his breath, the Central Pacific chief contractor, Charles Crocker, rode up.

"You shouldn't talk so roughly to the men," Crocker said. "They're human creatures."

"You cannot talk to them as though you were talking to gentlemen," Donovan said. "They're about as near brutes as you can get. Most of these micks will be off for the gold fields as soon as they've earned a grubstake. We started with five thousand men. Now I've got fewer than six hundred."

"There's a surplus of Chinese in San Francisco," Crocker said. "They're said to be quite reliable."

"I will not boss Chinese!" Strobridge declared.

Crocker looked down the line. The work was sloppy and the workers, indifferent. Abe dumped another load at Donovan's feet and they eyed each other rancorously.

In June 1864, Ethan and Margaret elbowed their way to the front of an agitated crowd before a mercantile store on Denver's main street. Ethan was carrying a camera on a tripod over his shoulder.

The mutilated bodies of a white family were on display. Father, mother, and two blond-haired daughters, aged three and six, stared out with frozen death masks at the horrified voyeurs. Each of their throats had been cut from ear to ear.

A tall man in his early forties, with piercing blue eyes and a booming voice that had been cultivated in the pulpit, addressed the crowd. "Look ye upon this outrage to all civilized people. The Hungate family cruelly murdered on their own land—land only twenty-file miles east of where we stand. Sacrificial lambs slaughtered by godless Cheyenne dog soldiers, their bodies cast like Joseph's into a well."

"Not exactly the vistas I was hoping for," Ethan said.

"Don't worry," Margaret said. "We did not give up San Francisco society life for nothing. The images you seek are beyond the cities, still waiting for you on the plain."

Ethan nudged a spectator. "Who's the speaker?"

"Why, that's Colonel John Chivington," the man said, surprised that Ethan did not know. "They call him the Fighting Parson. Whooped the rebels at Glorieta Pass, and now he's gonna give them redskins the what for."

"Brothers and sisters of Colorado," Chivington said, "our territory is poised on the very cusp of statehood. But there can be no statehood without order, and there can be no order while a single savage is allowed to occupy one sacred inch of our precious soil."

The crowd began to murmur, then shout for justice.

Chivington held up his hands. "Governor Evans has authorized me to muster a new regiment for our self-defense," he said. "To the Third Colorado Volunteers will fall the noble task of pursuing all hostile Indians on the plains, and destroying such hostiles wherever they may be found. Who of you will join me in this righteous enterprise?"

A roar of approval. Chivington extended his arms to the crowd, like an Old Testament prophet. Margaret shuddered while Ethan took a photo.

The Overland stage rolled along the South Platte River, leaving Denver. Ethan's camera and equipment were stored in the rear boot, and more luggage was lashed on top. Margaret and Ethan were crammed shoulder to shoulder with six other passengers; Margaret was the only woman. Dust seeped in through the drawn leather curtains.

"Grisly business, that," Ethan said.

"Why must you insist on making a record of it?" Margaret asked.

"The human appetite for the sensational is rather insatiable, I'm afraid," Ethan said. "And quite lucrative."

A garrulous frontiersman opposite them suddenly decided to impart wisdom on his captive audience. "Helluva price to pay for some mangy cows."

"Sir?"

"The Cheyenne and the army been goin' at each other since April," he said. "Some fool rancher loses his herd, blames the Indians. The volunteers ride out and shoot a few for sport. Then the braves up and kill the first white man they find."

"Please," Margaret said, "let's not talk about it."

"They say old man Hungate was out lookin' for strays when it happened," the frontiersman continued. "Saw the smoke from the ranch and rode back. That's when they butchered him."

"Ethan," Margaret said.

Ethan leaned forward to speak to the frontiersman. "I'll thank you to refrain from this line of conversation, sir."

"Beggin' your pardon, ma'am," the frontiersman said. "You just leave everything to the Fighting Parson. When he wants to do something, you can bet it gets done."

The frontiersman tipped his hat; then the stage lurched forward violently, picking up speed. Margaret was all but thrown into the frontiersman's lap.

Ethan fumbled to lower the leather shade. The frontiersman yanked down the shade on his side and craned his head out the window.

"Driver!" he called. "What in blazes?"

There was a high-pitched whining sound, then a sickening thud. The frontiersman slumped forward, shot by an arrow. Margaret screamed.

A party of mounted *hotamitanio*—Cheyenne dog soldiers—was gaining on the coach.

"I count maybe twenty," the expressman shouted.

A warrior leaped from the saddle and scrambled over the coach's luggage boot.

They could hear the warrior walking across the top of the stage as he advanced on the driver. The expressman turned and fired both barrels of his shotgun, blowing the warrior from the stage like a leaf in the wind.

The warrior fell in the path of the war chief, whose spirited horse jumped the slain warrior and kept running. The chief's name in Cheyenne was Broken Nose, but because he was fiercely handsome, whites called him Roman Nose. Around his waist he wore the long sash of the dog soldiers.

While the passengers fought desperately with his warriors, he rode beside the coach and exchanged glances with Margaret. Then Roman Nose put his heels to the horse's flanks. He shot forward, then threw himself from the horse onto the driver. He cut the man's throat and pitched the body aside. Out of ammo, the expressman swung the shotgun like a club at the chief. Roman Nose grabbed the butt, jerked it away, and cracked the expressman's skull with the barrel.

Then Roman Nose brought the stage to a halt, his warriors shouting with victory. They pulled Margaret and the others from out of the stage, and Roman Nose inspected them. Catching a glimpse of the amulet, he pulled it free of Margaret's dress, then snapped it away from her neck.

Ethan moved to protect his wife, but the dog soldiers beat him to his knees. One drew a knife and placed it across Ethan's throat, and Roman Nose indicated with a nod of his head to go ahead and kill the foolish white man.

"Stop!" Margaret screamed in Lakota.

Roman Nose was astonished. "You are Lakota," he said to her in sign language.

"This man is my husband," Margaret signed back. "He possesses great medicine. He has taught me how to make people's spirits visible. Spare us all and I will show you."

Later, Margaret focused the image of the dog soldier in the ground glass at the back of the camera. Ethan handed her a plate. She slid the plate into the camera, cleared the holder, and removed the lens cap.

She began to count. "One, two, three . . . that's right, hold still."

Then she replaced the cap, set the holder, and removed the plate. The stage had been pulled beneath a tree, and tarps were draped around it to keep out the light. Inside the stage, she worked feverishly to develop and then fix the image on the glass. Roman Nose was amazed for the second time that day.

While warriors milled about the camera, one of the dog soldiers cut loose two of the ponies and led them over. Roman Nose smiled and spoke to Margaret.

"Well, what does he say?" Ethan asked.

"The others are free," Margaret explained. "He wants us to go with him."

"That wasn't the bargain," Ethan said.

"The bargain's changed," Margaret said, smiling.

The camp on the banks of Sand Creek, Colorado, was bustling with life, and Margaret and Ethan used their supply of plates not on vistas but on portraits. Meanwhile, Roman Nose conferred with Chief Black Kettle outside his lodge.

"Your raids must stop," Black Kettle, a wise chief in his fifties, said. "We have made a promise of peace."

"I did not sign the soldiers' paper, old man," Roman Nose said.

"You will only do harm to your own people," Black Kettle warned.

"My warriors and I will never tear at the ground like farmers," Roman Nose said in disgust. "That is women's work."

Roman Nose turned his back on the chief and swung onto the back of his horse. Then he led his dog soldiers out of the camp. As he passed, Margaret saw the necklace bouncing on his bronzed chest.

That night, Margaret and Ethan were summoned to Black Kettle's lodge. The chief wanted to see the photographs.

"What do they call you in the white man's world, granddaughter?" Black Kettle asked in stiff but careful English.

"Margaret," she said. "My Lakota name is Light Shines."

"It is a fitting name," Black Kettle said.

Medicine Woman Later, Black Kettle's wife, pointed to a photo of the chief and laughed.

"She says that I am not so ugly in your magic box," Black Kettle said.

"We call it a camera."

Black Kettle tried pronouncing the word, but shook his head.

"The white man's words have no music in them," Margaret said, "but you speak them well."

"So many white men have come," Black Kettle said. "They fill our land with noise. But I do not like their language. Their words have no meaning. Walking the white man's road as you have done is a difficult thing. The spirit does not know where to rest."

"Sometimes," Margaret said, "I feel a hole in my heart."

"White men are like locusts," Black Kettle said. "They fly so thick that the whole sky is like a snowstorm. We are only little herds of buffalo left scattered."

"They will keep coming," Margaret said. "They are

building a railroad to carry them from one ocean to another. In a few years, it will be done."

"I have heard of this thing," the chief said. "When the white father told those who wished peace to come to this place, this reservation, we came. But there is nothing here for us. Without the buffalo, our boys cannot become men. They seek war to prove themselves."

"In Denver," Margaret said, "we saw a family. They had been butchered. Some said it was your people."

"This is a lie," Black Kettle said. "There are bad white men and bad Indians. The bad men on both sides brought about this trouble. But I am determined that this fighting should end." He searched her eyes. "Will you help me, granddaughter?"

Margaret was stunned by the request.

"You understand the white man's thoughts," the chief said. Then he indicated the photographs. "Yet in these shadows, I see your true heart. Will you take my message of peace to the tall chief in the fort?"

On the parade ground outside Denver's Fort Weld, Black Kettle sat in a circle of chiefs. Margaret sat beside him, and the white soldiers and politicians were unsure whether she was his captive or collaborator. When they inquired to her welfare, she simply said her husband was waiting for her back at the Cheyenne camp. Among the whites were Governor Evans and Colonel John Chivington, the Fighting Parson.

Black Kettle stood and began to speak. "We have been traveling through a cloud. The sky has been dark ever since the war began. We want to take good tiding home to our people, that they may sleep in peace. I want all the chiefs of soldiers here to understand that we are for peace, that we may not be mistaken by them for enemies. I have not come here with a little wolf bark, but have come to talk plain with you."

Black Kettle sat down. Evans and Chivington were stonefaced. After a moment, Evans rose.

"While we have been spending thousand of dollars making preparations to feed, protect and make you comfortable, your young men are on the warpath," Evans said.

"I have always done my best to keep my young men quiet," Black Kettle said, "but some will not listen."

"The war among the whites is nearly through," Evans said. "The Great Father will have nothing to do with his soldiers except to send them out after the Indians. We cannot live together on this land. Your people must make their peace with us and let us look after them."

The chiefs nodded. White Antelope stood up. A silver medal hung from his neck.

"The Cheyenne, all of them, have their ears open," he said. "White Antelope is proud to have seen the chief of all the whites in this country. Ever since I went to Washington and received this medal, I have called all white men my brothers."

"Whatever peace you make," the governor said, "must be with the soldiers and not with me."

Recognizing his cue, Chivington rose from his chair and planted himself in the middle of the circle of chiefs and whites. Even before he had said a word, his towering size and his wild look commanded attention.

"The shiny eye looks like a buffalo that has lost its reason," White Antelope said to Black Kettle in Cheyenne.

"I am not a big war chief," Chivington said. "But all the soldiers in this country are at my command. My rule of fighting white men or Indians is to fight them until they lay down their arms and submit to military authority. When you are ready to do that, the soldiers at Fort Lyon will see to your needs." Then Chivington strode away.

The parley was over. The chiefs were uncertain whether peace had been made or not, but the governor handed an American flag to Black Kettle.

"The tall chief says that as long as the flag flies above our camp," Black Kettle told Margaret, "no soldiers will harm us."

Margaret sat cross-legged opposite Black Kettle. More glass plates were arrayed before him. Medicine Woman Later looked fondly at another portrait of her husband. "When will you go?" Black Kettle asked.

"Tomorrow," Margaret said.

"You have brought us much happiness, granddaughter,"

Black Kettle said. "But it is well that you should return to your people."

"We will return with the glass shadows we have made here," Margaret said. "Many white people will see the Cheyenne as they really are. They will understand that your spirits are peaceful."

Black Kettle picked up one of the portraits of himself. "This one I will keep." He leaned forward. "For my wife."

"Of course," Margaret said.

Before dawn the next morning, Colonel Chivington addressed the seven hundred men of the Third Colorado Volunteers. Stoked by some inner fire, he seemed impervious to the November chill.

"Off with your coats," he told the men. "You can fight better without them. Remember the Hungates. Look back on the plains of the Platte, where your mothers, fathers, brothers, and sisters have been slain, their blood saturating the sands. Take no prisoners. Kill and scalp all."

"And the women and children?" an officer asked.

"Nits make lice," Chivington said.

In the Cheyenne camp, Ethan paused from lashing the photographic equipment to one of the ponies. A large cloud of dust seemed to be blowing into the village from the south. The American flag that hung outside of Black Kettle's lodge, however, was limp.

"Buffalo!" women said excitedly. "The buffalo have returned!"

The village began to wake. Black Kettle and the other chiefs, including White Antelope and One Eye, stepped out of their lodges to see what the fuss was about.

The cloud on the horizon was growing bigger, and through it could be seen metallic flashes.

"Soldiers!" Ethan said.

The camp erupted in panic. While women sought their children, the men rushed back into their lodges for weapons.

"Do not be afraid," Black Kettle called. "The soldiers will not hurt you. The flag will protect us."

When they reached the edge of the village, the troops opened fire.

"Stop!" White Antelope screamed in English. "Stop!"

With bullets kicking up the dirt around his feet, White Antelope ran toward the creek. He waded out into the center, then folded his arms across his chest and began his death song.

"Nothing lives long," he chanted, "only the earth and the mountains." A hail of bullets knocked him into the water.

With a pistol in one hand and a saber in the other, Chivington rode about the camp, dealing death and chaos. When he spotted One Eye attempting to nock an arrow, he wheeled his horse and ran him down.

Ethan and Margaret scrambled for safety. The pony on which the plates had been secured was caught in a cross fire, and it went down, screaming. As the animal hit the ground, the shattering of glass could be heard above the gunshots.

Ethan released Margaret's hand and ran to salvage what he could of the photographs. As he reached them, a trooper raised his pistol and fired it point-blank into Ethan's face. Ethan fell backward into a cooking pit.

Margaret screamed. Overwhelmed with rage, she grabbed a lance from a fallen warrior and swung it at the trooper, knocking him from the saddle.

Then a howitzer shell exploded nearby, and Margaret ran with the mad rush of the Cheyenne toward the safety of a nearby ravine, which led to the sand hills beyond. On the ground around her, she saw the faces of the men, women, and children she and Ethan had photographed in the camp: mothers, fathers, brothers, sisters, grandparents. All were dead.

A handful of Cheyenne warriors prepared for a last stand. Black Kettle, carrying his wounded wife on his back, led the refugees toward the ravine. As he passed Margaret, he said, "When you return to your people, tell them a great shame fills my heart."

"You are my people now," Margaret said.

Behind them were the mutilated bodies of two hundred Cheyenne, most of them women and children.

THIRTY-NINE

Lakota Winter Camp
The Dakotas
One Hundred Whites Killed (1866)

"Whose voice was first sounded on this land?" Red Cloud asked. "The voice of the our people, who had but bows and arrows! What has been done in my country I did not want, did not ask for. I have only a small spot of land left, and I want the white man to make no iron roads through it."

At forty-three, Red Cloud—a charismatic leader and holy man—had accomplished what none before him dared. He had united the five nations of the Lakota, Ogallala, Minneconjou Brule, Cheyenne, and Arapahoe. As White Crow and Red Lance listened to him speak, they felt their hearts swell with pride. Here, finally, was a leader who understood how to deal with the whites.

"Got a problem?" Abe asked.

A Chinese worker in his late twenties named Chow-Ping Yen eyed him closely. "Men say you are an Indian."

"Yeah. What of it?"

Chow-Ping gestured to his road crew. "They've never seen an Indian. They are very afraid you'll eat them."

"Haven't had a celestial before," Abe said. "Might like to try one." Abe made a face at the workers, who scattered to avoid being eaten. "Name's Abe Wheeler." They shook hands. "What bad luck brought you here?"

"Before here, *Gam San*. Gold mountain," Chow-Ping said. "*Fan gway* steal claim. Gold not for Chinese, he say."

"Fan want?"

"*Fan gway*," Chow-Ping said. "White ghost. Demon. They stand, talk, tell us what to do. Call us coolies. They hit, cheat, steal."

"Then you hit back."

"No," Chow-Ping said. "Better to hide anger, look blank—like this—so they not see inside you."

On the Union Pacific side, in Nebraska territory, Daniel Wheeler and his sons were busy repairing wheels for the endless line of wagons that supported the track layers. Most of these men were army veterans, and they displayed a variety of blue and gray jackets.

"Two rails every thirty seconds, one on each side," Daniel said admiringly. "Four rails to a minute. Three strokes per spike, ten spikes to a rail. Four hundred rails to a mile, eighteen hundred miles to San Francisco. Twenty-one million times they'll have to swing those hammers. Listen."

The hammers rose and fell, rose and fell. Clang—clang—*clang!*

"That's money, money, money," Daniel said, and the boys looked in doubt at the line. "Won't be long before this enterprise gets beyond the reach of any town. Men deprived of their diversions are inclined to get restless. If they can't come to town, why, then, the town will have to come to them."

Daniel smiled while thinking of the possibilities.

Jackson looked around him at the bleak landscape. "Sure doesn't look like much."

"Not now, maybe," Daniel said, "but you're going to have thousands of boomers coming up here to North Platte from Omaha. Men with nothing to do once winter sets in. Right here is where we stake our own little empire."

While Robert took the inventory by lantern light, Clara assisted. Still in her teens, she was already beautiful although a frumpy dress and severe hair made her look spinsterish.

"Take me with you," she said suddenly.

"No womenfolk allowed," Robert said. "It'll just be Father, Jackson, and me. Thomas is going to mind the business here. You're to help look after Ma."

"I can work as hard as any of your brothers," Clara said.

"Harder, I expect."

"So why, then?"

"You know Father."

"You're not like him," Clara said. "You're decent."

"He is who he is," Robert said. "No use trying to change him. Family's family. You know what it's like . . ." Before the words were even out of his mouth, he realized his mistake.

"They were taken from me," Clara said.

Then something inside of her snapped. She began to sob. She clutched his shoulder, and Robert held her there.

"Out here," he said, "we make our own way in life."

"Some of us haven't got a choice."

"We've all of us got a choice," Robert said. "When the first Wheelers came out, it was all wild country. We've tamed a lot of it. I figure the railroad will tame what's left. There won't be much of a west when it's finished. Guess I'd like to see it before it goes."

"Let me see it with you," Clara pleaded. "You're all I have. My only family."

Robert studied her face in the lantern light. "Father'll have himself a proper fit when he finds out."

"Then you'll help me?"

"I can't make any promises," Robert said.

The amulet dangling form his neck, Roman Nose conferred with Red Cloud during a war council at his lodge.

"I have tested these bluecoats," Red Cloud said. "It is easy to trick them. Their officers are too hot-blooded. It makes them stupid."

"The soldiers inside the fort will protect the supply train if my people attack them," White Crow said.

Red Cloud considered the strategy. Using a map drawn on a buffalo hide, he said, "We will set a trap for them. Here. Two young men from each nation will have the honor to lead the bluecoats into this trap."

"I would like this honor," Red Lance said.

"My son is eager to count his first coup," White Crow observed.

Red Cloud nodded. He turned back to Red Lance. "Crazy Horse will lead you."

"I was only thirteen when I took my first horse," seventeen-year-old Crazy Horse boasted. "Tomorrow you, too, will become a man."

"I will take many scalps."

"We will kill them all," Crazy Horse said.

On December 21, 1866—the day of the winter solstice— warriors of the five nations staged an ambush three miles east of Fort Phil Kearny. Captain William J. Fetterman and eighty men were sent out to rescue a besieged wagon train on Long Trail Ridge. Seeing only a small number of Indians attacking the wagons, Fetterman pursued the warriors over the ridge, where more than a hundred warriors waited for him.

A bugler was one of the last soldiers to stand toward the end, and Red Lance charged him, wielding his coup stick. The bugler took aim with his pistol, but the hammer fell on an empty chamber.

Red Lance caught the bugler across the forehead with the stick. Then he was upon him with his knife, while the soldier tried to fight him off with the only thing left to him, his bugle. Again and again he parried Red Lance's thrusts with the instrument until finally Red Lance overpowered him and pinned his arms.

Looking into the Indian's eyes, the bugler realized the boy was about his age. "Please."

Red Lance plunged the knife into the boy's heart.

Later, after the soldiers had been stripped and mutilated in the same manner that the Cheyenne had been at Sand Creek, Roman Nose sought out Red Lance. Roman Nose removed the buffalo amulet and placed it in Red Lance's palm. Then White Crow handed Red Lance the bugle, creased in many places by his knife, as a war trophy.

The following April, General George Armstrong Custer rode through the tent city of North Platte, in eastern Nebraska territory. Custer, a Civil War hero, had been breveted to brigadier general on the battlefield; after the war, as a lieutenant colonel, he was assigned the newly formed

Seventh Cavalry, but retained the right to be addressed as general. He was twenty-six years old.

Custer rode through the muddy streets at the head of his detachment, taking in the slack-jawed families in their Conestogas, the drunken railroaders, the pickpockets, card sharps, and swaggering young men. The few women on the streets appeared to be prostitutes. The signs on one of the saloon said WHEELERS.

Custer picked out a blue uniform among the throngs drifting from saloon to gambling hall to brothel, and he pointed a gloved hand toward the man. His troopers surged forward and arrested the drunken soldier.

Over at the gambling hall known only as the Big Tent, Daniel Wheeler was doing a land office business in sin. He preferred to watch the profits roll in from the gambling tables and left the wheelwright shop to his son, Robert. Nearby, Daniel rented a tent to Clara Wheeler (no relation, he was always quick to say). Clara was making herself a name as a seamstress, and there were always clothes that had been torn in work—or in fights—to mend. And, just as he had promised years ago, Robert continued to look out for Clara.

The deserter was hauled back to the Seventh's camp outside North Platte and strapped to a wagon wheel. Then Custer assembled the company to witness the flogging. Among the motley collection of scouts in Western garb was Jacob Jr., who was a year older than the general. Custer did not approve of how lightly the scouts regarded military discipline.

"Desertion and dereliction of duty are serious crimes," Custer warned the scouts. "Any other officer would have this deserter shot, but I have too few men to spare."

"Don't reckon this display will help morale any," one of the scouts offered.

"The men's morale will improve once they've been given Indians to fight," Custer said. "For that, gentlemen, I have relied on your good offices—to no avail, it seems."

"Funny thing about Indians, General," Jacob Jr. said. "They ain't so easy to find when they don't want to be."

The scouts laughed, but Custer did not. Instead, he said, "Let me offer you another explanation, Mr. Wheeler. As a half-breed yourself, perhaps you have not applied yourself to the work with the requisite enthusiasm."

In the background, the bullwhip cracked, and Custer continued talking. "The Seventh Cavalry has been entrusted to clear these plains between the Platte and the Arkansas. All depredations on the lands being opened up by the railroad are to cease. You will oblige me by performing your duties without further delay."

FORTY

Medicine Lodge Creek, Kansas
1867 (They Surrounded the White Tents)

In war paint, Roman Nose and his contingent of dog soldiers sat apart from the Indian delegations. Black Kettle wore a dragoon hat and a blue robe, with Margaret as his adviser. Leading the peace commission for the whites was General William Tecumseh Sherman, who was more famous for waging war than petitioning for peace.

"The iron horse is now crossing the land between the Arkansas and the Platte," Sherman told the Indians. "But there is land south of the river in the place called Oklahoma, and before it is all taken, we wish to set aside a part of it for your home. On that home, we will build you a house to hold the goods we will send you. To that home we will send a doctor to live with you and heal your sick. We will send you a farmer to show your people how to grow corn and wheat, and we will make a mill for you to grind your meal and flour."

Roman Nose stood. "Why do you come here?" he asked in Cheyenne. "Because Red Cloud has killed many bluecoats—that is why. This is the time for fighting, not for talking."

Sherman frowned as the message was translated. "We have prepared peace papers. Tomorrow morning at nine o'clock, we want your chiefs and head men to meet with us and sign these papers."

Later, Black Kettle walked with Margaret along the creek. "Our ancestors lived all over this country. They did not know about doing wrong. Since then they have died and gone I don't know where."

"We have all lost our way, Grandfather," Margaret said.

"I do not understand this young man's world," the chief lamented. "I fear it will come to a bad end. What must I do, granddaughter?"

"I cannot see clearly," Margaret said. "I have looked too long at men's shadows through the spirit box. But the camera does not reveal the thoughts behind their eyes. It only hides them."

"Many wrongs have been done to my people," Black Kettle said. "But still I live in hope. Unlike you, I do not have two hearts."

The next day, he signed the peace papers.

The railroads moved, and the Wheelers moved with them. Coming from the East, in the wake of the Union Pacific, Daniel Wheeler and his sons kept moving west and in 1868 eventually reached Cheyenne, Wyoming territory. There, Daniel Wheeler continued to trade in pleasure while Robert made wheels and Clara minded the dry goods store. From the West, Abraham Wheeler blasted through the Sierra Nevadas with the Central Pacific and, now among a crew that was eighty percent Chinese, found himself laboring in the scorching hell of the Great Basin.

"A jackrabbit would need a canteen and a haversack to get across this desert," Abe said to his friend, Chow-Ping. "Almost makes me wish we were back in the mountains."

Strobridge, the labor boss, rode along the line, offering encouragement in the form of elaborate curses.

"Goddammit!" Strobridge shouted. "Put your backs into it! Every mile we make, the mother-loving Union Pacific makes four. Work as though heaven itself were before you and hell behind!"

Riding up to Abe and Chow-Ping's crew, Strobridge flew into a rage. "This isn't a sewing circle, Donovan!"

"Begging your pardon, sir," Donovan said. "If I push these men any harder, you won't have a single one left. The heat, sir."

"Get those cursed celestials digging," Strobridge muttered as he rode off.

Chow-Ping stared at Strobridge for a long moment, then

threw down his shovel. Abe followed suit. Chinese workers up and down the line dropped their picks, shovels, and wheelbarrows.

"They want their pay raised to forty-five dollars a month," Abe said, "and a ten-hour day."

FORTY-ONE

Antelope Hills
1868 (They Traded Many Mules)

Jacob Jr. led Custer on horseback toward a ridge over-look. Custer, riding a black stallion, wore a gaudy uni-form, including scarf, stars, and fringed buckskin.

"They cut this trail around sunup," Jacob Jr. said. "War party, headed south. One hundred, one hundred fifty. Not more than a day, maybe two days old."

He motioned for the general to dismount, and together they approached the crest of the ridge. While other scouts kept lookout, Custer trained his field glasses on the Chey-enne camp in the valley below.

"The Indian is at his most vulnerable in winter," Custer said. "His ponies are weak, his ardor cooled. Find him in his lodges and he can be dealt a decisive blow."

He lowered the glasses. "We will overrun them in converg-ing columns. Our attack will be swift and simultaneous."

"Begging your pardon, General, but we haven't scouted that river bottom," Jacob Jr. said. "Suppose we find more Indians down there on the Washita than we can handle?"

"All I am afraid of," Custer said, "is that we won't find enough. Better to risk uncertainty than to sacrifice advantage. I did not take the time to count Confederate uniforms at Appomattox Station when we seized Lee's supply trains."

Custer turned to his officers. "Absolute silence must be maintained. No fires, no stamping of feet, not so much as a cough to betray our position."

The officers looked skeptical but did not object.

In the morning, a dense fog shrouded the Antelope Hills, but Venus shone brightly.

"See that, Mr. Wheeler?" Custer asked. "A presentiment of victory."

"Heaven-sent, General."

"Fine work," Custer said. "I will send for you if I need you." Then Custer signaled the band. "The 'Garry Owen,' if you please."

To the quick time of the old Irish drinking song, the cavalry fell upon the village.

In the camp, Margaret woke from uneasy dreams to find herself pondering the weird music that seemed to be drifting with the fog. Then she realized it meant soldiers, and she rushed to Black Kettle's lodge. She met him as he stepped outside, firing a rifle into the air to wake the village.

"Soldiers!" she said. "All around us."

"See to the women, granddaughter," the chief said. "Save as many as you can."

"It can't be happening," Margaret said.

"We live in a nightmare from which we never wake," the chief said.

Black Kettle and his wife were among the hundred that Custer estimated he killed at the Washita, although Indian accounts placed the number at closer to fifty. An additional fifty Cheyenne, mostly women and children, were captured and taken by Custer to Camp Supply, Indian territory. Fifty-one lodges were burned, along with the camp's winter supply of food, and some eight hundred horses and mules were killed.

Margaret shared the stockade with the other women and the children. When Custer brought his wife, Libby, to examine the captives, Margaret stared at the couple with hate. She also hated the white scout who accompanied them although she knew him well.

Libby clucked her tongue at the sorry state of the captives.

"You see," General Custer explained patiently, as if he were speaking to a child, "as a race, the condition in which we find the Indian today is not one step above his condition three centuries ago. If any change has taken place, it has taken place for the worse."

"Surely something can be done for them, Armstrong," Libby said.

"The savage and the enlightened of the species cannot live peaceably together, or with equal prosperity," he said. "The weaker must give way to the stronger."

Libby crouched down in front of Margaret. "This one doesn't look like such a bad sort, does she?"

"Many of their women possess a fierceness not found in our more refined sex." Custer's roaming eye appraised several of the younger women, but Libby pretended not to notice. "Those who have not been too degraded by being mere chattels may yet learn some rudimentary manners."

"And what's your name?" Libby asked.

Margaret was silent, but Jacob Jr. stepped forward. He had long ago realized that his sister was among the captives taken on the Washita. "This one goes by Margaret, ma'am."

"Margaret," Libby said. "That's a lovely name. I'm pleased to have met you, Margaret."

As Custer and his wife passed on, Jacob Jr. lingered behind a moment. "I'm getting you out of here."

That night, while Margaret slept on the cold ground, a guard grasped her hair and pulled her to her feet. He hauled her out of the stockade gate, to where Jacob Jr. waited.

"You keep your eyes skinned for this one, scout," the guard said. "Them as had her say she's a regular wildcat."

"She's not for me," Jacob Jr. said. "She's for the lieutenant."

Jacob Jr. half led, half dragged his sister away. "Stop fighting me! Ain't nothing going to happen to you."

"Take me back!" she said. "You're a murderer like the rest of them."

"No!" Jacob Jr. said, pulling her into the darkness between the barracks. "I'm marching you through that gate. There's a pony waiting on the other side. You're getting on it and you're going to clear out of here—understand me?"

"I won't," she said.

"Like hell you won't."

She fought him, then found the butt of his revolver and pulled it from his belt. She pressed it hard beneath his chin, pinning him to the wall. "Take me back."

"You don't belong with those women," Jacob Jr. said.

"They're my sisters," she said. "My mothers. My children. My *brothers*. I won't leave them."

"You're not talking sense," he said. "How can I ever face Ma or Pa again if I don't see you safe out of here?"

The barrel of the pistol slowly fell. "Tell them their daughter died at Sand Creek. Tell them that Light Shines lived to see the white man keep his promises on the Washita. Tell them that the hole I have in my heart is now filled with sorrow. Tell them that I can never go back to who I was. Tell them that I love them."

Both were crying now, and she asked, "Will you tell them that, Jacob?"

"Yes, I'll tell them." He took her back to the stockade.

The guard winked and asked, "What'd I tell you? Wildcat."

Jacob Jr. walked away.

"The lines will meet at Promontory Point," Daniel Wheeler told his son. He was wearing a tailored black suit and hat; he had a copy of the *Cheyenne Leader* beneath his arm. He looked for all the world like part of the railroad establishment.

"So?" Robert asked.

"Utah's Mormon country," Daniel said. "But they say Brother Brigham appreciates the worth of a gentile dollar. When they drive that last spike, the real opportunity begins. We'll have our pick of the spur lines and hauling contracts."

"I don't want any part of it," Robert said.

Daniel stopped. He looked at Robert as if his son were something alien.

"I had hoped to bestow upon you our family's good fortune," Daniel said. "That is no more or less than my obligation, as it is yours to respect and serve our business here."

"I'll carry out my duties until the rails meet," Robert said. "I owe you that much. Once it's done, I'm striking out on my own."

Daniel looked across the street to the dry goods store.

In the window, he could see Clara adjusting a mannequin. "You demonstrate no aptitude for enterprise. That girl's got a better head for business than you'll ever have. I underestimated her."

"Clara gives people nice things," Robert said. "Taking advantage of their weakness doesn't seem much of a business to me."

"Different times call for different methods," Robert said.

"If that's progress," Robert said, "then I don't care much for it." Robert walked away, toward the dry goods shop.

"You'd better think hard on the future, boy!" his father called after.

On May 10, 1869, the Union Pacific's Engine No. 119 and the Central Pacific's *Jupiter* touched cowcatchers amid a jubilee at Promontory Point, Utah. The transcontinental railway was complete, shrinking the time it took to cross the continent from six months to six *days*. But men like Abraham Wheeler, who had risked their lives under brutal conditions to achieve what many thought was impossible, were rewarded with unemployment.

Years passed beneath the hoop of the sky.

Then, in July 1874, an expedition led by George Armstrong Custer penetrated the Black Hills, ostensibly to locate a new fort in order to protect northern railroad expansion. Custer, with his flowing locks and buckskin jacket, delivered a running commentary to the reporters attached to the expedition.

"You may report to your readers that this expedition has thus far exceeded my most sanguine expectations," Custer declared. "We have discovered a rich and beautiful country. There is abundant game, fertile land—in short all the bounties necessary to the establishment of civilization."

"The Laramie Treaty of Six-eight made this Indian land, General Custer," a reporter observed. "Part of the Great Sioux Reservation. The Sioux might not take too kindly to trespassers."

"I shall recommend extinguishment of Indian title at the earliest moment practicable for military purposes," Custer said. "Should Congress give its support to the settlement of the Black Hills, gentlemen, you may rest assured the military will do its duty."

Custer paused, allowing the reporters to get his words down exactly. They were standing on top of a low hill, beneath the great medicine wheel, which troopers of the Seventh Calvary were using as baseball diamond, despite Jacob Jr.'s protestations that the wheel on the hilltop was a Lakota church. Down below was a stream, where a pair of prospectors attached to the expedition were panning for gold.

A shout went up from the stream.

Custer and the reporters looked down.

One of the prospectors was waving his hat over his head.

The prospector showed his pan to the general. Custer picked out a small nugget of glove with the tip of his calf-skin glove, then showed the gold to the reporters.

Hillsgate, Dakota Territory, was a ramshackle town that looked as if it had fallen from the sky. Fortune hunters speaking different languages flocked the streets. Wood-frame structures and Army tents defied the elements, and stenciled and hand-lettered signs were in abundance.

One of the signs said, "Wheeler's General Store."

Inside, thirty-one-year-old Robert Wheeler was using a crowbar to open a crate of shovels for anxious prospectors and immigrants.

"One at a time, gentlemen," Robert said. "Please don't shove. There's enough to go around."

"Is it true," one of the prospectors asked, "that there are nuggets as big as a man's knuckles all over the ground for thirty miles?"

"That's how the papers tell it," Robert said. "Just step over to the counter and hand the missus your money."

Clara, now twenty-six, unfurled a bolt of cloth for a group of women.

"This is English calico," Clara said. "Very pretty, yet very durable. Feel it."

"If you've no cash," Robert said, "I'll give you these tools on credit. Payment due in full on your first strike."

"How do you get to the Black Hills?" another prospector asked.

"Freedom Trail," Robert said. "Ten dollars will get you a ride on my wagon."

"Ten dollars?" the prospector groused. "Cost me half that by train from Chicago."

"Well, sir, you can wait until they build a railroad to the Black Hills, or you can hand over ten dollars and hop on. The price includes a simple meal and armed protection."

From behind the counter, Clara watched Robert with concern.

Later, in their simple home, Clara and Robert ate supper and dared some conversation.

"There's a fortune to be made," Robert said. "There are camps and towns spread out all through those hills. Those who got rich in forty-nine were the ones who mined the miners."

"Even the Army can't protect itself in the Black Hills," Clara said.

"I trade with the Lakota at the agency," Robert said, referring to the Red Cloud Agency. "They know me as a friend."

"You'll just be another treaty breaker to them," Clara said. "I don't like the whole business."

"A man's got to do better for himself, Clara. I wouldn't want any son of mine to ever say—"

Silence fell between them.

"We promised never to speak of that again," Clara said.

"Clara. What happened to the baby wasn't your fault."

"Let's say no more about it."

Robert Wheeler's arms and shoulders ached, his clothes were covered with dust, and the wagon bed behind him was piled high with goods from the store. On the seat beside him was the prospector who had asked about transportation to the Black Hills.

The prospector slumped forward, dead.

A moment later came the sound of the rifle shot that had killed him.

Craning his head, Robert saw three horseman riding fast toward him. Robert stopped the wagon, grabbed a rifle case, and scrambled beneath the wagon. The horseman had split up to cover both sides. Bullets began to ping off metal goods and kick up splinters from the wagon bed.

Robert removed the Sharps from the case, opened the

breach, and chambered a massive .50 caliber round. He sighted down the barrel, placing the "V" of the rifle sight on a horseman that was still three hundred yards away. Robert squeezed off the round and the horseman dropped from the saddle.

As Robert reloaded, the second horseman continued to pepper the wagon with rounds from his repeating rifle. Robert lowered the barrel and killed the second horseman as easily as the first.

While he reloaded again, the third horseman wheeled his horse and rode hard in the opposite direction. Robert placed the gun sight on the horseman's back, then thought better of it. Then the rider glance back, and Robert decided he did not want to take the chance of meeting this badman on the trail ever again. He shouldered the rifle and squeezed the trigger. The slug hit the third rider in the back.

As Robert climbed out from beneath the wagon, he was already hating himself.

The Red Cloud Agency was a handful of ugly log buildings squatting at the foot of a high, striated bluffs. An American flag hung from a pole. Tipis dotted the prairie around the agency.

On the parade ground, Indian elders had gathered to discuss politics. While he listened, twenty-three-year-old Red Lance idly touched the buffalo-and-medicine-wheel amulet that hung from his neck. Beside Red Lance sat his adoring thirteen-year-old brother, Voices That Carry. Next to them sat their father, White Crow, now forty-two, and his father, Running Fox, sixty-two. Nearby was Dog Star, also in his sixties, with his son, Sleeping Bear, and grandson, White Bird.

"The white father has sent me a message on the talking wire," the warrior and statesman Red Cloud said in Lakota. The chief had waged the most successful Indian war in history against the United States and the efforts to open up the Bozeman Trail. "The soldiers will chase away the men on the Thieves' Road," Red Lance said. "The peace talkers will come."

"Red Cloud once drove the bluecoats from their forts," White Crow said with thinly concealed contempt. "Now he lives on the white man's reservation and speaks the white man's words."

"I have been to see the Great Father," Red Cloud patiently explained. "I rode many suns in the houses pulled by the iron horse. The white man's villages are too many to be counted."

"These are our lands," White Bird said with anger. "We will not move our lodges because one man makes a mark on the white man's papers."

White Bird's outburst startled Dog Star. A murmur of discontent overtook the gathering. Red Cloud held his hands up in an attempt to stifle it.

"Those who think we can still make war with the white man as we did seven winters past," Red Cloud said, "speak like young men seeking to take their first scalp."

"Sitting Bull and Crazy Horse will fight!" White Crow said. "And so will we."

Many of the warriors shouted in agreement. White Cloud stood and led an exodus from the council, with Dog Star and Red Cloud looking on with dismay.

Later, inside a warm lodge, Voices That Carry listened as the elders of the Dog Star and Running Fox clans debated the right course.

"Better to die a warrior naked in death than to be wrapped up with a heart of water inside!" Running Fox declared.

"You dare to speak to me this way?" Dog Star asked.

"Even White Bird, your grandson, wishes to fight."

Dog Star glanced at White Bird.

"I am sorry, Grandfather," the boy said. "I saw myself kill bluecoats in a vision."

"A man cannot ignore his vision," Dog Star said. "But be sure it is your *vision*, and not that of another."

"My clan will follow Sitting Bull," Running Fox said.

"Voices That Carry is too young for battle," Dog Star said. "Let him stay with me to learn the art of the winter count."

As Running Fox's clan prepared to ride out of the Red Cloud Agency, Voices That Carry watched intently as his older brother readied his horse.

"I have never taken a buffalo," Voices That Carry said. "I have never taken a scalp. I want to hold my head high, like you."

"Your time will come to be a warrior," Red Lance said.

Then Red Lance removed the amulet and placed it around his little brother's neck.

"The great Cheyenne warrior Roman Nose gave me this," Red Lance said. "Be worthy of it."

Then Red Lance mounted up and rode off with the clan. Voices That Carry watched them go until they were all out of sight.

At the Wheeler Store in Hillsgate, Clara walked among the aisles between the desks made from fruit crates and quizzed the immigrant children on the lesson in their copies of *McGuffey's Fifth Eclectic Reader*. In this setting, she was less guarded, and more willing to reveal something of her younger self.

" 'The war is actually begun!' " a boy named Hans recited.

"You see the exclamation point Mr. Patrick Henry placed after 'begun'?" Clara asked. "Strong next time, Hans. Mr. Kurchenko."

Another blond-headed boy stood and took a nervous breath.

" 'Our brethren are already in the field!' " he said, giving the punctuation all that it deserved. " 'Why stand we here idle?' "

"Excellent," Clara said. "Mr. Kurtz?"

" 'Is life so dear, or peace so sweet, as to be purchased at the price of chains and slavery?' " another boy asked. " 'Forbid it, Almighty God!' "

"Good," Clara said. "Alvetina?"

Alvetina nodded, took a breath, and launched into it. " 'I know not what course others may take but as for me, give me liberty or give me death!' "

The students applauded.

"That's enough for today," Clara said. "Time for you all to be getting home. I'll see you next Sunday."

As the class broke, the children swarmed over Clara, hungry for her attention. The boys brought gifts of appreciation: a piece of cloth, food, even a live chicken.

"Mr. Kurchenko, Mr. Kurtz, gentleman," Clara called. "Your gifts are sweet but not at all necessary. Away with you now. Shoo!"

Clara playfully chased them out. The children scattered, laughing. As Clara watched them go, the longing was plain on her face. Safe at home, she pulled out a trunk from beneath the bed and removed a set of baby clothes. She caressed them and held them to her cheek before she returned them to their box.

"You put in paper like this," the salesman said, rolling a piece of paper into the new Sholes & Glidden typewriter, which had been designed by a gunmaker and was being produced by the Remington Arms Company. "You touch the keys—and *presto!*—out comes a letter with all the quality of newspaper print."

Clara was impressed as the salesman tapped out a message on the machine, which had quickly been set up on the counter of the general store.

"With this device, and a little manual prestidigitation, the tedious labor of business correspondence may be cut in half," the salesman said.

"Very . . . ingenious," Clara said.

"May I put the lady proprietress down for a model?"

The salesman was an affable forty-year-old by the name of Douglas Hillman, and his smile suggested that he only had Clara's best interests at heart.

Clara considered briefly, then nodded. As the salesman began to write up the sale with a pencil and pad, Clara gingerly tapped the keys. Then the door chime sounded as Robert Wheeler walked in.

Later, when he had Clara alone, he told her about his trip to the Black Hills. "The pickings were good there, Clara. Better than I imagined. Ran out of supplies before I ran out of customers. I figure it'll require a trip to Omaha, maybe Kansas City to restock."

"I won't have you going into those hills again," Clara said. "I couldn't sleep for the worry. Not knowing whether you were alive or—or moldering on the plains somewhere."

"I didn't mean to cause you grief, Clara. It's just that I have ambitions. For both of us." Robert took her hands in his. He glanced down at the plain band around Clara's wedding finger. "One day you'll have a proper gold band, not an old saddle ring."

"Iron is stronger than gold," Clara said. "I wouldn't

trade this ring for the world. This ring was made for a simple purpose. Like the man who gave it to me."

Robert's face clouded.

"Clara," he said. "There's something—"

"What is it? What's wrong?"

"I killed three men."

"Oh, Robert . . ."

"I looked down the barrel of a loaded gun and thought I might never see you again. I shot, and kept shooting, even when I didn't have to."

Clara was silent.

"So much for purpose, I guess," Robert said.

The peace talkers foretold by Red Lance came in September 1875 to the Red Cloud Agency. Leading the four-man commission was Iowa senator William B. Allison, a tin-eared bureaucrat in his forties. Seated around Allison, beneath a tarpaulin that had been strung beside a lone cottonwood, were General Alfred Terry, a missionary named Samuel Hinman, and Grabber, a half-black, half-Indian translator. A hundred twenty of Terry's men were drawn up in a line behind the shelter.

The Indian elders, including Red Cloud, sat in a semicircle opposite the commission. Few of them had seen the treaty that made the Lakota the keepers of the *Paha Sapa*. But they all knew that the treaty could not be changed without the marks of three of every four Lakota men.

Sitting Bull and other chiefs who were still at war and refused to meet with the peace talkers had sent warriors to be their messengers. Among the hostiles were Dog Star, Sleeping Bear, White Bird, and Voices That Carry.

"We have now to ask you if you are willing to give our people the right to mine in the Black Hills, as long as gold or valuable minerals are to be found, for a fair and just sum," Allison said in his best oratorical voice. "If you are so willing, we will make a bargain with your for this right. When the gold or other minerals are taken away, the country will again be yours to dispose of in any manner you may wish."

Red Cloud and the other chiefs laughed uproariously. Then Red Cloud replied in Lakota, "Would the white man give the Lakota mules for his wagon with the same promise?"

The plain erupted in laughter. Grabber translated, and Allison and the others exchanged worried looks.

"It will be hard for our government to keep the whites out of the hills," Allison said. "To try to do so will give you and our government great trouble, because the whites who may wish to go there are very numerous."

"I want our Great Father to give us meat," Red Cloud said. "I want flour and coffee, sugar and tea, and bacon, and cracked corn and beans, and tobacco, and soap. I want this for all the people, for their children and seven times their children."

In the middle of this speech, White Bird led a procession of warriors into the open space between the commissioners and the chiefs. Some were on ponies and all brandished rifles.

"The Black Hills is my land," White Bird chanted in Lakota, and was joined by the warriors. "Whoever interferes will hear this gun."

Then, at the same moment, the warriors discharged their rifles in unison. Some of the cavalry horses were spooked, and the troopers waited for the signal to fire.

Terry motioned them to stand down.

White Bird led the warriors out of the circle. Both sides were aware that the council had gone beyond their control. Red Cloud began to resume his speech, but Allison cut him off.

"Our firm offer is four hundred thousand dollars each year for the mineral rights," Allison said. "Should you wish to sell the Black Hills outright, the price will be six million dollars, payable in fifteen annual installments."

"We will go to the White Father in Washington," Red Cloud said reflectively. "We will smoke a pipe with him."

Allison did not encourage him.

"You have heard his words," the senator said, "which cannot be altered, even to the scratch of a pen."

That night, in Sitting Bull's lodge, the warriors related the events of the commission to the impressive and charismatic Indian leader.

"What was Red Cloud's answer?" Sitting Bull asked.

"He would not sell," Red Lance said.

"Not yet," Sitting Bull said. "But he will. Our brothers have made themselves slaves to pieces of fat bacon, some hardtack and a little sugar and coffee. The whites may get me at last, but I will have a good time until then."

The warriors laughed, and Sitting Bull picked up a pinch of dust. "The government will not have our land, not even this much."

The dust drifted from Sitting Bull's fingers, and Red Lances watched it rejoin the earth.

At the Wheeler General Store, Robert began to buy the buffalo hides, tongues, hoofs, and horns offered by the foul-smelling "stinkers" who followed the buffalo hunters. The buffalo were getting harder to find, and the southern herd was all but gone. Driven by oversupply, the price for buffalo hides had also plummeted. Douglas Hillman, the type-writer salesman, offered Robert Wheeler one dollar for each of the hides piled behind the general store.

"I consider that more than fair," Hillman said.

"And I consider that robbery with a smile under a high-top hat," Robert said. "Last time, the price was six dollars."

"The rage for buffalo bedspreads and other accoutrements back east has ended," Hillman said apologetically. "Leave the buffalo to their extinction, sir. They've served their purpose. On the train from New York to Hillsgate, I saw the future."

He paused.

"Bones."

"Bones?" Clara asked.

"Bones," Hillman said. "Buffalo bones. The detritus of sporting men lured by a three-dollar rail ticket and the promise of game there for the taking. The carcasses left to rot create a mighty stench, but in that smell an enterprising man may detect the odor of money."

Robert became interested.

"Bones can be ground to make fertilizer and fine china," Hillman said. "And this is only the start of the possibilities. A man could earn himself eight, nine, perhaps as much as ten dollars a ton."

"How many wagonloads in a ton, would you say?"

"I am told a ton consists of approximately one hundred carcasses."

Clara could see that Robert was calculating the possibilities.

Later, when the store was closed, Clara sat at her typewriter and pounded out correspondence and purposefully avoided Robert's gaze.

"I broke away from my father so we could have a life together," Robert said. "I mean to make it a good one."

"I know," Clara said, still typing. "But your dreams are still your father's. Not your own."

"Clara, all that money we made on the miners we lost on the hides, and then some. I wouldn't be gone long."

"You're gone too often."

"Then . . . give me a reason to stay."

The typewriter fell silent. Clara looked up at Robert sharply.

"You spend all your time with those . . . those square-head children."

"Don't be cruel," Clara said.

"Makes me sick to see it, sometimes," Robert said. "Wet-nursing those brats when you're too damn afraid to try to have a child of your own."

Clara bolted from the chair and slapped Robert across the face. After a long silence, Robert said, "I'm sorry. I didn't mean—"

"Yes," Clara said. "Yes, you did."

Clara returned to the typewriter. Soon, the keys were clacking again.

"Damn it," Robert said.

FORTY-TWO

Red Cloud Agency
1876 (Horses Were Taken Away)

A detachment of Buffalo Soldiers stood guard over a group of captive women and children while the white officer thrust a set of forms at the Indian agency.

"Can't feed them as I've already got," the agent said, "and now the government sends me more."

The agent grudgingly signed in triplicate; then the officer nodded to the soldiers to loosen the bonds of the new arrivals. Among them was Margaret Light Shines. Five years of captivity and being shuttled from one miserable camp to another had hardened her features. With Margaret were three orphan children, who clung desperately to their adopted mother for protection.

Robert Wheeler braked the supply wagon to a halt in front of the agency. He took in the long lines of women and children waiting for the distribution day handouts, the men who lurked some distance away because they were too proud to receive charity personally, and the group of newly arrived women and children.

"Ain't buying hides," the agent told him.

"Not selling 'em," Robert said.

With that, he started to unload the wagon, tossing hide after hide onto the parade ground. At first, the Indians just watched. But when they realized Robert was making a gift of them, they began to gather up the hides with gratitude.

The white officer, Captain William Henry Pratt, touched his hat in greeting as he rode up alongside Robert, who stood in the bed of the wagon. At thirty-five, Pratt was a dedicated, principled soldier who had worked his way up from private.

"I commend you, sir," the officer said. "Pratt, Tenth Cavalry."

"Robert Wheeler."

"Allow me to say, Mr. Wheeler, that you are the exception which proves the rule."

"What rule is that, Captain?"

Pratt shifted uncomfortably in the saddle. "I find the majority of traders to be unprincipled, unscrupulous rogues. A pack of veritable scoundrels, if you don't mind my saying so."

"Afraid I do mind, Captain." Robert continued to unload hides.

"Any one of those animals could feed an Indian family for half a year," Pratt said. "But the hunters take the hide and leave the rest to rot. The 'big kill' has done in more Indians in two years than the Army has done in thirty."

"Fine sentiments coming from a man who makes widows and orphans his stock-in-trade," Robert said, and jerked his chin toward the prisoners. "And you call me a rogue."

"Perhaps we both are, Mr. Wheeler."

Pratt regarded the captives with sympathy. "These unfortunates have been herded back and forth across the lines like so many head of cattle. Now, as you can plainly see, they are free to make a new home for themselves."

Robert looked around at the agency in disdain. "If you can call it that."

"We have denied these people fraternity," Pratt said. "We have driven them from their ancestral homes and forwarded death and depravity among them. It has cost the people of our government hundreds of millions of dollars and led to the present shameful impasse."

"Can't stop progress, Captain."

"What is progress but what men do?" Pratt asked, waxing philosophical. "Most men do what they will. Others, what they deem to be right. Where do you stand, Mr. Wheeler?"

Robert paused. "To be honest with you, Captain, sometimes I'm not so sure."

"Now that is a promising beginning to a man's education," Pratt said. "Good day, Mr. Wheeler."

Pratt motioned his column forward. The Buffalo Soldiers followed in tight formation. Robert continued to distribute hides, but he stared after the enigmatic Pratt.

"Too many damn Indians left, and no place to put them," the agent said, addressing the new arrivals in a rubble-strewn pocket on the agency's periphery. "This is the best I can do for you. Ration day is the first of every month."

"No," Margaret said, speaking for the group. "We will not beg."

The agent shrugged. "Suit yourself. Only make damn sure you and the other squaws stay put. The order's gone out: any Indian not on agency land by January thirty-first is to be considered hostile. You savvy that?"

"We will not make trouble for you," Margaret said.

"Hell," the agent said, "you already have." He stalked away, leaving the women and children to their fate.

As the orphans clustered around Margaret, she said in Lakota, "This is our home now."

"But," the boy named Kit Fox protested, "there's nothing."

Margaret knelt. "Can't you see it?"

"See what?" Kit Fox asked.

"All the mothers working," Margaret said. "All the children playing. If you listen, you can hear them."

The orphans looked around, trying to conjure up the image. Margaret's determination lifted the spirits of the other women.

"We will make a good life here," she declared. "And we will depend on no one. No one. Do you understand?"

The children nodded. Margaret stood. The other women looked to her.

"There are many on this land who have lost their sons to war," Margaret said. "There are elders with no family left to provide for them. Let us all work to help these people. We will make our own way, and not rely on what the white man calls charity."

Winter came and conditions in the camp grew more crowded. Supplies were even more scarce, and even the cattle grew sick. At Dog Star's camp, Voices That Carry watched in disgust as his great-uncle slaughtered the cattle to keep them from suffering . . . and to provide a few meager meals.

That night, Voices That Carry gathered his things—a few boyish weapons, a food pouch, and a medicine bag—and with a final look of farewell slipped beneath the cover of Dog Star's tipi into the night.

Many weeks later, when the winds of spring were whispering in the grass along Rosebud Creek, Voices That Carry arrived at Sitting Bull's camp. Red Lance seized the boy by the ear and flung him at his father, White Crow.

"You will go back to Dog Star," White Crow said.

"I won't!" Voices That Carry protested. "On the reservation they do not *live* like men—and I am a man!"

His father and brother could not help but smile at the boy's determination.

White Crow knelt beside him. "So you are, my son," he said.

"Where are the soldiers?" Voices That Carry asked.

"What soldiers?" Red Lance asked.

"Dog Star said if you didn't return to the agency," Voices That Carry said, "then soldiers would come."

"When is this to be?" a deep voice asked.

Voices That Carry turned to see Sitting Bull approaching, walking with a slight limp from an old wound. The boy was thunderstruck by his first sight of the great chief.

"Speak, boy," Sitting Bull said. "It is only Sitting Bull before you, not *Wakan Tanka*. When are the soldiers to come?"

"After the Moon of Popping Trees," the boy said.

"It is good that you have brought us this message," Sitting Bull said. "You are welcome to our camp."

Sitting Bull placed his hand on the boy's head. Voices That Carry stared as the chief walked off in deep contemplation. The chief found a ridge overlooking the encampment and offered a medicine pipe to the four directions.

"Wakan Tanka," he said. "In the name of the people, I offer you this sacred pipe. Save the people, I beg you. We want to live. Guard us against all misfortune. Pity me. Pity us."

Sitting Bull sat on the ground, legs outstretched, leaning against the trunk of the sacred cottonwood tree. His hands and feet were painted red, and blue stripes ran across his shoulders.

The chief prayed as an assistant, using an awl and knife, sliced small squares of skin from Sitting Bull's arms. Quickly, the assistant moved up the arm from wrist to shoulder, slicing away the skin and placing the offerings in a medicine bag.

"Sitting Bull sensed the spirits of the bluecoats who had been sent to capture him and his people and force them to live like white men," the chief said, referring to himself in the third person to give his words the proper gravity. "He sought a vision to prepare himself for the great struggle. He promised to offer a scarlet blanket of his own blood to *Wakan Tanka*."

Blood trickled down Sitting Bull's arms and dripped from the tips of his fingers, but the chief never cried out. The assistant daubed at the wounds with balls of sage.

In his lodge, Sitting Bull related his vision to a group of warriors that included Crazy Horse, Running Fox, White Crow, Red Lance, and White Bird. Among the Lakota were representatives of the Cheyenne and Arapaho.

"The sky was black with them, like grasshoppers," Sitting Bull said. "They fell into our camp. Endlessly they fell."

Outside the tipi, Voices That Carry listened to the vision.

"A voice in the sky said to me, 'Take these soldiers. They will not listen. They have no ears.'"

The warriors murmured their approval.

"'Kill them,' the voice said," Sitting Bull continued. "'But do not take their guns or horses. If you set your hearts upon the goods of the white man, it will prove a curse to this nation. These soldiers are a gift from *Wakan Tanka*. Hold the gift sacred.'"

A war cry went up inside the tipi, and Voices That Carry added his voice to the crescendo of war.

For many years, Loved by the Buffalo had wandered the nations without hearing the sweet, clear voices that sang to him in his youth. He had begun to see the truth of Growling Bear's vision, and it pained his heart. Loved by the Buffalo felt the loss of the power of *Wakan Tanka* and knew that the time was soon coming for him to return to his people, without having found the answer he had sought for so long.

He returned to the medicine Wheel in the *Paha Sapa*, the center of the world, and was dismayed to discover that through neglect and irreverence, the wheel's lines had become indistinct. Stone by precious stone, Loved by the Buffalo began to repair the wheel.

FORTY-THREE

Yellowstone River, Montana Territory
1876 (Horses Were Taken Away)

"Listen to this," Jacob Jr. said, then read from a copy of the *Bismarck Tribune*. " 'General George A. Custer, dressed in a dashing suit of buckskin, is prominent everywhere, taking in everything connected with his command with the keen, incisive manner for which he is so well known.' "

Trooper Long sneered. "Ain't every command that's got its own pet newspaperman tagging along." He took a nip of whiskey, then offered the flask to Jacob Jr., who waved him off.

Long gestured toward the command tent, pitched on a rise slightly above the camp. Through the tent flap, they could see Custer in conference with other officers.

"What d'ya think they're cooking up in there?" Long asked.

"Whatever it is," Jacob Jr. said, "I can guarantee it's all about the general."

Custer, who was wearing a bright blue shirt under his buckskin jacket, stood at a map table with his commanders, General Alfred Terry and Colonel John Gibbon. Also at the table were Custer's subordinates, Major Marcus Reno and Captain Frederick Benteen, who were both in their thirties. A young newspaperman, Mark Kellogg, scribbled notes.

"Major Reno's advance party located two abandoned villages up Rosebud Creek, between the Tongue and Bighorn rivers," Terry said. "The hostiles appear to be moving north, unaware of our present position."

"All the better, sir," Custer said. "Hit them swiftly and they'll fly like quail." He turned to the newspaperman. "Given a choice, Mr. Kellogg, the Indian will always run rather than fight."

While Kellogg dutifully scribbled down Custer's words, Reno and Benteen exchanged uneasy glances.

"Exactly what we anticipate," Terry told Custer. "I want you, Reno, and Benteen to follow their trail up the Rosebud. Gibbon and I will march up the Yellowstone to a blocking position here, at the mouth of the Little Bighorn, cutting off any escape to the north. I leave the particulars to your well-known discretion."

"Now don't be greedy, Custer," Gibbon said. "There are Indians enough for all. Wait for us."

Custer paused before replying. "No, I don't think I will."

"You may take three of our Gatling guns," Terry offered.

"That won't be necessary," Custer said. "The men of the Seventh Cavalry are capable of handling any force the enemy may hurl against us. Gatling guns would only slow us down."

Custer spoke slowly enough to make sure that the reporter would quote him exactly. Now it was Terry's and Gibbon's turn to trade worried looks.

"Answer me something," Long said, interrupting Jacob Jr.'s reading of the *Tribune*. "If you think Custer's so infernal bad, why do you ride with him?"

"Better to know a devil and confound his purpose than leave him be," Jacob Jr. said. Then he continued reading: " 'The general is perfectly ready for a fray with the hostile red devils—' "

"Uh, Jake?" Long was looking past him.

" '—and woe to the body of scalp lifters that comes within reach of himself and his brave companions in arms.' " He lowered the paper. "Guess that means us."

"Jake—" Long pointed.

Jacob Jr. turned to see Custer standing beside them.

"When you're quite finished, Mr. Wheeler," Custer said. "Two of our men failed to report for this morning's roll call. Take a small detachment with you and find them. Quickly."

As Custer walked on, Jacob Jr. stared after him and cursed softly under his breath in Lakota.

At sunset, Jacob Jr. found the deserters making a meal of hardtack in the cover of some brush on the Bighorn plains. Their horses were ground-tied nearby, and the skittish animals sensed something a moment before the troopers heard:

"Saddle up."

The deserters sprang to their feet, weapons drawn. Jacob Jr. stepped out from his hiding place, his carbine in front of him. Three troopers, including Long, backed him.

"Next time you desert," Jacob Jr. said, "you might want to stick to the creeks. Fewer tracks that way."

"You know what Old Hardass will do to us, Jake," one of the deserters pleaded.

"Should've thought of that before you hightailed it," Jacob Jr. said.

"I ain't going back, Jake," the other deserter said.

"Me neither," the first one said quickly. "I'm tired of marchin', Jake. Thirty-three miles one day, twenty-eight the next."

"All the man thinks about is how he's gonna be a major general again, on our backs," the other deserter said.

They began to back slowly toward their horses.

"You didn't take to the killin' of squaws and kids at the Washita no more than we did, Jake," the second deserter continued. "I seen it. And Lakota blood runs in your veins."

"That don't signify anything," Jacob Jr. said, but it was plain from his face that the man had touched a nerve. "Don't," Jacob Jr. said as they reached for the reins of the horses.

"Kill us if you have to, Jake," the first deserter said. "Rather be in hell than with Custer."

The deserters mounted up slowly. Jacob Jr. shouldered his rifle, but he allowed the pair to reign their horses around and ride off. He lowered his rifle to find Long and the other troopers looking on in sympathy.

"Even the best scout gets lost sometime," Long said.

*   *   *

On the outskirts of the Red Cloud Agency, Margaret and the other women had managed to make a home for themselves and their children. There were tipis in straight rows, hides stretching on rough frames, a small garden plot—and the laughter of children.

Margaret sat in a sewing circle outside her lodge, while the orphan girl Star Woman watched in fascination at her feet. Margaret handed her the needle.

A group of male riders approached, leading a horse bearing the carcass of a freshly killed deer. There were also boxes of agency rations. Margaret and the other women hustled inside their lodges and reemerged with various handiworks, which they spread on blankets.

The men eyed the impressive collection of war shirts and necessities. They huddled briefly, then made their selections. The leader walked over with the horse carrying the deer and rations.

Margaret nodded, and the deal was done. The women quickly accepted the payment while the leader and the men loaded up their purchases.

Margaret stepped over to have a word with the leader. "Many have come for war shirts," she said in Lakota.

"Sitting Bull has had a great vision," he said. "Soldiers falling from the sky."

The leader mounted up and rode out, his men following behind them. Margaret stared after the departing riders, a worried look on her face. Turning, she saw the agent watching warily from the compound buildings.

At Sitting Bull's camp, the circle of tipis grew ever larger, so the chief moved the village to the banks of the Greasy Grass River, where game was plentiful. There, the warriors readied themselves, waiting for the day the sky would rain bluecoats.

"What did you see, Mr. Wheeler?"

"Horses," Jacob Jr. said.

Jacob Jr. and the lead Crow scout had been summoned to Custer's tent in the Seventh Cavalry encampment at the place called Crow's Nest on the Little Bighorn River. At dawn, in a valley to the west, the scouts had spotted a large village.

"Horses?" Custer asked.

"More than I could count, sir," Jacob Jr. said. "Like a brown wave across the hills on the other side of the Little Bighorn."

"Were you spotted?" Custer asked.

"Don't think so."

"Can you be absolutely sure, Mr. Wheeler?"

"No, sir. I can't."

Custer straightened as he came to a decision.

"We will strike the village at once."

Jacob Jr. and the Crow scout shifted uncomfortably.

"Might be better to hold off until our reinforcements arrives," Jacob Jr. suggested.

"I will not risk the chance of our quarry escaping," Custer said, then leaned over a table to consult a map. "Major Reno will lead his men across the river with all due haste and flush out the hostiles. I will ride north with five companies to cut off the Indian's retreat. Instruct Major Reno to report to me immediately."

"Yes, sir." Jacob Jr. threw a sloppy salute and hurried out of the tent with the Crow scout.

Jacob Jr. finished writing a hurried letter. As he folded it and scribbled an address, the Crow scouts around him were peeling out of their Army uniforms and into traditional war clothes. The lead Crow scout saw Jacob Jr.'s puzzled look.

"If I go to the other side," the scout said, "I want to go as a Crow, not as a white man."

Custer rode into the middle of the group. He handed a dispatch down to Jacob Jr. "Deliver this to Captain Benteen on our left flank. He is to join the attack after we have engaged and routed the enemy."

"Yes, sir."

Custer took note of the Crow scouts' transformation. "What are they doing?"

"Bad omens, sir," Jacob Jr. said. "They see death."

The defeatist attitude angered Custer. "You've done your work!" he shouted to the Crows. "You've found the Sioux! If you're so afraid of them, go now. Leave the fighting to us!" Custer galloped off. The Crows continued their transformation, with Jacob Jr. watching. For a moment, he considered joining them. Then he strode away to ready his horse.

The Crow scouts stared after him and shook their heads.

As the troopers readied for battle, Jacob Jr. found Trooper Long in the tumult.

"Looks like us Reno boys get the honors today, Jake," Long said. "The major's offering thirty days' furlough to the man who takes the first scalp."

"I want you to have this," Jacob Jr. said.

He pulled the letter out of his pocket and handed it to Long. The letter was addressed to Mr. and Mrs. Jacob Wheeler.

"If anything happens, make sure it gets delivered to my folks," Jacob Jr. said.

"Sure thing, Jake. At least we're not ridin' with Ol' Hardass today."

They shook hands.

"Good luck to you," Jacob Jr. said.

"You, too."

Jacob Jr. reined his horse around and headed off to deliver Custer's message to Benteen.

In Sitting Bull's camp, the inhabitants went about their daily activities. Voices That Carry helped Red Lance and White Bird tend to the horses. Suddenly, two boys raced through the camp shouting.

"Soldiers!"

Sitting Bull emerged from the council lodge. Crazy Horse was with him, as were Running Fox and White Crow. Across the river, they could see the Seventh Cavalry materializing on the crests of the hills.

In an instant, the camp took on a warlike cast. Painted warriors jumped on their horses to meet the bluecoats. Sitting Bull rallied them from horseback, a Winchester rifle in one hand and a Colt's .45 in the other.

"Warriors!" Sitting Bull called. "We have everything to fight for. Let us fight like the brave men we are!"

Voices That Carry watched in admiration as Running Fox, White Crow, and White Bird rode out across the river. White Bird looked back and shook his coup stick in farewell.

*   *   *

Later that day, Voices That Carry crawled along the bank of a ravine just outside the village. He carried a coup stick in one hand and a knife in the other. The furious sounds of battle came from beyond the rim of the Medicine Tail Coulee.

The coulee rumbled with the thunder of galloping hoofbeats, and Voices That Carry saw a flicker of approaching soldiers. As he ducked behind some brush, Custer and a company of Seventh Cavalry raced past, retreating.

A shot boomed dangerously close. A bluecoat dropped out of the saddle and fell to the ground in front of Voices That Carry. The boy stared in the dead trooper's glassy eyes.

Indians pursued the retreating cavalrymen, closing ground fast. Voices That Carry recognized White Bird among the war party. Soldiers and Indians streaked past Voices That Carry's hiding place in a blur of horseflesh and dust.

As the hoofbeats grew fainter and fainter, Voices That Carry crawled out of hiding. He prodded the dead trooper's face with his coup stick, then advanced more confidently.

He removed the trooper's hat and put it on his own head. Then he laid claim to the soldier's Colt and his binoculars. The view through the binoculars startled him at first. Then he carried the binoculars up the rim of the coulee and hunkered down behind some brush and surveyed the battlefield. At various points, he saw a lone officer covering Custer's retreat, firing deliberately into a band of pursuers. Then he swung the binoculars around and saw White Bird being blown out of the saddle. The boy lowered the glasses, stunned. Then he raised them again, unable to take his eyes from the battle.

Jacob Jr. rode down an embankment and splashed into the creek. Shots rang out on both sides of him, and his horse went down. Jacob Jr. scrambled from beneath the dying animal and tore off on foot. He could hear voices in pursuit, but he could not determine their location, so he took some cover amid some scrub.

Inside the brush, he remained absolutely still. The voices bypassed him, then returned a moment later. Knives slashed into the brush with terrifying fury. One of the blades slashed Jacob Jr. across the face, and he struggled to keep from crying out.

Outside the brush, a young Indian boy looked at the bloody knife and whooped. Other boys came running.

Voices That Carry hurried to a new vantage point and lifted the glasses. In the curious oval floating in a field of black, he could see Custer and his men fall back toward the top of a knoll overlooking the coulee. Many had dismounted and were holding their horses' reins in one hand while firing at the pursuers with the other.

Crazy Horse appeared on the ridge directly behind the soldiers. He rode back and forth across the rear of their lines, daring the troopers to shoot him. The soldiers' carbines popped, the report trailing the muzzle flashes by a few moments. Crazy Horse was just out of range of their single-shot carbines.

As Voices That Carry watched, the shadow of a horseman fell over him. The boy turned in alarm. Sitting Bull was looking down at him.

The boys chased after Jacob Jr. He drew his revolver, but held his fire; after all, these were just Indian boys. Lakota women and children joined in the chase, their ululating cries echoing in Jacob Jr.'s ears.

"I am Lakota!" Jacob Jr. shouted, in their language.

An arrow struck him in the lung. Another pierced his thigh. Jacob Jr. rolled down the embankment, snapping off the shafts of the arrows while grimacing against the nearly unbearable pain. Then he crawled along the riverbed.

"Not like this," he prayed. "Please, God. Not like this."

The boys, women, and other children surround the wounded and dying Jacob Jr. The lead boy drew his scalping knife.

"How do you do it?" he asked in Lakota.

"Like this," another boy said.

The second boy pulled Jacob Jr.'s head back and put the knife to his forehead. As the blade skittered across his skull, Jacob Jr. ground his teeth in pain beyond endurance and his eyes rolled back in his head.

*   *   *

Voices That Carry, now sitting behind Sitting Bull on the chief's horse, stared through the binoculars. Custer's men trained their fire on Crazy Horse, and on a final pass, they realized too late that, as with the Fetterman Fight, it was an ambush. Warriors hiding in the thick sagebrush assaulted the troopers from all sides. The close-quarters fighting was savage. The Army carbines overheated and began to foul. Warriors struck down the troopers with clubs and tomahawks. Custer took a bullet to his breast, another to his left temple. Then the dust and the powder smoke rendered the scene infernal, apocalyptic. It terrified Voices That Carry.

As the sounds of battle gradually diminished, Voices That Carry lowered the binoculars and handed them to Sitting Bull. The chief lifted the glasses. The smoke and dust cleared to reveal the dead bodies of Custer and his men.

Custer had been ahead of the man column led by General Terry, and he had separated his force into three. The groups led by Major Reno and Captain Benteen had managed to fight off the attack in three day's desperate fighting. But Custer, leading 261 troopers, was cut off and had faced four thousand warriors.

Kellogg, the reporter for the *Bismarck Tribune*, was among the slain.

At sunrise the next day, a pair of Cheyenne women came across the body of Custer. A look of recognition passed between them. The women knelt beside the body. One of the pulled a sewing awl from her bag. She grasped the awl tightly and jabbed it into Custer's ear.

"Now you will hear us better in the afterlife," the woman said as she yanked out the awl.

FORTY-FOUR

Red Cloud Agency
1876 (Horses Were Taken Away)

An Indian rider made his way solemnly toward the camp of the Dog Star clan, leading another pony. A corpse, wrapped in a buffalo robe, was draped across the back of the second pony.

Dog Star stepped out of his lodge. His wife, Yellow Hawk, looked over his shoulder.

"Stay inside," Dog Star said, then walked out to meet Voices That Carry.

For a long moment, the boy could not meet the eyes of his elder. Dog Star pulled back the buffalo hide to confront the blue face of White Bird.

"He was first in battle," Voices That Carry said. "There are no wounds on his back."

"Are you proud of this?" Dog Star asked. "Will you use such fine words when your own sons lie dead?"

Dog Star wept in despair. Soon, the entire clan was weeping as well.

Hillsgate
1876 (Horses Were Taken Away)

"This town got a postmaster?"

"That'd be me," Robert Wheeler said.

"You're the first civilization we've seen since—" The limping trooper could not finish his sentence.

Robert placed a consoling hand on his shoulder. "What can I do for you, trooper?"

"Promised a friend his folks would get this," the trooper said and pulled a beaten-up letter from his back pocket.

"I'll see to it."

"He was a good man," the trooper said. "Always spoke well of his family."

As Clara gave the trooper a kerchief of food and the trooper limped back into formation, Robert walked into the general store and stamped the letter with only a cursory glance and dropped it into a bag of outgoing mail. He did not notice that the letter was addressed to Mr. and Mrs. Jacob Wheeler.

*   *   *

Dearest Mother and Father,

I am off on a fool's mission and cannot be certain of the outcome. There is no time for me to write all the things I wish to tell you. Many a time have I thought to abandon my charge here rather than submit to the willfulness of others who have been placed above me.

I want you to know that I have always tried to act according to the lessons of duty and honor that have been your legacy to me. If I have ever given you cause to be ashamed, please forgive me. I have traveled far and seen too much, but always I think of home. You are both in my prayers. I remain forever your loving son,

Jacob

*   *   *

Several months later, the letter was carried back to Hillsgate by an elderly man and woman who stepped down from the rear of a passenger car. Jacob Wheeler was now sixty-five, and Thunder Heart Woman was sixty-one. They made their way to the general store.

"May I help you?" Clara asked.

"We're looking for the man who sent this," Thunder Heart Woman said as she pulled the letter from her bag and handed it to Clara.

"He was your son?" Robert asked later, as they sat on the porch of the Wheeler home in Hillsgate.

"Yes," Jacob said.

"I'm sorry."

"He didn't tell you anything, the man who gave you this?" Jacob asked.

"Only that your son was a good man," Robert said. "And that he loved his family."

Jacob nodded, jaw clenched. Thunder Heart Woman stepped out from inside with Clara.

"I want to see the place where it happened," the older woman said.

"The battlefield's two days by wagon," Robert said. "That's a perilous country. The Army won't vouch yet for its security. And there's no telling where your son might lie."

"We'll pay you anything you ask," she said. "Please."

Robert and Clara exchanged looks.

"Keep your money," Clara said.

"I've heard tell of a Jacob Wheeler," Robert said as they sat around a campfire on the prairie. "They say this one took off with a mountain man. Married an Indian woman. My grandfather used to tell me stories about him."

"What kind of stories?" Jacob asked.

"About how he rode with Fremont to California and struck it rich."

Jacob glanced at Thunder Heart Woman.

"If a man lives long enough, son, he gets to hear the legends folks tell about him."

"So you're the same."

"I reckon I've lived that long," Jacob said. "Maybe too long."

On the other side of the campfire, Thunder Heart Woman asked, "You have no children?"

"I had a son," Clara said. "A beautiful boy. He was stillborn."

"Life is very fragile," Thunder Heart Woman said. "I have lived to see most of the things I ever loved taken away from me." She glanced at Jacob and Robert across the fire. "Do you hold your husband in your heart?"

"With *all* my heart," Clara said.

"Always hold tight to that love," Thunder Heart Woman said. "Let it sustain you."

Thunder Heart Woman plucked a clump of sage from the ground and gathered it into a bundle. She touched the tip of the bundle to the fire and blew on it, drawing smoke.

"You are young yet," Thunder Heart Woman said. "The Creator holds out many thing before us. We must learn to accept his simple gifts." Then she blessed Clara with sage smoke.

At sunset the next day, at the Little Bighorn, Thunder Heart Woman offered a prayer. "Find my son, *Wakan Tanka*. Take his hand and lead him on his journey across the hanging road. Let his spirit, and the spirits of all the young men who died before their time, shine like the stars in the sky. There may we mothers find them and say: 'There. That is my son.' "

Then she began to sing a Lakota death song.

The American people demanded retribution for what had happened to Custer, and Congress was only too quick to oblige them. Because the Army could not find Sitting Bull and the war chiefs to punish, the retribution fell on those closer to hand. The Great Council in Washington decreed that henceforth the reservations would be considered the responsibility of the War Department. General Sherman ordered that all persons thereon be regarded as prisoners of war. Because the Indians had made war on the United States, the government said they had violated the Laramie Treaty of Sixty-eight, and that their claim to the Black Hills was null and void.

Some chose to continue the fight. But by the spring of 1877, even the great Sitting Bull was weary of war. He took his people, including Running Fox, White Crow, and Red Lance, north across the border to Canada, the "Grandmother's Land" of Queen Victoria. There, he said, he would live out his days as a free Indian.

Settlers took possession of the Black Hills. They robbed the land not only of its gold, but also of its ancestral spirits. The most sacred of sacred lands, the *Paha Sapa*, promised forever to the Lakota people, now belonged to the white man.

And he would never give it back.

FORTY-FIVE

Hillsgate
1879 (Spotted Wolf Was Killed)

Robert Wheeler was rolling a finished wheel against the wall of the wheelwright shop, next to the general store, when a valise-carrying stranger in civilian clothes stepped up.

"Mr. Wheeler."

"Captain Pratt."

"You remember," Pratt said, pleased.

"Not likely to forget our last encounter," Robert said. " 'An exception to the rule,' you called me."

"Not only that, I see, but a man of many skills."

"This just keeps breath and bone together," Robert said. "I come from a family of wheelwrights."

"Your business prospers?"

Robert shook his head. "The ice storm last year killed most of the cattle and destroyed most of the wheat. Drought finished off the rest. Farmers who bought goods on credit had nothing to sell or barter."

"Nature can be a stern taskmaster."

"The whole idea of a general store is becoming obsolete," Robert said. "A man can find everything he wants nowadays in the Montgomery Ward, and Sears Roebuck catalogues."

"Everything but purpose, Mr. Wheeler."

After supper, Pratt spun his proposal to Robert and Clara. "An enormous settler army pours continually into our Eastern seaports to spread itself over the West," Pratt said. "The Indian is quite unable to withstand this onslaught. We must either butcher them or civilize them, and what we do we must do quickly."

He paused to make sure Robert and Clara were listening. "It is a great mistake to think that the Indian is born an inevitable savage. He is born a blank, like the rest of us. Left in the surroundings of savagery, one naturally becomes a savage. But transfer the savage-born infant to the surroundings of civilization, and he will grow to possess a civilized language and habit. As the Lord Himself said, 'And a little child shall lead them.' "

Clara nodded and Pratt continued. "President Hayes and the Congress have at last seen the wisdom of such a policy. They have granted me the use of barracks in Carlisle, Pennsylvania, for a model Indian school, and authorized me to recruit one hundred twenty-five children here and in the territories for its inaugural class."

"So far away," Clara said. "Surely the reservation would be a better place—"

"The reservation works to colonize the Indian, not individualize him. The reservation says: 'You are Indians, and must remain Indians. You are not of the nation, and cannot become of the nation. We do not *want* you to become of the nation.' No, Mrs. Wheeler. If the Indian is going to be assimilated, he must be gotten into the swim of American citizenship. He must feel the touch of it day after day, until he becomes saturated with the spirit of it. In this belief I am more Baptist than Methodist. Immerse the Indian in the waters of civilization and hold him there until he is thoroughly soaked!"

When Robert smiled, Pratt said, "This great experiment will rely on *people*—people who share the principle of our common humanity. I believe I detected that quality in your conduct at the agency, Mr. Wheeler."

"Clara's the teacher, Captain," Robert said. "Not me."

"Perhaps you yourself are unaware of these qualities," Pratt said. "Or perhaps I am wrong. I am known to have been so occasionally."

Robert looked at Clara. She took his hand.

At the Red Cloud Agency, with the help of Grabber the translator, Pratt delivered the same speech to Red Cloud and the subchiefs, including Dog Star.

"In short, sirs, by being placed in good schools, taught our language and industries, and sent out among our people, your children can become useful Americans. You see yourselves the evidence that this is now the white man's land. His railroads and towns and farms are everywhere, and there is nothing left for you and your children but to become part of it all."

Pratt sat and waited. Red Cloud conferred with his subchiefs, then rebutted. "The white man is very smart. He makes many promises, more than I can remember. But he keeps only one. He promised to take our land—and he took it."

Pratt was unfazed. "And why was that land taken? Because you can neither read nor write. Because you were not educated, these mountains, valleys, and streams have passed from you."

"The people who have taken these things are thieves and liars," Red Cloud said.

"If you were all as smart as the white man, you would have known that there was gold in the Black Hills and led your people to dig it out," Pratt said. "You leave your affairs in the hands of the white man, and this is why you come to grief. The white man will walk right over you unless you get up and stand in front of him as his equal. The way to do this is to get his education. You see that I do not come with soldiers to remove the children from your very arms. I believe that there are wise men among you who will themselves allow their fortunate sons and daughters to partake in the white man's learning."

In Dog Star's lodge, a council took place to discuss Pratt's proposal. Rainbow, White Bird's young widow, was suspicious of the white man who talked like a preacher, and of Red Cloud, who urged white education for the Indian children.

"Red Cloud has no children to send to the white man's school," she said. "By what right does he ask us to send ours?"

"The whites are never satisfied," her brother-in-law, Sleeping Bear, said. "They possess the very earth we walk upon. Now they want our children, too."

"*Wakan Tanka* has sent this man Pratt to us," Dog Star

said. "I believe he speaks from the heart. Our children must do better than we have done."

Silence fell over the lodge. None dared to question Dog Star, who said, "My grandchildren will go to the school. Voices That Carry will watch over them."

"You cannot make me go," the boy said. "I am not your son."

"No," Dog Star said. "My son and grandson are dead."

Voices That Carry lowered his head, and Dog Star continued. "Only with the white man's knowledge can we keep what little we have left. Do you understand?"

"Yes, Grandfather," the boy said.

That same night, in Margaret Light Shine's lodge, the orphans and other children of the fringe camp clustered around her.

"Why can't we go to school?" the orphan girl Star Woman asked.

"There is power in the white man's knowledge, but also great danger," Margaret said. "We must take from it what we need, but we must always remain true to ourselves."

"The man at the agency says there won't be any Indians pretty soon," Kit Fox said.

"Don't believe this," Margaret said. "Never believe it. Let me hear you say your names."

The children shouted out their names, overlapping one another, in a kind of spontaneous Lakota poetry.

"In each of your names you carry the spirit of your people," Margaret said. "In your language is all the wisdom of the earth and the sky. Hold on to it."

"Will you be our teacher, then?" an orphan named Eagle Woman asked.

Margaret smiled and nodded her consent.

The children were gathered together at dawn on the parade ground of the Red Cloud Agency. Pratt stood with Red Cloud and the subchiefs; instead of soldiers, a group of Indian policemen supervised the loading. Robert and Clara manned one of the three wagons designated to carry the "recruits" away. Although the proceedings were voluntary, many children were wailing while mothers sobbed.

Rainbow started to load her youngest son, Two Horns,

into the back of the wagon where her other children, Good
Iron and Talking Bird, were already squirming. But at the
last moment, she reconsidered and pulled Two Horns away,
protesting loudly to Pratt in Lakota.

"Not this one!" Rainbow said. "Let me keep one son!"

Dog Star interceded. Gently, he lifted Two Horns from
his mother's arms and placed the boy back in to the wagon.
Then Voices That Carry climbed aboard, alongside his
young charges.

"Remember your promise," Dog Star said, and Voices
That Carry nodded.

Dog Star stepped away from the wagon while the Indian
policemen lifted up and fastened the tailgate. Clara was
near tears; try as she might, she could not shut out the
sounds of the overwhelming sadness. When some of the
children began screaming, her resolve weakened.

"Clara?" Robert asked.

"I'll be all right."

They mounted the wagon box, and Pratt swung up beside them.

"Fortitude, Mrs. Wheeler," Pratt said. "Our task awaits."

FORTY-FIVE

Carlisle, Pennsylvania
1879 (Spotted Wolf Was Killed)

The campus was forbidding, with stone barracks facing one another across a drab parade ground. In between were a classroom and administration building and, just outside the perimeter, a Revolutionary War–era guardhouse.

Inside an assembly hall, the boys and girls were segregated into groups and shown lists of Anglo names on blackboard. The rule was immersion: only English would be spoken.

Pratt indicated the blackboards and asked the children, "Do you see these marks? Each word is a white man's name. You will choose one of these names for your own. Begin please."

He nodded to Robert and Clara. They handed pointers to the first children in line. Baffled, the children stared at the blackboard, then pointed to names at random. Each name was called out, transcribed on tape, and then slapped on the child's shirt. When the pointer passed to Voices That Carry, he pointed at random.

"George," a proctor said.

As the boy surrendered the pointer to the next in line, he said his Lakota name under his breath: "Voices That Carry."

When they tried to cut his hair, Voices That Carry bolted. With proctors and matrons chasing behind, the boy ran out onto the quad. The whites formed a circle around the boy. Voices That Carry whirled around, unable to find an escape route.

"It is to be expected with some of them," Pratt said, looking on from the boys' dorm with Robert. Clara joined them. "An Indian man only cuts his hair in times of great mourning."

"But if that's their tradition, Captain—"

"Old habits must be unlearned, Mrs. Wheeler," Pratt said. "The sooner, the better."

Voices That Carry lunged against the circle of whites, but could not break through. Finally, his fury spent, he simply sat down in the middle of the circle.

Pratt dispersed the proctors and matrons and allowed Voices That Carry to continue sitting on the ground, looking to the west. He sat there until sunset, and then he began to chant something that sounded like a death song. The children flocked to the windows to watch, and soon were wailing in sympathy. The whites waited uneasily.

Then Voices That Carry produced a knife and began to hack away at his long black hair.

At the Red Cloud Agency, Margaret Light Shines was conducting an outdoor lesson for a group of orphans. She urged each of them to draw a large circle on the ground with sticks. In each of the circles, she had them draw a cross, making a medicine-wheel symbol.

"The universe is made of circles," she said. "The earth around the sun. The moon around the earth. The seasons of nature, and of life."

She switched to English. "The cross touched the circle four times," she said. "Four is a sacred number. There are four directions. Four races of men. And four virtues. Who can name them?"

"Courage," Kit Fox said.

"Strength." Star Woman.

"Wisdom," an orphan boy said.

"Generosity," Eagle Woman said.

"Each of us is born with one of these," Margaret said. "All of you must work to find the other three within you."

One of the orphans pointed with his stick to the center of the circle. "And here, Auntie?"

"In the center sits the Creator, holding everything in perfect balance," Margaret said. "We must all seek to find this balance within ourselves."

The boys at the Carlisle Academy were made to wear uniforms and the girls Victorian dresses. They were taught to make wheels by Robert Wheeler and barbed wire and other goods prized by the whites. Clara taught them to write in longhand and even to type. When they spoke Lakota, Pratt scrubbed their mouths with lye soap.

Voices That Carry continued to rebel. At night, he shinnied down a drainpipe and found a secret place in the pasture beyond the academy, where he established a mock Indian camp. Soon, he was bringing his young charges there as well. He stole barbed wire and fashioned it into medicine wheel amulets, like the stone one he wore, and urged the others to wear them under their uniforms so they would not forget their heritage. Eventually, he was caught stealing a horse from a neighbor's barn so that he could ride wild and free at night, even though he was imprisoned during the day.

When the academy staff and local police caught him with the horse, they threw him into the Revolutionary War–era guardhouse. Although Pratt was in favor of giving up on the boy, Robert Wheeler had grown increasingly disturbed by the school's draconian practices, and he received permission to speak to the boy.

The first thing that Robert saw when the door of the guardhouse clanged shut behind him was the medicine wheel that the boy had drawn with chalk on the bricks of the back wall.

"George," Robert said.

"My name is Voices That Carry," the boy said in Lakota.

Though Robert tried to pronounce the name, he failed to get his tongue around the unfamiliar syllables. But the attempt pleased the boy, and Robert was urged to sit cross-legged on the floor with him.

After an uncomfortable silence, Robert began. "I know you can understand some of what I say. Whatever you think, Captain Pratt means well for your people."

"No," Voices That Carry said.

"I'm a simple man," Robert said, "but I know this much:

knowledge is power. If you don't study our ways, how will your great-grandsons know the meaning of your holy wheel? How will they know of your history? Your great victories?"

"We will tell them of these things."

"It isn't enough, George," Robert said. "What we call history is written by those who win the battles. You must make your voice heard. You must preserve your culture. You must write it down. In English. Not for Pratt. For your children and their children."

"Why should I do what you tell me?" the boy asked. "The white man says many things, but means nothing."

"That's true of some white men," Robert said. "And some Indians, I expect. You're young, George. Believe me, I know the nature of a young man's dreams. Don't stop dreaming." Robert stood and added, "But remember, when you wake up, you're back in the white man's world."

Voices That Carry nodded, almost imperceptibly. "And you, Rob—Rob—?"

"Robert."

"Do you have dreams?"

"I've still got a few left," Robert said. "Maybe it's not too late to make them happen."

Months later, at the end of the school year, the Carlisle student body assembled before a proscenium arch to view a commencement pageant presented by the class of Clara Wheeler. Robert and Clara, who was quite pregnant, watched from the audience while the students performed the theatrical in English for Pratt and assorted dignitaries.

Midway through the pageant, a teenage Indian girl wrapped in an American flag and portraying the goddess Columbia took the stage. She was followed by Indian boys portraying Columbus, Captain John Smith, Miles Standish, and other white heroes, including pioneers and settlers.

Suddenly, the pioneers gasped as a savage took the stage. It was Voices That Carry, in native dress, and the medicine wheel amulet was on his naked chest.

"You have taken our rivers and fountains, and the plains where we loved to roam!" Voices That Carry said with authority. "Banish us not to the mountains, and the lonely wastes for homes!"

Pratt shifted uncomfortably in his seat.

"Our clans that were strongest and bravest are broken and powerless through you," Voices That Carry proclaimed. Then, much weaker, he added, "Let us join the great tribe of white men as brothers to dare and to do."

The next morning, in the administration office, Robert Wheeler and Captain Pratt faced each other in stony silence.

"You disappoint me, Mr. Wheeler."

"You're not the first man to say that, Captain, and I expect you won't be the last. Comes from my trying to please people too much. But a man's got to stand for something or he doesn't count for much."

"And do you know what you stand for, Mr. Wheeler?" Pratt asked. "Do you even know yourself?"

"I do now, sir," Robert said. "It's time for me to go home where I can do some good—my own way."

FORTY-SIX

Nevada

The Winter the Sun Died (1888)

On December 22, the day after the winter solstice, the young man called Wovoka danced against a backdrop of desert wasteland while Loved by the Buffalo beat the sacred drum and chanted. Wovoka, a Christianized Paiute mystic, was covered in sweat and dust and his eyes were lost in a trance. A Lakota elder, Good Thunder, looked on with curiosity.

Loved by the Buffalo was now seventy-two, about the same age his grandfather Two Arrows had been when he had painted the terrifying vision of Growling Bear on the winter count so long ago. The world no longer seemed real to Loved by the Buffalo, but instead seemed a counterfeit world, made of promises turned to lies.

Above, the silver moon slid over the golden disk of the sun. The landscape was swallowed in shadows and the corona of the sun blazed like a halo above Wovoka.

"When the sun died, I went up to the Milky Way," Wovoka said. "I saw the Great Spirit. I met all the ghosts who had ever died. God told me to come back to earth and tell my people they must be good and love one another and not fight or steal or lie. He gave me this dance to give to my people so that they can talk to their departed."

FORTY-SEVEN

Pine Ridge Agency
South Dakota
1890 (Big Foot Was Killed)

Voices That Carry, now twenty-seven, wore a hat and a three-piece suit. He sat beside Robert Wheeler on the seat of the wagon, and behind were assorted blankets, sacks of food, and a crate marked BOOKS: MR. GEORGE VOICES THAT CARRY.

"Senators came and negotiated with Sitting Bull himself," Robert was explaining. "The head of every Indian family gets 160 acres of land. Individuals get eighty acres. The surplus land was opened up to the settlers."

"Surplus land?" Voices That Carry asked.

"That's what they call it," Robert said. "All horses, except those that pulled wagons, were confiscated."

"No."

"And sold at auction."

"And the proceeds?"

"Supposed to be returned in wagons and farm equipment."

"And Sitting Bull agreed to this?"

"Sitting Bull walked out."

"They wanted him to approve their thievery," Voices That Carry said. "They know we still look up to him as our chief."

"That's how Sioux land was divided into six separate parcels."

"If my brother is alive," Voices That Carry said, "he will be with Sitting Bull."

The wagon moved past a family of Indians burying a child. Many other graves were marked with barrows and feathered sticks.

"Funeral scaffolds are no longer allowed," Robert said.

Farther down the road, the wagon neared a group of Indians walking in the road. A man was leading his family, all laden with bundles of sticks for firewood. The man stood in front of the wagon.

"You give something."

"You must get your supplies from the agent," Robert answered, slowing the wagon.

The father spat onto the ground in disgust.

Voices That Carry turned away in sorrow.

"I'm sorry for your plight but there's nothing I can do," Robert said.

"When your children cry for food—you will do nothing?" the man responded.

Robert secured the reins, then stepped into the bed of the wagon. He glanced around to make sure no soldiers were watching, then placed his hands on a fifty-pound sack of cornmeal. He jettisoned the sack over the side. It was followed by more cornmeal, slabs of bacon, and blankets.

Then Robert returned to the wagon seat. He felt criminal. He started the horses and continued on his way.

Later, at the Pine Ridge Agency, Clara greeted George Voices That Carry in her schoolroom. She listened proudly as he told her students about his plan to put down the Lakota traditions and stories on paper.

That evening, in the Wheeler home, Robert said, "Lord, we thank you for the safe return of Voices That Carry to the land of his birth."

"We'd love for you to stay with us," Clara said.

"Thank you, but I hope to find my brother, Red Lance," Voices That Carry said. "When I was a boy, he went to Canada with Sitting Bull."

"The Bull's been living outside Standing Rock," Robert told him. "That'd be the place to start."

Voices That Carry nodded in gratitude.

*　　*　　*

Margaret Light Shines moved through the Pine Ridge Agency, keeping a close eye on her orphans.

"No distribution until the line is straight!" bellowed an agency worker. "Can't you people understand what straight means?"

Daniel Royer was a forty-year-old, officious Indian agent appointee with a streak of paranoia, and he was making the rounds. He observed the Indian police, all dressed in blue Army uniforms, trying to organize the women and children into a line. Farther down, an Indian lieutenant was addressing new police recruits.

"If you want to join the Indian police," the lieutenant announced, "no long hair. No more than one wife. No heathenish ways. No old religion. No drinking. No language but English."

At the warehouse, a white agency worker opened the top half of a Dutch door, and the first woman handed him her ration card. He punched it. An Indian worker placed a small sack of coffee, a bigger sack of flour, and a shoddy blanket on the shelf built into the bottom half of the door.

"Only flour, coffee, and blanket this week," the white man said. "Next."

"No meat?" the Lakota woman asked, her voice breaking.

"No meat, no sugar," the man said tiredly. "Flour, coffee, blanket. Next."

"No bacon?"

"Bacon is meat," the man said. "There is no meat. Next."

"Our men want meat."

"Tell your men there's no meat. Flour and coffee. Take it or leave it."

The woman took it, with anger.

"Ingrates," the man said. "Next."

For lack of buffalo hides, Dog Star's lodge at the edge of the Pine Ridge Reservation was a ragged patchwork of canvas and fabric and blankets. Inside, Dog Star and Red Lance listened attentively to Good Thunder.

"The messiah's medicine is powerful," Good Thunder said. "Many saw their relatives in the next world."

"This dance will make many problems," Red Cloud said.

Outside, Old Coyote and Yellow Earring—members of the Indian police force—skulked past. Peering through the door of the lodge, they eyed the gathering suspiciously. When they had moved on, the council resumed.

"Let the dance be taught to our people," Dog Star said.

"You believe in this man Wovoka's vision?" Red Cloud asked.

"I believe in hope," Dog Star said.

After they spoke, Good Thunder painted his face with red ocher and demonstrated the ghost dance. Royer, the agent, watched the Indians gathered around Good Thunder and felt a growing sense of unease.

An old man with shoulder-length hair and a full beard and his wife slowly approached the Wheeler home, where young Jedediah Wheeler pretended to be a swashbuckling pirate. Looking on from the doorway, Clara recognized Jacob and Thunder Heart Woman immediately. She promised to help them find Margaret Light Shines, who was rumored to be on the reservation.

An Indian teamster drove the wagon while Voices That Carry sat beside him on the seat. In the bed of the wagon were piled Voices That Carry's luggage and crates of books.

As the wagon stopped in front of a cabin, several young men, who considered themselves Sitting Bull's bodyguards, looked on suspiciously.

"I am looking for Red Lance, son of White Crow, grandson of Running Fox," Voices That Carry announced.

"Brother?" Red Lance asked, stepping forward. "Is it truly you?" Red Lance pulled his brother down from the wagon.

"Look at you!" Voices That Carry said.

"No, look at you!" Red Lance exclaimed.

They laughed and hugged each other for a few moments.

"I have come back to stay, brother," Voices That Carry told Red Lance.

Red Lance nodded. "This is good."

FORTY-EIGHT

Standing Rock Reservation
1890 (Big Foot Was Killed)

Later, in the cabin of Red Lance, on the Standing Rock Reservation, Voices That Carry sat at a desk made of a board placed across two barrels and wrote, oblivious to his immediate chaotic surroundings. From the roof of the cabin hung scores of dried plants, each with a carefully handwritten tag, and books and papers flowed from the makeshift desk to cover much of the floor.

"What good are the white man's books if you don't know when you are cold?" Red Lance asked as he knelt by the fireplace and stoked the fire.

"I'm sorry," Voices That Carry said, apologizing for having been so absorbed in his writing that he did not notice how cold the cabin had become. "I'll gather more wood."

Red Lance walked over and picked up one of the books on Voices That Carry's desk. He thumbed through the pages. "You read all these books?"

"There is much to be learned from them," Voices That Carry said.

Red Lance looked doubtful. "What good is this knowledge?"

"You have many question, Red Lance, but you have no desire to hear my answers," Voices That Carry said.

"And *you* do not wish to learn."

"I've told you," Voices That Carry said tiredly. "The ghost dance is only superstition. Spirits won't help our people. Only we can do that for ourselves."

"You do not have ears," Red Lance shot back. "You do not listen."

There was a hard look between them. Then Voices That Carry softened a bit, realizing there might be truth in what his brother said.

Thinned and aged by too many Canadian winters, Sitting Bull, now nearing sixty, listened patiently while Kicking Bear urged him to believe in the ghost dance. Red Lance sat with Voices That Carry, and the latter's white clothes attracted skeptical stares from the other men present at Sitting Bull's camp.

"I bring you the promise of a day when no white man will lay a hand on the bridle of an Indian horse," Kicking Bear proclaimed. "Our fathers, the ghosts, have told me so."

"It is impossible for a dead man to live again," Sitting Bull said. "The white hair at the agency—McLaughlin—says soldiers will stop this dance."

"The soldiers will harm no one," Kicking Bear said. "The messiah has sent me a vision."

Kicking Bear held out a simple white cotton shirt, painted blue around the V-neck collar, and adorned with magic symbols. The shirt passed around the circle. Red Lance examined it and handed it on to Voices That Carry.

"This shirt is powerful medicine," Kicking Bear said. "Whoever wears it is protected even from the soldiers' guns."

Voices That Carry spoke out. "Cotton will not stop a lead bullet."

Kicking Bear stared with anger at Voices that Carry. "Red Cloud's people are dancing. So are Big Foot's. Sitting Bull's people must also dance."

The shirt passed to Sitting Bull. He fingered the fabric, unconvinced. A knowing look passed between the chief and Voices That Carry.

At the Pine Ridge Agency, Royer warily fingered a ghost shirt as Robert Wheeler said, "If you leave it alone, likely as not the whole craze will die out on its own."

"Mr. McLaughlin at Standing Rock believes that as long

as a single malcontent like Sitting Bull remains at large, we cannot be secure," Royer said. "I concur. Lock up the ringleaders—"

"And you'll have a real problem on your hands, not just in your imagination."

"What was it you wished to see me about, Mr. Wheeler?"

"I'd like your permission to post these around the agency," Robert said, passing the other man a handbill. It bore an engraving of Margaret Light Shines as a young girl.

ANYONE WITH INFORMATION AS TO THE WHEREABOUTS OF MARGARET LIGHT SHINES IS KINDLY REQUESTED TO REPORT SUCH INFORMATION TO ROBERT WHEELER, HILLSGATE GENERAL STORE.

"It would sure mean everything to her folks," Robert added.

Royer gave the handbill the once-over, then dismissed Robert with a wave.

"Thank you," Robert said. "You . . . might not have seen her around yourself?"

"I do not keep track of faces, Mr. Wheeler."

Robert stepped out, leaving Royer to ponder the ghost shirt.

Inside the agency warehouse that night, Royer aimed a pistol. Lit by a shaft of moonlight was the ghost shirt, tacked against the wall. Royer fired, then hurried to the wall to examine the shirt. He saw the bullet hole, then pushed a finger through it.

At the edge of the Pine Ridge Agency, Margaret sat outside her lodge, her group of orphans nearby. Passersby, including a pack of newspaper reporters drawn to the agency because of rumors of the ghost dance, paused to inspect the array of wares for sale. In addition to the traditional items, there were purses, wallets, belts, and other accoutrements catering to white buyers. One of the older orphans worked to finish painting a store-bought man's shirt. Shaking it out to dry, she placed the fancifully decorated shirt on a blanket.

One of the reporters, with a Kodak snapshot camera slung beneath his arm, paused outside Margaret Light Shine's lodge, looking at the goods she had for sale. He whistled when he saw the painted shirt. "Is that a ghost shirt?"

Margaret sized him up and played dumb. "Ghost . . . shirt?" She nodded, exaggerating her movements in the same way she had faked her English.

The reporter, whose name was Lang, smiled. "What'll you take for it?" When Margaret stared blankly, Lang resorted to mime and pidgin English. "You, me. We . . . make . . . trade."

"Trade," Margaret repeated.

Confident of his bargaining skills, Lang smiled. But Margaret surprised him when she pointed to the camera, then to herself. "You want my camera?"

Margaret slowly pronounced the word, as if it were unfamiliar.

"Now what would a squaw know about taking pictures?" Lang asked. Then he reconsidered; cameras were easy to come by, but where was he going to find another genuine ghost shirt? "Lady," he said finally, "you've got yourself a deal."

He motioned for Margaret to hand over the shirt. Then Margaret gestured for the Kodak. Lang gave her the camera and snatched away the shirt.

Alongside the agency building, Margaret suddenly stopped in her tracks, her eyes drawn to a handbill that displayed a portrait of a young woman. It was a picture of her in the clothes of a white woman. Beneath was the legend, which she read to the orphans trailing behind: " 'Her family would be grateful. Report any information to Robert Wheeler, Hillsgate General Store.' "

When Margaret was reunited with her mother, Thunder Heart Woman embraced her with silent gratitude.

Agent James McLaughlin sat astride his horse looking down from a ridge at Sitting Bull's camp on the Red Rock Reservation. A spirited ghost dance, led by Red Lance, was reaching a peaked frenzy. McLaughlin lowered his binoculars.

"These old troublemakers are crafty," he said. "There's mischief afoot. First we'll talk. After that . . ."

The ghost dance was interrupted when McLaughlin rode toward Sitting Bull's cabin with a small contingent of Indian policemen.

Sitting Bull's followers, including Red Lance and Voices That Carry, converged on the arriving agent and policemen. A handful of them carried guns, but McLaughlin refused to be intimidated. He calmly dismounted and headed for the cabin door, where Sitting Bull stood waiting. Together, they passed inside.

"Your practicing of this absurd messiah doctrine is making a good number of people uneasy," McLaughlin told the chief. "I've come to ask that it be stopped."

"Sitting Bull cannot stop the wind from blowing."

"I remind you that you are on an Indian reservation at the sufferance of the government," McLaughlin said. "You are fed by the government, clothed by the government. Your children are educated by the government, and all you have and are today is because of the government. If it were not for the government, you would be freezing and starving in the mountains."

"I do my best to walk the white man's path," Sitting Bull said.

"And still you allow your people to dance a war dance," McLaughlin said.

Outside, Red Lance and Voices That Carry were listening at the window. The Indian police and Sitting Bull's followers had come to an uneasy truce. Kicking Bear was among them, and Loved by the Buffalo watched from a short distance away.

"No," Sitting Bull said firmly. "Not a war dance."

"What else can it be, with people's faces painted bloodred?"

"Red is the place where the sun is born," Sitting Bull said, "where life rises up each day."

"You don't believe a word of this prophecy, do you?" McLaughlin asked.

Sitting Bull looked away, unwilling to answer the question directly. "You and me," the chief suggested. "Let us take the train. We will find this messiah and ask him to show us his medicine. If he is no good, then I will come back and stop dance."

"A novel proposition," McLaughlin said, before walking away. "But I can see I'm wasting my time."

Sitting Bull's followers stood aside as McLaughlin came through the door.

"Your time is short, long hair," Kicking Bear taunted, in Lakota.

"Remove that man," McLaughlin said to the Indian police. "Escort him off the reservation, and see that he does not return."

Two Indian policemen seized Kicking Bear. As the situation escalated toward violence, Sitting Bull gave Kicking Bear a look that said, *No more.* Kicking Bear allowed himself to be placed under arrest, and as his hands were bound, he spoke in Lakota to Loved by the Buffalo.

"You danced with Wovoka," Kicking Bear said.

"Yes," Loved by the Buffalo said. "But no vision came to me."

"Dance," Kicking Bear said. "The vision will come."

Dancers covered the parade ground at the Pine Ridge Agency. Dog Star had joined Good Thunder in the center of the circle; both wore red face paint and carried a staff used to urge the dancers on. The circle of dancers was so large that there was little room for the agency's daily activities. Work had come to a standstill. The staff, civilians, and police could do little but watch and worry.

As the ghost dance reached a fevered pitch, Royer turned away from the agency window and snapped the shade down.

"What do you say now, Mr. Wheeler?" he blustered. "Do you think this 'craze,' as you call it, is dying out? I've put up with quite enough of this lunacy, and I intend to do something about it."

Before Robert Wheeler could answer, Royer stalked away to the telegraph office. There, he dictated the following:

TO THE COMMISSIONER OF INDIAN AFFAIRS IN
WASHINGTON.

SIR, THE GHOST DANCE HAS NOW ASSUMED SUCH PROPORTIONS BOTH IN NUMBER AND THE SPIRIT OF ADHERENTS THAT IT IS ENTIRELY BEYOND THE CONTROL OF THE AGENT AND POLICE FORCE, WHO ARE OPENLY DEFIED BY THE DANCERS. EMPLOYEES AND GOVERNMENT PROPERTY AT THIS AGENCY HAVE NO PROTECTION AND ARE AT THE MERCY OF THESE DANCERS. WE NEED PROTECTION, AND WE NEED IT NOW.

The United States government responded to the Ghost Dance threat by sending the Seventh Cavalry, Buffalo Soldiers of the Ninth Cavalry, and a battery of Hotchkiss guns for good measure. As a result, many frightened Indians left the reservation for the Bad Lands. Despite Red Cloud's assurances, the government chose to regard the exiles as hostile.

At the Wheeler home, Voices That Carry sought the council of Thunder Heart Woman. "The buffalo spoke to me. I did not hear it with my ears, but inside."

Voices That Carry was shaken by the mystical experience he had had shortly before. He had been sitting on a hill overlooking the Wheeler ranch, writing in his journal, when a buffalo bull with a distinctive crescent scar came close to graze. Suddenly, the buffalo bull was startled by the presence of Voices That Carry and charged. Voices That Carry found himself on the ground, with the bull looming over him, snorting, mucus streaming from its nostrils and onto Voices That Carry's face. As Voices That Carry looked up into the obsidian eyes of the bull, he knew he was looking into the ancient eyes of *Tatanka*.

Voices That Carry lowered his head and prepared for death.

From the top of the hill, ten-year-old Jedediah Wheeler had shouldered a Sharps buffalo rifle and placed the bead carefully on the shoulder of the buffalo, where the .50 caliber slug would pierce the animal's heart. But Voices That Carry had pleaded for Jedediah not to shoot. Voices That Carry had looked into the beast's eyes one last time. Then it turned and walked away, grazing once more.

"What did you hear?" Thunder Heart Woman asked.

"I heard all hooves . . . gunshots. I heard the buffaloes'

last breath," he said. "It was as though he was . . . chiding me somehow."

"*Tatanka* came to say you have forgotten his power," Thunder Heart Woman said, "that you have neglected the knowledge and wisdom of your grandfathers. Learn to see again with the eye of the buffalo and you will find the right path."

Voices That Carry looked at Thunder Heart Woman, affected by her certitude. He touched his chest, feeling something beneath his shirt. Then he pulled out the medicine wheel amulet and allowed it to dangle from his neck.

Thunder Heart Woman recognized it immediately. "Who gave you this amulet?" she asked.

"My brother, Red Lance," he said. "It was a gift from the Cheyenne warrior Roman Nose."

"May I see it?" When Voices That Carry lifted the amulet from his neck and handed it to her, Thunder Heart Woman said, "The sacred medicine wheel. It once belonged to a great holy man named Growling Bear. He passed it on to my brother Loved by the Buffalo, who gave it to me. My husband and daughter wore it for many years, and then it was lost to us."

"It's been looking for you all this time," Voices That Carry said.

Thunder Heart Woman nodded. "A circle."

FORTY-NINE

1890 (Big Foot Was Killed)

Around the Pine Ridge Agency, a contingent of soldiers pitched their tents protectively around the agency headquarters. Indians who had been ordered onto the reservation set up their tipis along the perimeter. Inside the agency office, Royer watched approvingly through a window. He read and reread a telegram with satisfaction. It informed him that General Miles had authorized Sitting Bull's arrest.

At Sitting Bull's camp on the Standing Rock Reservation, Voices That Carry placed some books on a makeshift desk.

"See what I have made for you." Red Lance pulled up a loose floor plank and removed a bundled ghost shirt. "Put it on."

"I can't," Voices That Carry said.

When Red Lance tried to force the shirt into his brother's hand, Voices That Carry refused to take it.

"You are false to your people if you do not put on the ghost shirt," Red Lance said.

"That way is the way of death," Voices That Carry said. "But maybe there is another road. Maybe we can find our own destiny again."

Red Lance crossed to the desk, picked up a handful of books, and then tossed them into the blazing stove.

"What are you doing?" Voices That Carry cried.

"You have too many *wasichu* ways," Red Lance said.

When he returned for another load of books, Voices That Carry tried to restrain his brother, but Red Lance threw him off and tossed more books onto the flames.

"You even think like a *wasichu*," Red Lance said.

Then he screamed and charged his brother. They fell to the floor fighting. Voices That Carry attempted to shield himself from the blows that Red Lance rained down upon him, and then he fought back. The brothers fought until both cried in pain, and resentment seemed to pass from them. Brothers again, they embraced.

At dawn on December 15, 1890, forty Indian police rode into Sitting Bull's camp on the Standing Rock Reservation. A dog began to bark as they headed for the chief's cabin.

Inside, Sitting Bull was asleep on the floor with his wife and sons. The door burst open, and Sitting Bull squinted into the darkness, trying to make out the shadowy figures streaming inside. Then someone struck a match, which illuminated the face of Bull Head.

"What do you want here?" Sitting Bull asked.

"You are my prisoner," Bull Head said. "You must go to the agency."

Sitting Bull's wife began to wail. A policeman grabbed Sitting Bull and lifted him, half naked, off the floor. They attempted to thrust Sitting Bull out the door, but he braced himself against the frame.

"Let me go," the chief said, and the policemen began to lose their nerve. "We were warriors together," Sitting Bull told Bull Head. "Now you come for me." Then the chief asked his wife to fetch his clothes.

Roused by barking dogs and the cries of Sitting Bull's wife, a large number of the chief's followers converged to confront the Indian police. Some of Sitting Bull's followers carried guns, while others had knives and clubs. Red Lance raced to the scene, rifle in hand; he pushed past the onlookers. Voices That Carry remained a few paces behind, unarmed, on the edge of the action.

As Bull Head emerged from the cabin, gripping Sitting Bull's arm, the crowd hurled a cacophony of insults.

"Release our chief," Red Lance said.

"Sitting Bull is under arrest," Bull Head said.

"No," Sitting Bull said, "I will not go."

While Bull Head attempted to convince Sitting Bull to surrender, the chief's followers cheered and pressed hard against the police line. Voices That Carry watched as Catch the Bear raised his Winchester.

Lurching forward, Voices that Carry cried out: "No!"

Catch the Bear shouldered his Winchester, took aim, and fired. The bullet struck Bull Head in the right side. As Bull Head fell, he discharged his gun, shooting Sitting Bull in the chest.

At the same instant, Red Tomahawk raised his pistol and fired into the back of Sitting Bull's head. The chief fell to the ground as his outraged followers surged forward.

FIFTY

The Badlands
1890 (Big Foot Was Killed)

Voices That Carry and Red Lance rode a forbidding maze of barren hills, narrow valleys, ravines and buttes, all but devoid of vegetation. With them were the remnants of Sitting Bull's followers: thirty-eight men, women, and children, including fewer than a dozen warriors on horseback.

As they approached Big Foot's camp, they saw a medicine man leading a ghost dance. The chief, who was suffering from a dangerous bout of pneumonia, watched the dance from the bed of an open wagon. Although he was in his fifties, the sickness gave him the wizened appearance of a much older man.

The dancers shuffled in their steady, right-to-left rotation. The more desperate the times became, the more frenzied the dancing was.

As Red Lance and Voices That Carry brought the refugees into camp, Big Foot raised himself up from the wagon and squinted at them through watery eyes.

"Where do you come from?" he asked.

"Standing Rock," Red Lance said, "where Sitting Bull lies dead."

The news shot through the camp, prompting a communal wail of grief. Later, as the refugees conferred with Big Foot, the chief said he intended to lead his people to Pine Ridge, to join Red Cloud's camp.

"We saw signs of many bluecoats," Red Lance warned.

"Let there be no fighting," Big Foot said, then paused to cough up a bit of blood into a rag. Despite his illness, none dared question the chief, to the disappointment of Red Lance and the warrior Yellow Bird.

On Christmas morning, at the Wheeler home, there were piles of open boxes and torn wrapping paper. While Robert, Clara, Jacob, Thunder Heart Woman, and young Jedediah looked on, the orphans laughed over their presents.

"Thank you," Margaret said.

"It's the least they deserve," Jacob said. "Poor kids."

"No," Margaret said. "Not poor. Not poor at all."

"Reckon you're right," Jacob said.

Thunder Heart Woman handed a present to Jedediah. "This is for you—from Grandpa Jacob and me."

Jedediah eagerly unwrapped the gift. Inside the box was a finely carved and painted wooden buffalo. Jedediah lifted the carving out of the box and gazed at it in wonder. The orphans gathered around, and Jedediah proudly showed off the carving.

"*Tatanka*," Jedediah said to them.

"*Tatanka!*" the orphans chimed.

"Thank you," Jedediah said to Thunder Heart Woman.

FIFTY-ONE

Pine Creek—Badlands
28 December 1890

Big Foot's caravan was stopped at the edge of a dry creekbed, the sick chief still in the back of a wagon. On the other side of the creek, blocking the path, was the Seventh Cavalry.

Colonel James Forsyth rode out with a small contingent of officers, and Big Foot's wagon rolled forward, accompanied by riders, including Red Lance and Voices That Carry. Big Foot struggled to sit up as Forsyth approached.

"Are you Chief Big Foot?" Forsyth asked.

"Want peace," Big Foot said in a hoarse whisper.

"I won't parley with you," Forsyth said. "It's either unconditional surrender or fight. What is your answer, sir?"

"No fight," the chief said.

Forsyth was relieved. "Where were you headed?"

"Pine Ridge," Big Foot said. "Make peace."

"If it's peace you want," the colonel asked, "why do you give shelter to Sitting Bull's renegades?"

"They brothers," Big Foot said. "Relatives. Cold, hungry. You do same for your people."

Forsyth nodded. "I'm glad to find you peaceable. You and your people will follow us to our camp. We'll provide you with blankets and rations."

"We go with you," Big Foot said.

As he spoke, blood dripped from his nose and splashed on the wagon.

"We'll have an ambulance brought forward," Forsyth said. "You'll ride more comfortably." Then he nodded to his officers, and they turned back toward their lines.

"How far is the camp?" Voices That Carry asked.

"A few hours' ride," Forsyth said. "The creek called Wounded Knee."

Wounded Knee Creek
28 December 1890

The ice-covered creek meandered through a flat ground bordered by steep slopes on three sides and a deep ravine on the fourth. All was layered in snow.

Robert drove his wagon loaded with supplies into a flat area, over the tracks made by the Army's four Hotchkiss guns. Those weapons belonged to Battery K of the First Artillery; each was loaded with grapeshot and aimed at the makeshift Indian camp.

Inside Big Foot's tent, Indians packed the stove with dry wood and lit a fire. Others brought food. Robert Wheeler came with a pair of woolen undergarments.

"This is good medicine," Robert said.

"Of all the things whites make," Big Foot said, "the wool underwear is best."

"They say you've got some of Sitting Bull's people with you," Robert said. "I'm looking for a friend of mine. Young, speaks English. His name's Voices That Carry." Robert repeated the name, in Lakota.

Big Foot stared a moment, attempting to decide how far he could trust him. "I know this man."

Robert and Voices That Carry greeted each other warmly and walked together.

"I cannot go back with you," Voices That Carry said.

"I don't understand."

"I thought it was possible to bridge the Indian world and the white man's," Voices That Carry said.

"You are that bridge," Robert said.

"No," replied Voices That Carry. "When I was back east, people looked at me as an educated Indian. Something different. A curiosity. I see that now. I lived among white men, but never belonged."

"And you belong here?" Robert asked.

"I belong nowhere now," Voices That Carry said. "This is what I have learned. This has been my real education."

"What will you do?"

"I must walk my own road," Voices That Carry said.

"So must we all," Robert agreed.

"I am grateful to you for everything, my friend," Voices That Carry said. He offered his hand, and Robert shook it.

"George . . ." Robert said.

"Goodbye."

Their hands slipped apart. Voices That Carry turned back toward the camp.

Wounded Knee Creek
29 December 1890

Colonel Forsyth ordered Big Foot and his warriors to surrender all weapons, which they did reluctantly. Forsyth, however, thought there were more to be found.

"You are deceiving me," Forsyth said. "You have nothing to fear from us, Chief. We will treat you kindly. But do not deceive me any longer."

"We do not deceive you," Big Foot said.

"Did I not put you in an ambulance and have my doctors care for you? Did I not put you in a good tent with a stove to keep you warm and comfortable? Did I not provide more rations to feed your people? Now where are those guns?"

"We have no guns except what you have found," Big Foot said.

Forsyth ordered the cavalry to search each man. In the midst of this charged atmosphere, Yellow Bird began singing the sacred song. His singing ignited the Indians and set the cavalry men's nerves on edge.

"Sir," a soldier said, pointing, "I think that Indian has a gun under his blanket."

Soldiers circled the young Indian wrapped in the blanket. They asked in English for him to surrender the rifle, and when he refused, one of the soldiers snatched away the blanket. A Winchester .73 repeating rifle was across his lap. The Lakotas around him started talking excitedly.

"They say his name is Black Coyote," Robert yelled. "He's deaf. They say he gave a lot of money for that rifle, and he is willing to give it up, but he wants a fair price."

Two of the soldiers grabbed the barrel of the rifle and tried to wrench it away. Black Coyote resisted. In the struggle, the gun went off, firing into the air.

Forsyth wasted no time. "Fire!"

"No!" Robert Wheeler cried. "It was an accident."

The troopers fired into the group of Indians.

Red Lance and Voices That Carry dove for the pile of confiscated weapons, but it was too late. A hail of bullets had ripped through Red Lance's ghost shirt and pierced his chest. Voices That Carry howled in grief and anger.

The four Hotchkiss guns barked, and the grapeshot ripped through the tipis, breaking lodge poles and scattering the fires. Women and children were killed where they stood. While the tipis burned, the Hotchkiss guns were reloaded with exploding shells, and the soldiers rushed into the camp, shooting at everything that moved through the smoke. They were also poorly placed, and unintentionally shot one another in the cross fire.

Then the Hotchkiss guns opened up again, and this time many of the white soldiers fell bloody onto the snow as well. What Indians were left in the open rushed their families toward whatever safety they could find.

Suddenly, a shell exploded behind Robert Wheeler, and the pristine canvas wall of the Army tent was splattered with his blood. He had taken a piece of shrapnel in the legs. As an officer called for the Hotchkiss battery to cease fire, Voices That Carry bore Robert Wheeler on his back through the carnage to a wagonful of the wounded.

"I have to leave you here," Voices That Carry said. "Goodbye, my friend."

Under the cover of the smoke from the cannon and the burning lodges, Voices That Carry slipped away.

The worst of the fight had lasted only ten seconds, when the soldiers opened fired and the Hotchkiss guns spoke. One hundred fifty Indians, including Big Foot, were killed, and another fifty wounded. Twenty-five soldiers died, mostly in the cross fire of the first confusing moments.

Soon, Robert was carried toward the field hospital at the Pine Ridge Agency, where he was reunited with Clara.

New Year's Day 1891

The snow continued to spiral down from the gunmetal sky, covering the corpses of the dead and the brightly colored ghost shirts with their hopeful images.

Loved by the Buffalo moved slowly through the landscape of cold and death, a bundled blanket in one hand and a knife in the other. He stumbled and found the grotesquely frozen body of a warrior.

The Indian looked as if he had fallen on his back and was trying to prop himself up with his elbows. His face was contorted by a death grimace, and he still wore a strip of white cloth around his head to keep his ears warm.

Loved by the Buffalo knelt in the snow.

With numb and clumsy fingers, he took a lock of hair and tied it in a knot. Then he cut it off with the knife and dropped it in the blanket.

Not far away, another old man, Jacob Wheeler, walked a silent pilgrimage through this graveyard of lost hopes.

Nearby, soldiers noticed Loved by the Buffalo moving from corpse to corpse.

"Hey, what are you doing?" a soldier demanded.

Loved by the Buffalo ignored them.

"Indian, I asked you a question," the soldier said, climbing out of the pit. "What are you doing here?"

Jacob looked at Loved by the Buffalo's face and believed he recognized him. He nudged his horse to follow the old Indian's serpentine path through the corpses.

Loved by the Buffalo came upon other soldiers, stacking the frozen Indian corpses like wood onto the back of a wagon. One frightened young soldier aimed his rifle at Loved by the Buffalo.

"Back off, or so help me . . ."

Loved by the Buffalo ignored the threat and proceeded to cut a lock of hair from each of the bodies. The young soldier approached and slammed the butt of his rifle into

Loved by the Buffalo's stomach, knocking the old Indian to the ground. Loved by the Buffalo lost his grip on the bundle and the blanket unfolded, spilling more than a hundred knots of dark hair onto the white snow.

Jacob rushed over and grabbed the young soldier by his collar. "What's wrong with you? He's doing you no harm. He's a Lakota holy man performing the death rites."

Jacob pushed the stunned soldier back against the wheel of the wagon. Then Jacob walked over to where Loved by the Buffalo lay. The Indian studied the old white face that loomed over him, but did not recognize it.

Then Jacob removed the amulet that Voices That Carry had returned to Thunder Heart Woman. He held it out to Loved by the Buffalo, who placed it around his neck.

Jacob pulled Loved by the Buffalo to his feet. They regarded each other for a moment, and then all of the corpses around them. They embraced like the spiritual brothers they were. Both wept, unable to find words.

Thunder Heart Woman joined them. "Now the circle is complete."

FIFTY-TWO

Pine Ridge Agency
A Few Years Later

Loved by the Buffalo sat in the center of a medicine wheel atop a hill not far from the Wheeler home. Sacred smoke from a bundle of sage wafted toward the sky. Surrounding him were Jacob, Thunder Heart Woman, and Margaret's orphans.

"On that day, I, Loved by the Buffalo, saw Growling Bear's prophecy come to pass," Loved by the Buffalo said. "My heart filled with blackness. But in the end, there was a new beginning, too. Our people still live. Not like before. But in living, there is still hope."

The orphans listened carefully as the old man continued. "Remember who you are. Remember our stories. Tell them to those who come after you. When you tell your story, you touch your grandfathers and grandmothers, and all the ancestors who walked before them. And when others ask how you know these things, tell them that Loved by the Buffalo was spared so that I might live to give you this story. Now it belongs to you."

Loved by the Buffalo turned to Thunder Heart Woman. She stepped forward with a specially folded cloth and opened it. Three eagles feathers rested inside.

"We cannot perform the ceremony with only three," Loved by the Buffalo said. "We need four."

A shadow passed over the hillside and everyone looked up. An eagle was circling over the hillside. Something fluttered from the bird, and it spiraled to earth.

One of Margaret's orphans ran with glee, retrieved the feather, and brought it to Loved by the Buffalo. He examined the eagle feather, and found it perfect in every way. Loved by the Buffalo placed the feather together with the other three in the bundle, and his spirit was seized by a sense of awe: of the eagle, of the sky, of the world and all of the forces the govern it.

The eagle glided like a dream on a thermal.